For Mary

[signature]

11/27/18

PRISONER MOON

by John Van Roekel

2012
Triptych Press

This is a work of historical fiction. Apart from the well-known actual people, events and locales that figure in the narrative, all names, characters, places, and incidents are the products of the author's imagination or are used fictitiously. Any resemblance to current events or locales, or to living persons, is entirely coincidental.

Published in the United States by Triptych Press

JohnVanRoekel.com   Facebook.com/johnvanroekel
jvr@johnvanroekel.com

Cover design by O'Brien Design and John Van Roekel

First Edition, June, 2012
8/17/16

Triptych

A picture on three panels. Each panel tells its own story and contributes to the picture as a whole.

Each of John Van Roekel's novels tells a story from three intertwined points of view.

A portion of the reverse side of the Stefaneschi Triptych by the Italian painter Giotto. Pinacoteca Vaticana, Rome.

For Pam

The camp held more than 600 inmates and I had been one of them … We were all German soldiers—part of the more than 425,000 of us who were captured in North Africa and Europe and brought to America in captivity.

—Georg Gaertner with Arnold Krammer, *Hitler's Last Soldier in America*

Tension continued to run high for some time after the killing, and perhaps it was for this reason that the military authorities were inclined to take seriously the tale of a Polish informant who came forward to report the existence of "an organization" in the camp called the Heilige Geist—or Holy Ghost.

—Wilma Parnell, *The Killing of Corporal Kunge*

Non so se 'ntendi: io dico di Beatrice;
tu la vedrai di sopra, in su la vetta
di questo monte, ridere e felice.

Do you understand me? I mean Beatrice.
She will appear above here, at the summit
of the same mountain, smiling in her bliss.

—Dante Alighieri, translated by John Ciardi, *The Divine Comedy*, Purgatorio, Canto VI

Table of Contents

Chapter One

So far today, *die Monstren*—the monsters—had left him alone.

Fifteen-year-old Edwin Horst, his German uniform dirty and torn where the Americans had ripped away the insignia for souvenirs, cowered alone with his back to the railroad car window, oblivious to the verdant fields of Michigan sweet corn rolling past outside. He was exhausted, terrified, and bored. His eyes twitched back and forth beneath half-closed lids, scanning the car filled with other prisoners and the single guard, watching and waiting.

Edwin's thoughts again drifted to his mother, alone in their apartment back in Düsseldorf. His father had died of tuberculosis six years before, his older brother Stefan was serving on the Eastern Front, and just four months ago, when the call came for volunteers as young as fourteen, Edwin had enlisted.

He had left his mother alone in a time of war.

Edwin squeezed his eyes closed as tight as he could, willing himself to suppress the tears he feared would come, trying to remember a happier time. Last year, when Stefan came home on leave, he let Edwin look through his army field glasses, and when Edwin squinted, he saw his own eyelashes pressing in from above and below, grazing the eyepieces.

Stefan had long eyelashes too. Both brothers had blond Aryan hair and hardly any beard. But Stefan was solidly built; he looked like a man, like an ideal German soldier. With Edwin's curly hair, thin frame, and slightly rounded hips, he knew his long eyelashes only added to his girlish appearance. If he could find some scissors, he could cut them. Maybe that would help.

He wondered what had happened to Stefan's field glasses. Were they buried in a snow bank outside of Stalingrad? Maybe one of Stefan's Waffen-SS comrades had them—or some oaf of a Russian soldier.

With a start, Edwin realized that he wasn't watching, guarding himself against the monsters he knew were all around him. His eyes popped open and he saw a large man, another prisoner, looming over him. Throwing up his hand and waving it back and forth, Edwin said, "Go away," trying desperately to sound tough and confident, and knowing at the same time that he was failing.

"My name is Henri Gelbert," the man said. "From Zwenkau. You know where that is?" His German was formal, educated. "It's near Leipzig, where my father went to university. You are wondering why I have a French name, yes?"

"Go away," Edwin repeated. He stared up at this Henri. He was older, perhaps nineteen or twenty, and at least two meters in height. He wore small eyeglasses with thick lenses that made his large head look even larger. The stubble-covered skin under his chin hung loosely, making Edwin think that he'd once been fat.

"And why should I do that?" Henri asked. "You've got this whole seat to yourself. If I want to sit here, why shouldn't I?"

"Sergeant Spinkel says I can have this seat." Spinkel was the German sergeant the Americans had put in charge of this car. He sat up front, next to the sleeping guard.

"Spinkel! And why should I care about him?" Henri shrugged dismissively. Then he leaned down a little, peering at Edwin through his tiny eyeglasses. "My mother was French, you see." He paused for a second, and then refocused on Edwin. "So, where were you captured? And what unit are you from? Me, I was in Battalion 999. Perhaps you've heard of it?" He cautiously slid down onto the far end of the seat.

Edwin tried to push himself back farther into the corner, ready to yell, ready to jump up and try to somehow get away. Beneath his fear, he remembered that Battalion 999 had been created to get military work out of men who couldn't be trusted as regular soldiers. "You're a communist!" he whispered, trying to sound superior. Then he winced, regretting he'd said anything. He had to avoid getting into a conversation with this Henri.

"A communist? Ah, and what's a communist?" Henri's eyes brightened with enthusiasm. "The Nazis think anyone who doesn't love that Austrian paper hanger Hitler is a communist. Now—"

"Be quiet!" Edwin hissed. "They might hear you." He pointed toward Spinkel and the guard.

"So?" Henri asked loudly. "Do you fear the Nazis here?" He waved his hands around, gesturing toward the windows and the passing farmland outside. "In the middle of America?"

Edwin peered over the seat in front of him and saw that Sergeant Spinkel had turned around to look at them. After a moment, he turned to face forward again.

"Listen!" Edwin said, "I don't care about politics. Leave me alone!"

Henri didn't leave. Instead, he slid fully onto the seat and stared dolefully straight ahead.

Edwin pulled up his legs so his knees were tucked under

his chin and hugged them tight. He wanted to look out the window, to turn away from this Henri, but he dared not. If only Axel were here.

Axel Schmidt had been big, taller than Henri, and heavier. They grew up together in the Carlstadt district of Düsseldorf, where Axel's family lived in the apartment directly below Edwin's. On Saturdays, they went to the cinema, greatly preferring the American horror movies with Boris Karloff and Lon Chaney. They'd enlisted together and stayed together during training, and to their mutual surprise and relief, they'd been assigned to the same artillery battalion. Axel, so big and strong, had been his protector. He'd kept the monsters away.

"You think you're a tragic case?" Henri said suddenly, still staring straight ahead. "Everybody on this train has a sad story to tell. Perhaps the American airplanes have bombed your family out of their home. Or your best friend died in your arms in a filthy bunker in France. You haven't heard from your pregnant wife for many months. We're all on our way to some miserable prisoner-of-war camp. In America! It's all very sad. When we were aboard ship, there were so many unhappy men jammed into such a small place, it must have been the highest concentration of wretchedness that the world has ever seen."

Of course Edwin remembered. The American guards had called the *Walter S. Mitchell* a "Liberty Ship" and claimed that hundreds were being built for the war. After carrying troops and supplies to Europe, the *Mitchell* returned to the United States with nine hundred German prisoners. The bunks in the deep holds stood six-high, so tightly packed that if there was a man in the bunk above him, Edwin couldn't roll over from his back to his stomach without having to slide out first. Barbed wire had been welded across the portholes.

There had been showers onboard. After three weeks in a hellhole prisoner camp in England, and after being sprayed with DDT powder as they boarded the ship in Liverpool, Edwin had been desperate to get clean. The DDT itched like fire, but he didn't shower. He didn't take off his clothes and join the other naked men when his turn came. Because he was dirty and stank and didn't care, the monsters stayed away; and because they thought he was crazy, it was almost as good as having Axel with him. When the ship docked at New York City, the guards finally forced him to wash. But in his heart he knew he would never truly feel clean again.

Edwin peered over at Henri. The man sat with his shoulders slumped, his hands on his knees, still staring straight ahead. Edwin had noticed him on the ship and on this train; it was hard not to because of the man's height. Henri liked to talk, and Edwin would like to talk to someone. Could he trust Henri? He had probably bored all the other prisoners with his stupid conversation, and now he had set his sights on Edwin. Maybe that was all there was to it. Still, if he were wrong …

A shudder passed over pretty, fifteen-year-old Edwin Horst.

Thirty minutes later, the train came to a stop at a small, stone-built station with a sign above the platform that read "Ann Arbor." When the American guard gestured to Sergeant Spinkel that they would get off, both Henri and Edwin stood, and as they waited, Henri bent back down and looked out the window, past Edwin.

"Look!" Henri whispered. "Girls! American girls."

Edwin looked. Standing on the platform next to the station doorway were two young women, one with dark hair and the other with fiery red. They were pretty, Edwin thought. And Henri said they were American girls. Well, of course they were.

A moment later, as the prisoners stepped off the train,

Sergeant Spinkel ordered them to fall in, pointing to an open area next to the station building. As Edwin automatically moved to obey, he saw Henri suddenly stop and turn, a glint of excitement in his eyes. He scurried across the short distance to the station and stood in front of the two girls. Watching Henri, it seemed to Edwin as if he were back in his Düsseldorf schoolyard, and he yearned to go stand next to Henri and talk to those pretty girls.

Henri seemed to be doing well. One of them—the brunette —giggled, and the redhead smiled. Both the American guard and Sergeant Spinkel shouted at the same time, and bidding a quick farewell to the girls, Henri hurried back to join the formation, falling into line next to Edwin. Both Sergeant Spinkel and the guard stood in front of Henri, Spinkel yelling at him even as he wrote in his notebook. The guard said nothing, merely nodding with approval. Watching through the corner of his eye, Edwin saw Henri's face twitching as he struggled to suppress a smile.

Fifteen minutes later, Edwin and Henri sat next to each other in a chartered city bus as it rumbled down a dirt road leading out of town. Edwin stared at Henri, but the big man said nothing. Finally, Edwin could contain himself no longer. "What did they say?" he asked.

Henri looked at him and grinned. "So now you want to talk to me, eh?"

"Come on, Henri. What did they say?"

Henri shrugged and said nothing more. Edwin glared at him for a moment and then turned away, his eyes drifting toward the front of the bus where the guard stood chatting with the civilian driver and where Sergeant Spinkel sat alone in the front seat. Spinkel was certain to punish Henri once they got to the camp, but Edwin guessed that Henri would consider his short conversation with those girls to be worth it. Spinkel stared ahead out the front window, and it occurred to

Edwin for the first time that even he was worried about his future, about this new camp.

"You know the remarkable thing?" Henri asked.

"What?" Edwin asked eagerly.

"The dark-haired one. She spoke German."

"That was pretty strange," the dark-haired girl said, turning to Doris.

"Yeah, I reckon," Doris replied. She'd arrived on the same train as those prisoners, having boarded it in Ypsilanti. Thankfully, this girl had been waiting to meet her, and they'd just started to introduce themselves when that tall boy had walked up to them.

"Doris Calloway, from Brooksville, Kentucky," Doris said, holding out her hand. "It sure is good to meet you."

"Hildegard Gruden. Everybody calls me Hildy."

They shook hands, and together they turned to look back at the formation of German prisoners, fifty feet away.

"That must've been German you two were talking," Doris said. "What'd he say?"

"He just told me where he was from," Hildy replied. "Look, you might as well know right now, my whole family was born in Germany. There are lots of German families here in Ann Arbor, but we're real Americans, see? My family has been here for fifteen years. We used to speak German at home, but not anymore. Well, hardly at all."

Doris stared back at Hildy. German? The clerk at the plant housing office hadn't said anything about living with a bunch of Krauts. When was the next train back to Ypsilanti? Maybe there was a bus. But they told her she was real lucky to get a place so close, and she sure didn't want to go back to that YWCA. She couldn't bear the thought of another night on a cot in the gymnasium with fifty other girls.

Hildy watched her, waiting. "And my brother is in the

army, fighting for our country," she added. "He joined up right after Pearl Harbor."

"Well, good on him," Doris said. So what if they came from Germany? Like she said, they were real Americans, after all. "I reckon it'll be okay."

Hildy looked relieved.

"Anyway, I sure appreciate your meeting my train," Doris added. "And for renting me a room. That's mighty kind of you."

"Just doing our part for the war effort," Hildy replied as she picked up Doris's suitcase. They started walking.

Doris glanced over at Hildy. She was slender, and her coal black hair framed a face that was lovely and sweet. She wore lipstick and a little color on her cheeks. When that tall German boy had walked up, his eyes had darted back and forth between them, and then settled on Hildy, who had preened and giggled. Doris reached up and ran her fingers through her unruly red locks and tried to push them back into some kind of shape. With her own rawboned figure and freckled complexion, she figured boys would always prefer this pretty girl who sauntered along beside her. She sighed.

"Our house is just a few minutes' walk," Hildy said. "We've got a nice enough room for you. On the third floor, kind of in the attic."

"A room to myself? That'll be jus' fine." Doris shook her head. "You rich Yankees ..."

"Oh, we're not rich!" Hildy said, horrified. "Papa, uh, my father, just has the store. He sells farm equipment."

"My daddy's a soybean farmer, back home." Not a very good one, she added to herself. "We've got eighty acres and this little ol' house with two bedrooms. My meemaw lives with us, so I share with her. In the summer, I sleep out on the porch."

"Meemaw?"

"Oh, my grandmother."

"No brothers or sisters?" Hildy asked.

Doris shook her head.

"I've got two brothers, Hans—he's the one in the army—and Karl."

They turned a corner onto a quiet street lined with old oak trees and a mix of large and small houses.

"I guess you'll take the bus to work," Hildy said. "The station isn't far."

"They got a special bus just for us war workers," Doris replied.

"I think you're awful brave," Hildy said. "Leaving your family to come to a strange new place."

"I reckon that's nothing compared with moving halfway around the world like you did."

Hildy shrugged. "I was only four. I hardly remember the old country. And I was with my family. You're all alone."

Doris reckoned Hildy was right. She was all alone. This was what she'd wanted, after all.

Last Sunday morning, as Doris and her family came out of church, they'd seen a young woman passing out pamphlets. The Ford Motor Company needed workers for its Willow Run plant in Michigan, where they built the big B-24 bombers. Doris grabbed a pamphlet, and Daddy had tried to snatch it away from her, but she'd fled down the street with him shouting after her. That night, she packed her suitcase while her momma and meemaw cried, and in the morning, she was on a Greyhound bus, heading north.

"Hey, I get two-fifty an hour," Doris said. "Up here I can live high on the hog and still send money back home. There sure ain't much war work back in Brooksville."

They walked for a while. It was cooler under the oak trees.

"You want some Juicy Fruit?" Hildy asked. "My big brother Hans sends me lots. He gets all he wants in the army."

Hildy stopped, set down the suitcase, and pulled a pack of gum out of her pocket. She offered a stick.

"Thanks," Doris replied, taking it. She tore it in two and gave half back to Hildy. They stood next to each other on the quiet, shady street, unwrapping their gum.

"So tell me about this here Hans," Doris said. "How old is he?"

Hildy grinned.

Sam Demsky crouched next to the rear wheel of his 1936 DeSoto Airflow, its dark blue paint, lovingly washed and polished just the day before, now covered with dust from the gravel road.

"Damn it," he muttered as the lug wrench slipped off the wheel nut again. He glanced at his watch. In twenty minutes, he had an appointment with Dr. Hooper, chairman of the History department, and here he was, stuck out in the country with another flat. He eyed the spare doubtfully, half flat and completely bald, leaning against the DeSoto's bumper. He just had to get some new tires.

Sam stood and pressed his hands into the small of his back, groaning. He was of medium height, with dark, curly hair and thin, aquiline features. At twenty-six, he wasn't officially too old for military service, but he knew there was no danger from the local draft board. When he walked, his right foot turned inward and dragged, especially when he was tired. His impediment, as his mother called it, had given him one positive gift during a lifetime of bother: a 4-F draft status.

He sighed and reached down to massage his foot. He'd just spent an hour standing at the front gate of the new prisoner-of-war camp, pleading with the guards to let him talk to the commanding officer. Sam worked part-time as a reporter for *The Ann Arbor News*—in addition to lecturing in European history at the University of Michigan—and this had been his third trip out to the camp. Captain Harris, the camp commanding officer, still refused to see him. What a waste of tire tread and rationed gasoline.

He hefted the wrench in his hand, and as he prepared to attack the stubborn nut again, he heard the rumble of a large vehicle coming up the road behind him. He glanced around, his hand shielding his eyes from the mid-afternoon sun. It was an Ann Arbor city bus, a cloud of dust rising behind it. He wondered what it was doing this far out of town. When he picked out the word "Chartered" in the windshield, he dropped the wrench. Speak of the devil. It must be going to the camp.

As the bus drew close, he made out the driver and a guard standing next to him wearing a helmet, a rifle slung over his shoulder. When Sam raised his hand and waved, both the driver and the guard waved back, and the bus slowed. For a second, Sam thought it might stop, but it didn't. As the bus passed by, he saw dozens of drawn and haggard faces staring down from the windows.

There was a story out at that camp. He just knew it.

The house wasn't particularly different from the others on the street, not especially large or impressive, but neat and trim, and with a recently mowed lawn. Doris followed Hildy through the front door, where she dropped the suitcase at the bottom of a stairway leading up to the second floor and, presumably, to the third where Doris would sleep. There was a living room on the right and a dining room on the left. Hildy led the way through an open door at the rear of the front hall, beside the stairs.

In the kitchen, an older woman that Doris reckoned was Hildy's momma, hunched over the front of old-fashioned cast-iron stove. She used a big pair of tongs to select pieces of coal from the shuttle and carefully placed them inside the open fire grate. When she was satisfied, she closed the grate and straightened up, grimacing a little. Heavier and shorter than Hildy, her blond hair was streaked with gray. She wore no makeup and no jewelry except for a plain wedding band.

"Mutti, this is Doris Calloway," Hildy said. "She's from Kentucky."

Doris stepped forward and held out her hand. "I'm right glad to meet you, Mrs. Gruden."

Gertrud Gruden wiped her hands on a towel next to the stove and then wiped them again on her spotless apron. She looked Doris up and down. "In Kentucky, do young women wear pants?" she asked. She folded her arms across her chest and stared at Doris.

"I've got a nice dress," Doris said quickly. "I'll change right away." She dropped her hand back to her side.

"They're called slacks," Hildy said. "Doris was telling me that they're all the rage at the Willow Run plant."

"Change before dinner," Gertrud said. "And no smoking, not in the house. You understand?"

Doris nodded and said, "Yes, ma'am."

Gertrud stared at her for a second more and then her face softened. She reached out and Doris shook her hand, noticing how hard and rough it was compared to Hildy's.

"You cook?" Gertrud asked.

"I guess. Course our kitchen ain't nearly as nice as this one."

Gertrud showed a thin smile. "I teach you to cook hasenpfeffer, eh?"

Hasenpfeffer? Doris stared at the older woman.

"It's rabbit." Hildy wrinkled her nose. "Mother raises them out back."

"Hasenpfeffer is *gute* German food. You add some onions, some cloves."

"And meat is hard to get here, I reckon, just like home,"

Doris said. "Because of the war and all."

Gertrud's face went blank, and there was an awkward silence.

Doris guessed that she shouldn't mention the war, at least not to Mrs. Gruden. She said, "We eat rabbit back home sometimes. I bet my kin'd be glad for me to learn a new way to cook 'em."

"Okay!" Gertrud replied, clapping her hands together. "And you will show me how you cook rabbits in the state of Kentucky."

"Sure. And maybe some night I can cook up a mess of fried chicken for y'all."

"We will see," Gertrud said.

"Yes, ma'am."

"Come on," Hildy said. "I'll show you your room." As they headed for the stairs, she leaned toward Doris and whispered, "It'll be a while before she lets you cook by yourself in that kitchen."

"Hildegard!" Gertrud called out. "Did you write a letter to Hans today?"

"Not yet, Mutti. I will tonight, I promise."

"It's good, eh?" Henri said, as he shoveled potatoes into his mouth.

He and Edwin sat at a rough wooden table in the prisoner mess hall, the clean smell of pine from the raw lumber used in its construction mixing with the comforting aromas of their food. The doors were propped open, and an Indian summer evening breeze drifted through the room packed with prisoners. Just beyond those doors, they knew, stood a twelve-foot high barbed-wire fence, the innermost of two.

Edwin glanced down at his tin mess plate. There was a slice of something that looked like meat, some overcooked carrots, and a big dollop of those potatoes. They'd eaten plenty of "mashed" potatoes onboard the *Mitchell*, and Edwin had become tired of them. Apparently, Henri had not. Edwin cut a piece of the meat on his plate and cautiously tasted it. It was moist, tender, and salty.

"It's a sign, I think," Henri said. "Good food, ready when we got here. These Americans know how to run a camp."

"The cooks are German," Edwin said.

"Still, you've got to admit, this is Nirvana compared with the ship and that miserable camp in England."

Edwin didn't know what Nirvana was. He shrugged and tried the carrots.

"And," Henri added, happily waving a forkful of potatoes, "nobody is shooting at us! Right? Come on, Edwin. I think this will be an excellent place to sit out the remainder of the war."

Glancing around, Edwin hoped that nobody had heard, but next to him a chubby boy from Berlin named Hubert nodded in agreement. Edwin didn't know what to think.

"Spinkel doesn't look very happy," Henri said, glancing toward the front of the room.

Sergeant Spinkel sat with another man at a table near the door.

"He's sad because he's no longer in charge," Henri continued. He gulped down the last bit of potatoes. "Me, I'd be relieved. In fact, this is wonderful. No officers—just senior sergeants. These Americans, they put the officers in camps by themselves. And they leave us alone. At night, there aren't any guards inside the fence at all."

Edwin glanced around the room. Henri was right, there weren't any guards visible. He continued picking at his carrots. It was hard to understand.

The man with Spinkel was Staff Sergeant Gott. Earlier, after the new prisoners had piled off the bus and assembled on the small parade ground, Gott had welcomed them. Short,

barrel-chested and completely bald, he told them that he'd
fought in the Afrika Korps with Field Marshal Rommel and
had been in America for two years. As the senior sergeant in
the camp, Gott was the liaison with the Americans and was in
command. He expected good German discipline. They'd
work for the Americans on non-war related activities, he'd
said, and in return the Americans would provide the same
rations, accommodations, and medical care that they provided
their own troops. There would be time for sports, hobbies,
and classes. All of this was clearly covered by the Geneva
Convention, a copy of which was posted on the bulletin board
inside the mess hall.

Sports. Edwin remembered seeing a large, flat field behind
the barracks buildings. If we could only find a soccer ball.

There was a commotion near the mess hall door. When
some of the men leaped to their feet, their chairs tumbling
over behind them, Edwin and Henri glanced at each other and
stood up.

Two men stood stiffly at attention in front of the table with
Spinkel and Gott. They had their backs to Edwin and Henri,
but they seemed to be holding something between them.

Staff Sergeant Gott looked hard at Spinkel, clearly
expecting something. Spinkel stood up, straightened his
shoulders, and shouted, "Attention!"

All the men jerked to attention.

"Proceed!" Gott ordered, and the men carrying the
mysterious object marched to the wall beside the door leading
to the kitchen. As they turned around, Edwin realized that
they held a framed photograph of der Führer, Adolf Hitler.

"Salute!"

Edwin's right arm shot up automatically, outstretched in
front of him with the fingers pointed straight at the
photograph.

"I think maybe the Americans won't appreciate this,"

Henri whispered.

Edwin wanted to remind him that the American guards had left for the night, but he said nothing. Out of the corner of his eye, he saw that while Henri was also giving the Nazi salute, his arm was relaxed and his fingers drooped. Edwin wondered if Spinkel or Gott would notice, but their attention stayed fixed on the photograph.

"*Heil Dir im Siegerkranz, Herrscher des Vaterlands!*" Gott's voice rang out, singing the opening line of *Deutschland über Alles* with a flat and reedy voice. Sergeant Spinkel joined him, followed by the rest of the men. Edwin sang loudly. Group singing was one aspect of military life that he always enjoyed. He heard Henri beside him, and it seemed that as Henri sang, his arm lifted and stiffened.

When the song ended, the men with the photograph held it high, and then turned and hung it on a nail.

"They planned this all in advance," Henri whispered. "See, the nail was already there."

After a nod from Gott, Sergeant Spinkel shouted, "As you were!" and they returned to their seats.

Henri picked up his fork and then set it down again. When Edwin looked at his face, he saw confusion and maybe fear.

"I didn't expect that," Henri said.

"What?"

"To feel stirred. To feel German again. To feel proud."

"Even here, in the middle of America?" Edwin asked. "Like you said on the train?"

Henri shrugged.

Edwin glanced back over at Sergeant Spinkel and saw, as Henri had said, that he didn't look very happy. As Staff Sergeant Gott said something to Spinkel, slapping the table to make a point, Spinkel said nothing, only staring down at his plate, still filled with food. Gott stood, his face flushed, and Spinkel leaped up and came to attention. Stiffly, Spinkel reached into his uniform shirt pocket, pulled out his notebook, and held it out to Gott. But suddenly, Spinkel snatched it back, and turning on his heel, marched from the room. Gott, still fuming with anger, stared after him.

Edwin thought that Sergeant Spinkel was making a terrible mistake. Gott was clearly in charge at this camp. Would he punish Spinkel for his defiance? Perhaps, like Henri said, Spinkel was used to being in command. Probably he would come to his senses, remember his discipline, and do whatever Gott wanted.

Edwin had seen the notebook several times. Spinkel used it to record the names of anyone who committed an infraction, either major or minor. Henri's name was surely in it for the silly affair with the American girls that afternoon. Edwin looked across the table at Henri, who was eyeing Edwin's mashed potatoes.

"Go ahead," Edwin said. "Just leave the meat."

"It's called Spam," Henri said as he scooped the potatoes onto his own plate.

Later that evening, with Gertrud still working in the kitchen, Doris and Hildy stood behind their chairs in the dining room waiting for dinner to begin—Doris's mouth watering at the unfamiliar but delicious aroma wafting through the connecting door. She glanced around the room. There was barely enough space for them to sit between the heavy oak table and the other pieces of dark furniture that lined the walls. Dozens of framed photographs looked down on them, some very old. It felt to Doris as if dead people were peering over her shoulder.

Oskar Gruden strode into the room and moved directly to the head of the table. Hildy had introduced Doris to him a few minutes earlier, after they'd changed for dinner. Oskar had been working in his small study, just off the living room, and while he'd been polite enough, he'd also made it clear that he was busy. Now, as he stood next to her, she saw that he was about fifty, with gray peppering his walrus mustache and the fringe around his balding head. A gold watch chain hung across the front of his vest and—as he'd removed his suit coat —Doris saw he wore garters on his shirtsleeves.

"Miss Calloway, you will sit here, please," he said, pulling back the chair on his right. "This is Hans's place," he added. "My oldest son."

"Thank you, Mr. Gruden."

"Hans is fighting the Japanese in New Guinea."

"Yes, sir. Hildy told me."

Gertrud came in and stood behind her chair at the opposite end, near the kitchen. Hildy sat across the table, and there was an empty place setting on Doris's right.

"We'll not wait for Karl," Oskar announced, and he bowed his head.

Hildy did the same, along with Gertrud who, still standing behind her chair, clasped her hands over her chest.

Doris lowered her head, folded her hands on her lap, and closed her eyes.

"*Lassen Sie uns beten ...*" Oskar began.

This was the second time in her life that Doris had heard German being spoken. She wondered what Mr. Gruden was going on about. She heard him say "Hans" in a sentence that sounded serious. The son in New Guinea, wherever that was. Hildy had said that this Hans boy was twenty years old and had hinted that he was good looking.

Mr. Gruden droned on.

"Sorry I'm late ... oops!"

Doris opened her eyes. A fair young man with his shirttail hanging out stood next to Hildy, breathing hard as though he'd been running. He glanced across the table at Doris and blushed. Oskar said a few more German words, added

"Amen," and then looked up at Karl. Doris saw a flash of anger in the old man's eyes.

"Go clean up," he said.

Karl bent down and whispered something in Hildy's ear and then dashed from the room, bumping into a big sideboard and rattling the glass knickknacks on its top. Doris noticed that Karl had been clutching a paper bag.

"Go ahead and serve, Gertrud," Oskar said.

Gertrud disappeared into the kitchen and returned with a large, steaming platter. Cooked cabbage, Doris guessed by the smell. And rabbit too.

Oskar lifted a basket of rolls and offered it to her. As she smiled and took one, Doris saw for the first time that there was an oversized envelope sitting on the table next to his plate. Oskar didn't return her smile.

Karl came back into the room. His shirt was tucked in and his hair—sandy blond in contrast to his sister's—was neatly combed. He sat next to Doris, clasped his hands together on the edge of the table in front of him, and squeezed his eyes shut. He muttered something to himself for a few seconds and then looked at his father. Oskar continued eating, and Karl lunged for the basket of rolls.

"Karl," Hildy said, "this is Doris Calloway. She's the girl from Kentucky I told you about. She's working out at the Willow Run plant."

The boy mumbled something into his plate.

"Karl," Oskar said quietly.

Karl reluctantly stood up and, without looking directly at Doris, bowed stiffly at the waist. "I am very pleased to meet you, Miss Calloway."

"Likewise, Karl. Just call me Doris, okay?"

Karl shrugged and sat down. They all ate in silence for a while.

"The strangest thing happened to Doris and me this

afternoon," Hildy said.

"What was that?" her father asked.

"I was at the railroad station to meet Doris, and we saw this bunch of German prisoners. One of them came over and talked with us. He—"

"Hildegard," Mr. Gruden interrupted, his voice stern. "I've told you that you aren't have any contact with that camp."

"We didn't really talk to him. He just said he was from Zwenkau. Isn't that near—"

"No," Mr. Gruden said. "We'll not discuss it. Miss Calloway, while you live in our house, you will please obey me on this matter too. Do you understand?"

Doris nodded, not really understanding what "this matter" actually was. The others picked up their forks and resumed eating. Doris had a thought.

"Mr. Gruden and Mrs. Gruden," she said. "I know I just got here and all. But would you mind if I write a letter to Hans?"

Hildy and Karl both stared at her with surprise. Oskar's eyes narrowed and he asked, "And why would you want to do that?"

"I don't know," Doris said. "I thought it might be right nice for him to hear from someone new. If you don't want me to …"

"Yes," Gertrud Gruden said from the other end of the table, her voice firm. "You do that. Hans will be happy to get a letter from a nice girl like you." She turned toward her husband and fixed him with a steady gaze.

"He'd be happy for a letter from any girl besides his sister!" Karl said with a smirk.

Oskar suddenly laughed. And then Hildy, Karl, and even Gertrud joined in. Doris smiled and relaxed a bit. Maybe this would be okay. They were a real family.

Next to her, Oskar resumed eating. Doris noticed that he

kept his fork in his left hand, pointed down at the plate, and she thought that was strange. Glancing around the table, she saw that the others were doing the same. She guessed it must be some kind of German thing. Doris moved her fork to her left hand, turned it over, and stabbed at a carrot. It didn't feel right.

She glanced over at Oskar again, wondering if he was anything like her own father, whether he'd try to force her to his will—even try to change the way she ate. Oskar ignored her. She told herself to relax as she switched her fork back to her right hand and popped the piece of carrot into her mouth. Take it easy and give this a chance, she thought.

Again she noticed the envelope sitting next to Oskar's plate; it was a large business envelope. She reckoned it wasn't a letter from Hans.

A drop of sweat lingered on the tip of Doris's nose. Before she could brush it away, it fell onto the cheap *Big Chief* writing tablet that she held pressed against her knees. Her room, on the third floor of the Gruden house, was stifling. Tucked up under the eaves, it had only a single window, which looked out over the backyard and Mrs. Gruden's rabbit hutches. Doris had tugged the window open as far as it would go, but hardly a breath of air penetrated the room. She sat on the end of her narrow bed, hunched over with the back of her head grazing the inclined ceiling behind her, clutching her pencil, and went on with the letter to her mother.

"I was worried these Gruden folks might be stuck up cause they got money, but they seem OK," she wrote. "Hildy is my age and she says Mr. Gruden has a farm equipment store. It's doing real well with the war on. They sure have a nice house. I even got my own room, but it's awful hot."

What else? Other than a postcard sent the day she arrived at Willow Run, this was her first letter home.

There were footsteps in the stairwell outside her door, followed by a polite knock. Doris called out, "Come on in!"

Karl stuck his head inside.

"I said, come on in, Karl. It's okay."

As the boy stepped into the room, Doris saw that he carried a beat-up electric fan.

"I thought you could use this," he said. "I got it out of Hans's room."

"Why, Karl, that's mighty sweet of you."

The boy blushed and looked down at the fan, idly turning the blades with his fingers. "I'll plug it in for you," he said. "I can put it right in the window."

Doris was sitting at the end of the bed nearest the window. As Karl tried to squeeze past her, his leg touched her knee, and he leaped back, banging his head on the sloping ceiling. Doris smiled as she lifted her feet, tucked them beneath her, and slid back to give him more room.

Karl set the fan on the window ledge. It had a long cord, and he snaked it behind the dresser opposite the bed and plugged it into the single outlet next to the door. The fan slowly started to turn. Doris reached over and aimed it so the growing breeze blew directly on her face. "Back home, when it's hot like this," she said, "I sleep out on the porch at night."

Karl, back by the door, stared at her and blushed again. "I, uh, uh," he stammered. "I don't think Papa would let you do that here."

Doris shrugged and turned her face back toward the window. The fan was spinning faster now, and the air felt cooler. She ran her hand through her long red hair, pulling it back from her face.

"I don't think your papa likes me," she said.

"Oh, no. That's not right," Karl replied. "It's just that, well, he didn't really want us to take in a war worker."

"Lots of folks do it."

"That's what Hildy and I kept telling him. Of course, he finally gave in when Hans wrote a letter saying that we should do it."

"Hildy says your big brother Hans is twenty years old. That right?"

Karl thought for a second. "Yeah, last March."

"Twenty," Doris repeated, still facing the window and turning her head side to side so the fan-driven evening air caressed each cheek.

"Yes, ma'am."

"I done told you to call me Doris. I'm just nineteen, myself. And you're what, fifteen, sixteen?"

Karl didn't answer. She turned around and saw that his eyes were shadows, hidden in the dusky light from the window.

"Oh, that ain't right," she said quickly. "Now that I see you better I can tell you're at least eighteen."

Karl swallowed. "Next month," he said. "Eighteen next month."

"You see? So it's just not right for you to be calling me ma'am, is it?"

"Sure. Okay."

Neither said anything for a moment. Karl put his hand on the doorknob and mumbled, "I guess …"

"So what's gonna happen when you turn eighteen? You goin' in the army?"

Karl's face brightened. "The Air Corps—fighter planes, I hope. Hans joined up on the day after Pearl Harbor. Papa says that's enough for our family, so he doesn't want me to enlist."

"What about the draft?"

"I don't know. Papa keeps saying that's not going to be a problem."

Doris thought that was strange. "Back home," she said, "I got two uncles and three cousins drafted."

"Um …," Karl said. "Say, you want to come downstairs? Hildy and I are going to play some records."

"Why sure. That'd be real nice. Let me finish this letter, and I'll be right there."

After Karl had left, Doris picked up her writing pad again. She'd written less than a page. Well, the hell with it, she said to herself, and she scrawled, "I get paid next week and will send money then. Love, Doris."

She stood in front of the small mirror above her dresser and quickly ran a brush through her hair.

Later tonight she was definitely going to write a letter to this Hans boy.

"Hi, Mom," Sam said as he stepped through the back door into the kitchen.

Blanch Demsky leaned back from her potter's wheel and took a sip from the glass at her side. Her hair was tucked under a bandanna, and she wore a man's blue work shirt. When Sam was a child, she seemed the most beautiful woman in the world, but now eight years of widowhood had left her face gaunt and dry.

"So how was your meeting with Hooper?" she asked.

Sam put his battered reporter's notebook on the counter. "Interesting, actually. Dr. Hooper told me the damnedest thing." Sam took a glass from the cupboard, opened the Frigidaire, and filled the glass from the cold water bottle. "It seems I'm finally going to be making my contribution to the war effort."

"Oh?"

"Some genius in Washington had this bright idea. Since we've got so many German prisoners of war in the country, Dr. Hooper said there's at least two hundred thousand—"

"Oh honey, that can't be right."

"That's what he said, two hundred thousand, probably

more. Anyway, since we have them here, and the war is going to be over soon, we should start teaching them about democracy. We need to prepare these men to go back to Germany and help build a modern democratic country."

"And with your teaching experience and your flawless German, Hooper figured you're just prefect for the job."

"Well, my German isn't flawless. But with my visits to Germany before the war, I do seem like a pretty good fit. Actually, the idea is kind of clever. Instead of trying to force American democracy on them, we're going to teach them about German history and culture. We'll show the prisoners that they have their own tradition of freedom and democracy."

"But is that really true?"

Sam shrugged. "Sort of. But you've got to remember, most of these prisoners are just kids. We can mold them."

"Propagandize them, it sounds like," Blanch said as she gave the pottery wheel a kick. Sam watched patiently as his mother pulled a water-soaked sponge from the coffee can at her elbow and touched it to the spinning lump of clay in the wheel's center. The clay's surface glistened. Kicking occasionally as she worked, the wet clay surged up between her slippery fingers, seeming to defy gravity.

"Looks like another vase," he said, keeping his voice neutral.

"So you're finally going to get inside that camp," Blanch said.

"Yeah, but—"

"Don't say 'yeah,' Sam."

Sam sighed. "Yes, but I won't be writing about it for the *News*. Dr. Hooper was very clear about that. It's a secret program so I shouldn't even be telling you. And it's a full-time job. But maybe I can still turn in one story about the camp before I start."

"When is that?"

"Next week. But I had another flat today. It's funny. Now that I'm going to be able to get in the camp, I may not be able to drive there."

Blanch wet her forefinger in the coffee can and pushed it down into the center of the burgeoning vase. Again it grew magically taller, and Sam watched as his mother carefully formed its delicate walls. He knew that this was a skill in which she took particular pride. It had something to do with the consistency of the clay, the amount of water, and the timing of her actions. He held his breath until she grunted with satisfaction, leaned back again, and as the wheel coasted to a stop, a tall, gracefully fluted vase stood before them, its surface already drying and turning dull.

"Looks real nice, Mom."

"Thank you." She glanced at her now empty glass. "It's propaganda, you know. Your father, rest his soul, would call it that."

"I guess."

"Funny, I thought Hooper knew about him."

"He does. I don't think he's told the army, but he knows." Sam lifted the half-empty whiskey bottle that sat on the kitchen counter and poured an inch into his mother's glass.

"Thanks, hon. Look, you be careful. There's no reason to let those damned Nazis know that you're half-Jewish."

"Of course." Sam turned around, rinsed his own glass in the sink, dried it, and put it back into the cupboard. "It'll be interesting, but I won't be a fool."

"Speaking of damn Nazis ..." Blanch looked thoughtful. "Guess who I heard has black market tires at his store?"

Sam spun around. "Who?"

"Oskar Gruden."

Doris raced down the stairs two at a time: first, the twisting flight from her attic bedroom to the second floor, and then the main staircase into the front hall by the living room. The sound of *Chattanooga Choo Choo*, played by the Glenn Miller Band, resounded throughout the house, and she guessed that Mr. and Mrs. Gruden must have gone out for the evening.

Karl sprawled on the floor next to the big Victrola, and Hildy lay on the overstuffed couch, her bobby socks-clad feet on the cushions and her saddle shoes next to her. Both she and Karl stared into space, listening, and neither looked up as Doris bounced into the room.

"Hey, you swinging cats!" Doris said.

Hildy turned to her and smiled. "Pretty hep for a Kentucky girl."

Karl leaped to his feet. He took a step forward and then stopped, his mouth opening as if he wanted to say something. But nothing came out.

"Come on," Doris said to Karl. "Let's dance." She grabbed his hand and pulled him into the center of the room, the music swirling around them. Karl's eyes got big. Doris thought she could see the struggle going on in his head; signs of it played out across his face. She smiled, thinking he might turn and bolt from the room. His hand was limp and clammy in hers. "I'm easy to dance with," she said softly.

Karl stood next to her. As his face became still, impassive and serious, Doris tried hard not to giggle. He shifted his hand around so that it covered hers and then clamped down tight, as though he needed to prevent her from escaping. Doris stepped closer and his free arm slid up around her waist. His feet began to move and Doris followed.

"Atta boy, Karl!" Hildy cried.

They fox-trotted until the song ended. When Karl started to pull away, Doris held on and waited as Hildy flipped the record.

"Pretty good, Karl," Doris said. She reckoned that Hildy had taught him.

Karl's eyes had softened and taken on a dreamy cast. As the instrumental *I Know Why* began to play, slow and sweet, Doris gave his hand a squeeze. He didn't jump or look away. She smiled, thinking maybe she'd won his heart forever, poor boy.

When the song ended, Doris stepped back and fanned her face with her hand. "Hot, ain't it? Hildy, you want to dance while I sit for a spell?"

Karl scowled, and Hildy laughed. "No, that's okay," Hildy said. "Hey, Karl, what do you think? You want to play it?"

Doris looked at them both, wondering what they were talking about. A conspiratorial expression came over Karl's face, and he glanced up at the big clock that stood over the mantelpiece. It was just after eight.

"They won't be home for another hour at least," Hildy said. "Come on. I'll bet Doris hasn't heard it either."

Karl grinned at both of them, and Doris thought that he wasn't bad-looking when he smiled.

After quickly surveying the living room as though he expected his parents to jump out from behind the couch, Karl dashed for the front hall and up the stairs. He returned a moment later with the paper bag that Doris had seen him with at dinner.

"Look at this," he said, pulling out a phonograph record.

Doris took it and peered at the label. "*Der Fuehrer's Face* by Spike Jones and his City Slickers," she read aloud.

Karl watched her eagerly.

"I ain't heard it before," she said. "I like Spike Jones, though. His songs are so funny." She sat on the couch next to Hildy, guessing that this wasn't going to be a dance number.

"Just wait," Karl said. He slid the record from its paper cover and put it on the Victrola. A comic trombone started, and it led into a parody of a German oom-pah band. Then the singer began.

When Der Führer says, "We ist der master race"
We HEIL! HEIL! Right in Der Führer's face
Not to love Der Führer is a great disgrace
So we HEIL! HEIL! Right in Der Führer's face

Doris started to laugh. The famous Spike Jones sound effects and the exaggerated German accent were hysterical.

Are we not the supermen
Aryan pure supermen
Ja we ist der supermen
Super-duper supermen

Karl stood beaming in front of Doris, his smile brightening every time Doris laughed. The song wasn't long, and as the final chorus ended, both Doris and Hildy applauded.

There was a knock at the front door, and Karl jumped.

"Relax, Karl," Hildy said. "They wouldn't knock." She went to the window and peeked out. "Say, there's a real nice car outside."

Karl took a breath and went into the front hall, with Doris following and wondering who it could be at this time of night. Hildy stayed at the window. Karl opened the door to reveal a man in his mid-twenties with curly black hair and dark good looks. He wore a tired-looking brown suit.

Doris touched her hair.

"Have you seen the movie cartoon with Donald Duck?" the man asked.

Karl and Doris stared at him.

"Walt Disney made a cartoon with Donald Duck … Uh, you know, *Der Fuehrer's Face.*" He glanced back and forth between Karl and Doris. "I'm sorry. I heard the record. My name is Sam Demsky, and I'd like to talk to Mr. Gruden."

"My father is out for the evening," Karl said.

"Karl," Doris said quickly, "don't you think it'd be okay for Mr. Demsky to come in and sit a spell until your daddy gets home?"

Karl frowned at her and then reluctantly moved back so Sam could step inside.

Hildy came forward. Doris noticed that she'd put on a little lipstick, and Doris regretted that she hadn't had a chance to do the same. They introduced themselves.

"Please join us," Hildy said, and they all went into the living room. "Is that your car out front?" Hildy asked after they'd sat down, her voice sweet and demure.

Sam smiled broadly. "Why, yes, Miss Gruden, it is. A 1936 DeSoto Airflow. My pride and joy, I guess. Only five thousand were ever made."

"Oooh, it's such a beautiful car!" Hildy replied.

Doris thought Hildy was so obvious, it was embarrassing.

"We've got a '38 Chevy Master DeLuxe," Karl said.

"That's a nice car too," Sam said. "A good family car."

Karl slouched back into his chair, his hands stuffed into his pockets.

"Do you like to dance, Mr. Demsky?" Hildy asked, pointing to the phonograph.

Oh, Hildy, Doris thought, you're completely shameless.

"No, I'm afraid I've got this bum foot." Sam stretched his right leg out and wiggled his foot back and forth.

"Were you wounded in combat?" Karl asked, leaning forward.

Sam shook his head. "Born with it, I'm afraid. Kept me out of the army, though."

Karl sneered at him. "4-F," he said as he leaned back again and rolled his eyes at Doris.

Sam looked uncomfortable, and nobody said anything.

Doris glared at Karl. Boys were so immature at seventeen, almost eighteen. "So, Mr. Demsky, what do you do for a living?" she asked.

"I lecture at the university, and I'm a part-time reporter for *The Ann Arbor News*."

"Oh, a reporter. How interesting," Hildy cooed.

"Actually, it's pretty boring. Just civic events, obituaries, social occasions. Once the war is over and the regular reporters in the service come home, I'll probably lose my job. Still, there is this one story I've been working on." He told them about the prisoner-of-war camp and his attempts to get inside. He mentioned the new batch of prisoners he'd seen arrive earlier that day.

"We saw them too!" Doris said quickly, before Hildy could say anything. "One of them came up to us at the train station."

"Really?" Sam looked at her intently. "What was he like? What did he say?"

"He was tall," Doris said. "Nice looking, I reckon. Glasses."

Sam patted the pockets of his suit coat and pulled out a notebook. "How old?" he asked.

"It was hard to tell," Doris replied. Hildy seemed ready to butt in, so Doris hurried on. "Nineteen or twenty, maybe. He had a funny name for a Kraut—"

Doris stopped. That was dumb. Back home, everybody said "Kraut" or worse.

The room was quiet. The ticking of the mantle clock echoed around them. Hildy stared at her fingernails, a look of embarrassment or shame on her face. Karl, with a funny little smile, stood up and walked over to the Victrola, his back to Sam.

Sam sat in the big easy chair across from her. His eyes

hadn't left her face. They seemed soft and understanding. And amused. Doris wanted to look away but didn't. Sam finally gave a tiny shrug of his shoulders and cocked his head a little, seeming to say that it was okay.

"I'm sorry," Doris said. "That was a dumb thing to say."

"His name was Henri," Hildy said. "I guess there's lots of reasons a German soldier might have a French first name."

"Henri," Sam said, writing in his notebook. "Last name?"

Doris and Hildy glanced at each other and shook their heads.

"He said he was from Zwenkau," Hildy added. "I remember that because we have an uncle who—"

"Mr. Demsky doesn't care about that," Karl said suddenly. He glared at Hildy, and she didn't continue.

Doris remembered Oskar Gruden's stern warning at dinner.

Sam glanced at Karl and then shrugged. Turning back to Hildy, he said, "Well, thanks anyway, Miss Gruden. I guess that's something."

Hildy beamed, and Doris sat back against the couch cushion.

"So, Karl," Sam said, putting away his notebook. "What do you do for the war effort?"

Karl pulled himself up straight. "I'm an aircraft spotter," he said. "After school and on weekends."

Hildy smirked. "Yeah, like there's really a chance of an enemy bomber attacking Ann Arbor, Michigan."

"It could happen!" Karl said. "What if the Germans sailed an aircraft carrier into Hudson Bay? Then they could send bombers down to attack the Willow Run plant!" He glanced at Doris. "So it's possible, don't you see?"

Hildy laughed, and Sam joined her. Doris put her hand over her mouth, but she couldn't help herself. She laughed too.

Karl glared at them, his arms straight down at his sides and his hands clenched into fists. "It's important," he said.

"Karl, you're right," Sam said, trying to be serious. "It is important. I mean that."

"It's all Papa will let me do. When I'm eighteen—what's that?" Karl asked, looking around. "It's them. They're home early!"

Doris heard a noise in the back of the house. Mr. and Mrs. Gruden must be coming in through the kitchen.

"Quick, Karl," Hildy whispered. "The record!"

Karl lifted the Victrola lid and then slammed it back down as his parents walked into the front hall. He turned and backed up against it.

"Good evening, Mr. and Mrs. Gruden," Doris said quickly.

"Good evening, Doris," Gertrud replied, as she pulled off her white gloves and looked around the room, her mouth forming a thin line. As her gaze fell on Sam, her brow furrowed. Beside her, Oskar stood with an old-fashioned bowler hat in his hand. He stared at Sam too.

"Have we met?" Oskar asked.

"Papa, this is Mr. Demsky," Hildy said. "He came by to see you, so we invited him to come in and wait."

Mrs. Gruden said nothing more and left the room. Doris heard her slow steps on the main staircase.

Sam came forward, his hand outstretched.

"Demsky, did you say? Sam Demsky?" Oskar asked as he shook hands. "Is that your car outside?" His brow furrowed.

"Yes, sir. I'm sorry to bother you this late," Sam said. "But you see, I'm desperate for some new tires and—"

Mr. Gruden raised his hand and waved it back and forth slightly. "Not here," he said. "We'll talk in my study."

As both men left the room, Sam glanced over his shoulder, and his eyes met Hildy's for a second.

Damn it, Doris muttered to herself.

Hildy leaned casually against the couch cushions, smiling

sweetly.

As soon as his father closed the study door, Karl whirled around, threw open the lid to the Victrola, and pulled out the Spike Jones record. Spotting the cover and paper bag on the floor, he grabbed them and dashed from the room.

"Look," Doris said to Hildy, "I know it's got to be hard for your family, being at war with Germany and everything. But why's Karl so skittish about your father seeing that record?"

"You don't know Papa," Hildy replied. "It's more complicated than you might think."

"I reckon."

Doris remembered the mysterious envelope at dinner and Oskar's strange command that none of them have anything to do with the POW camp. Was all this somehow connected? And who was this man, this Oskar Gruden? Oh Lord, why hadn't she thought of it before? Was it possible that maybe Oskar Gruden was some kind of Nazi spy? Don't be silly, she told herself.

"Let me understand this fully," Henri said.

He and Edwin stepped out the front door of their barracks, towels wrapped around their waists and wearing their new GI cloth slippers to protect their feet from the gravel road. The sun had just risen, and the camp was still quiet as they headed, shivering, for the shower building.

"So you want me to stay nearby to protect you," Henri said. "But I can't get so close that I might see you naked. Do I have that correct?"

Edwin knew that Henri was kidding him, making light of the situation. He wanted to be able to joke with Henri about it, but he couldn't.

"Yes, please," he said.

"Okay! Now it's completely clear. You know, Edwin, you must have been truly miserable in the army."

Edwin said nothing. They walked together in silence until they reached the shower building. When they stopped outside, Edwin didn't hear any water running, and he guessed that meant that the building was empty.

"Henri …"

"You go first. I'll wait. Besides, I've got to piss." He headed for the nearby latrine.

Relieved, Edwin stepped through the door into the big shower room. Then he screamed.

Beneath the roof, the rafters were open above his head, and dripping water pipes ran along the beams leading to a dozen shower heads. What looked like an electrical cord had been thrown over one of the beams and beneath it, his neck canted to an impossible angle, his face dark and his blackened tongue sticking out, hung the lifeless body of Sergeant Spinkel.

Henri ran into the room and then stopped next to Edwin. Spinkel's body drooped surprisingly low, the toes of his polished boots just above a drying pool of urine. Nearby, a wooden chair lay on its side. When Henri stepped around the chair and stood before Sergeant Spinkel, their faces were almost level. "He's been dead for a while," Henri said, his voice calm.

Edwin guessed that Henri had seen death before, and that he wasn't surprised by it.

Henri leaned in and squinted through his eyeglasses, scrutinizing Spinkel's face closely, then he stepped around the body, examining it from every angle. "Suicide," he said. "Or that's what we're supposed to think."

Edwin wondered what Henri meant. He was reminded of an English Sherlock Holmes movie, with blurry German subtitles, that he and Axel had seen. Was this a mystery?

Henri tentatively reached out and touched Spinkel's tunic. Then he began to methodically pat at Spinkel's pockets, apparently looking for something. The body swayed and turned as he worked.

"What're you doing?" Edwin asked.

"Nothing," Henri replied. Satisfied, he stepped back from the body. "The notebook," he said. "It's gone."

Spinkel's notebook seemed unimportant to Edwin. Why did Henri care? Surely that minor matter with the girls that he'd been written up for yesterday wouldn't matter compared with Spinkel's death.

"I don't understand," Edwin said. "Why did he do it? Things were just getting better for us."

"Perhaps our good Sergeant Spinkel had more problems than we knew," Henri replied. "Or perhaps, it was the *Heilige Geist.*"

Chapter Two

Edwin still couldn't believe it. *Indians!* And they were
close by. As he worked his way down the row of corn, he
occasionally caught sight of them in the next field. Max
Lohmann, seventy-three years old and the owner of the farm,
spoke German reasonably well and had explained that his
wife of forty-seven years had been born in Bremen. When
he'd picked them up that morning, he told Edwin and the
others that some Indian farm workers had arrived the night
before. Edwin wondered if he could get closer, maybe during
the upcoming lunch break. *Indians!* What next? Cowboys?
Gangsters?

Edwin, Henri, and some other prisoners had worked on the
Lohmann farm all week. Every morning, Mr. Lohmann
arrived at the camp gate at five o'clock driving an old Ford
flatbed truck. The prisoners climbed onto the back and the
American guard, a friendly enough private named Martini,
rode up front with Mr. Lohmann. Martini promptly went to
sleep.

The first morning, they'd ridden on the bare truck bed, and
the splintery wooden beams had cut into Edwin's behind and
legs. As they bounced down the country road to the farm,
Edwin and the others were thrown about and Hubert, the
chubby boy from Berlin, almost fell off the back. Already

worried about spending weeks working under the hot sun, Edwin thought he might not even survive the ride out to the farm.

Late that afternoon, as they lay exhausted by the side of the cornfield they'd just harvested, Mr. Lohmann pulled up in his truck. He said nothing, but as Edwin groaned and climbed to his feet, he saw that the truck bed was now covered with hay. Lohmann had rigged ropes so they crisscrossed over the hay, holding it in place and—as Edwin quickly understood— providing handholds for the men. As they rode back to the camp, they all lay back in the fresh-mown hay and sang happy songs of home.

Edwin paused and took a swig from his American GI canteen. There was no hint of a breeze, the sun was blazing, and heat radiated up from the dark soil and from the close-packed cornstalks towering over his head. He glanced back over his shoulder, but he couldn't see Henri, who worked with less energy and enthusiasm and trailed behind.

It'd been a week since they'd found poor Sergeant Spinkel. For a few days, Henri talked about it incessantly, speculating as to whether Spinkel had committed suicide or if something more sinister had happened. One night, Edwin dreamed of finding Spinkel in the shower building again and woke up screaming. Henri agreed not to talk so much about Spinkel's death, but he pouted for a day.

Putting his canteen back on his belt, Edwin moved forward to the next stalk, automatically noting that it held three ripe ears of corn. He grasped the top ear, gave it quick twist, and then tossed it into the burlap bag he carried on his back.

"Hey, Eddy!"

Edwin glanced up. It was Hubert, working two rows over. For some reason Hubert had decided to call him Eddy.

"What do you think we'll have for lunch today?" Hubert asked.

Edwin gave an exaggerated shrug. There was a tension in his stomach, an almost pleasant sensation that told him that soon he'd be eating. It wasn't like real hunger, like the gut-twisting feeling that lasted for days back home. Here, farmers who contracted with the government for prisoner labor were required to provide lunch.

"Pretty lucky, huh?" Hubert continued. "Us being sent to a German farm with good German food."

Edwin smiled and nodded. It was all so unbelievable, really. He dropped another ear in his bag and looked down. His arms and the backs of his hands were brown from the sun and were getting darker every day. He knew the same thing was happening to his face, having looked at it in the barracks mirror that morning. Turning his hands over, he examined the growing calluses. In a few weeks, his hands would be rough and hard. Yes, this was a good place to be as the war finally wound down.

Edwin wrenched another ear from the stalk in front of him, flipped it high up in the air, and deftly caught it in the open mouth of his bag.

Hubert laughed and tried to do the same, but his ear of corn bounced off his shoulder and rolled into the next row among the corn that had already been picked. He looked at it for a second and then moved on to the next stalk.

A horn sounded in the distance.

"Lunch!" Hubert shouted. Dropping his bag, he took off running toward the edge of the field where Mr. Lohmann's truck was now visible. Edwin put down his own bag, marking the spot where he'd resume work in an hour. As the hunger rumbled in his stomach, he crossed over several rows, picked up the errant ear of Mr. Lohmann's corn, and tossed it over next to Hubert's bag.

"Lunch, Henri!" he shouted, looking back over the rolling field.

Henri, who was half the width of the field behind, came bounding up the row. His face was both joyous and determined as he joined Edwin. "Let's see what Frau Lohmann has for us today," he said, rubbing his blistered hands together.

As they hastened after Hubert, Edwin saw that the truck was parked near the edge of a dark thicket of trees. He averted his eyes from the dark wood and tried think about lunch. Off to the south, the sound of a train whistle rolled across the field, and Henri, now surging ahead of Edwin, suddenly slowed his pace, glanced over his shoulder in the direction of the train, and looked thoughtful for a moment. Then he hurried on.

"Can you see 'em?" Doris asked. She stood at the edge of the cornfield, her hand shading her eyes as she peered across the field.

Hildy stood next to her, doing the same. "Yeah!" she said as she squeezed Doris's shoulder and bounced up and down on her toes. "Look, they're walking toward the truck."

It was Doris's day off from work at the plant. Hildy had been pulling corn all week for Max Lohmann, and the evening before, when her father wasn't around, she'd told Doris about seeing the German prisoners in a nearby field. With nothing else to do, Doris figured she might as well join Hildy and earn a little extra money.

"You gonna eat your lunch?"

They turned and saw a man sitting with his back against an elm tree, his canvas jeans and worn work boots stretched out in front of him. Gray hair hung in two braids against his chest, each tied with a bit of rawhide at its tip. His eyes, tired and dark, stared at them from a wrinkled face that was the color of a dried winter apple. He held a clasp knife in one hand, its small blade open. Nearby, a dozen other Indians, including women and a few children, rested in the shade after a morning in the field.

"I'll take 'em, if you ain't," the man continued.

"Sorry, uh, mister," Doris said. "I reckon I'll eat mine."

"Me, too," Hildy added quickly. She edged away from the man. "Let's go sit over here, Doris."

"Name's Tatanka Sapa," the man said. "That means Black Buffalo. But you can call me George. We came in last night."

Doris wasn't sure what to say. There were a few Chickasaw living around Brooksville, and she'd seen them selling vegetables by the road. Her momma occasionally bought tomatoes from them and had always been courteous. If this man were standing, she reckoned she'd introduce herself and even shake his hand. But he continued to sit, his eyes on the wax paper-wrapped lunch in her hand. Hildy had moved away, and sat on the opposite side of another tree. Giving George a little shrug and a nod, Doris joined her.

"Do you believe that?" Hildy said as Doris sat down beside her. "Talk about being forward!"

They opened their lunches. Hildy got up and went to the jug that Mr. Lohmann had left and returned with two tin cups of cider. She carefully skirted the area where the Indians sat.

"This heat," Doris said, as she pulled off the scarf that held her hair back and shook her head. "I should cut my hair."

"Oh, no," Hildy said. "Your hair is your best feature."

"Thanks. I got it from my grandma Maureen, my daddy's momma. She came over from Scotland by herself with nothin' but some clothes and twenty dollars in her pocket. I never knew her, but Daddy used to tell me stories." She unwrapped her sandwich and took a bite. It was some kind of sausage on rye bread with mustard.

"You know," Doris continued, her mouth full, "how you expect a grandma to be all nice and warm and fun? Near as I can tell, Grandma Maureen wasn't nothin' like that. Daddy called her a tough old bird, and I reckon she had to be, coming here all on her own, with no family and nobody to stay with. Somehow, she ended up in Brooksville and met my grandpa there."

"Papa's mother is back in—" Hildy caught herself. She took a sip of cider.

Doris guessed that Hildy was going to say something about Germany.

"So, your grandma," Hildy continued, "she must have died before you were born, since you said you never knew her."

Doris took another bite. "Nope," she said, swallowing. "She left. When Daddy was twelve years old, she just took off one day. Nobody ever heard from her again."

They ate in silence for a while.

"You know," Hildy said, "that's the most you've ever said about your family."

"Yeah, I guess. They all weren't real happy about me coming up here."

"I can imagine."

"I used to fret about making them happy—tried to be a good girl and all that. Finally, I figured it out. It was like a big light bulb turning on in my head. No matter what I did, they weren't gonna be happy. That's just the way they are. So I might as well come up here and try something different."

"And here you are, building airplanes, living with us, and eating lunch with Indians!"

Doris laughed.

"You know," Hildy said a moment later, "I think I saw that tall German boy we talked to at the train station."

"Yeah?"

Hildy nodded as she swallowed the last of her sandwich. "Henri, that's his name. I think he might of taken a shine to you."

"What? Do you think so?" Doris asked.

"Maybe we should take a walk over there. What do you think?"

"I don't know. Your daddy ..."

"Oh, who cares? I'm nineteen, so he can't control every bit of my life, right?"

Doris said nothing. This was a side of Hildy that she hadn't seen before.

"Besides, I'm so damned bored, forgive my French. I hate working out here."

"Well, it don't seem so bad to me," Doris said.

Hildy finished her cider and stood up. "Come on," she said, holding out her hand to Doris. "I'm going to walk over and talk to those German boys."

Doris hesitated. She'd been careful to stay on the good side of both Mr. and Mrs. Gruden. Still, it might be fun to talk to this Henri.

"Oh, okay," she said, taking Hildy's hand and pulling herself up. "But listen, if you get into a fight with your daddy, you leave me out of it, okay? I don't need any trouble."

"Sure."

They took a minute to "freshen up" as Hildy called it, brushing out their hair and putting on a touch of lipstick. As they started over to the next field, they passed the resting Indians, and Doris glanced at George, wondering if he was watching them. But his eyes were closed, his head leaning to one side against the tree trunk, snores escaping from his wide-open mouth.

They approached the Ford truck and saw an American soldier smoking a cigarette and sitting on the running board in front of the open door. His rifle leaned against the front bumper, at least five feet away.

"Hi!" Hildy called out.

The soldier looked up and then jumped to his feet, snubbing out his cigarette and hurriedly tugging his uniform shirt into place. To Doris, he didn't look like much of a soldier.

"Afternoon, ladies," he said. "Private First Class James Martini at your service. What can I do for you pretty little things?"

Hildy stepped forward, her hand outstretched. "Private Martini, I'm Hildy Gruden. I'm very pleased to meet you."

"Please," the man said, "call me Jimmy." He looked into her eyes as he took her hand.

Hildy blushed. "And this is my friend, Doris. She's from Kentucky."

Jimmy Martini turned and looked Doris up and down. "Well, ladies, I've got to say that my day just got a lot more pleasant." He took Doris's hand, and even as he gave it a suggestive squeeze, he looked at Hildy again.

"So, Private Martini," Doris said. "Where are your prisoners?" She glanced at the rifle.

"Oh, don't you worry about them. They're racked out over by those trees."

"You see, Jimmy," Hildy said. "Doris and I would like to see them."

"Yeah?" Martini looked back at Doris. "And why is that?"

Hildy batted her eyelashes and shrugged. "Oh, I don't know. We're just curious."

"That's funny," Martini said. "In provost school, they told us about girls like you."

"What's that supposed to mean?" Doris asked, her eyes squinting. "What about 'girls like us'?"

Hildy took a half step back from Martini and added, "Yes, please explain that."

"Look, I don't mean nothing by it. Sorry. It's just that we were told that some American girls, well, they get kind of fascinated by prisoners. At some camps, there's been a problem with them trying to sneak in. Hard to believe, huh?"

Doris couldn't believe it. Of all the … He thought they were some kind of freaks!

Hildy crossed her arms over her chest and glared at Martini. "I assure you, Private Martini, we're nothing like that. Like I said, we're just curious. And Doris, here, well, she'd—"

Just as Doris was about to interrupt, she caught sight of two men approaching the truck. One of them was tall and wore glasses. It was Henri.

She ran her hand through her hair, pulling it back from her face.

"Halt!" Martini said, puffing out his chest. "You two stop right there." He stepped forward, placing himself between the prisoners and the young women.

The men stopped. Doris felt Henri staring at her. Beside him stood a short, slight boy who looked too young to be a soldier. His eyes flitted back and forth between Hildy and the ground at his feet.

"What do you want?" Martini asked. "Um, vas, uh, vollen, uh..."

"*Was wollen Sie?*" Hildy said. Everyone looked at her. She turned to Martini. "I speak German."

Henri said something to her.

"He says they want to see the Indians," Hildy said to Martini. "There are some Indian migrants working over in the next field."

"So you speak German," Martini said. Doris could practically see the wheels turning in his head.

"Don't you?" Doris asked.

"Hey, think about it. How many German-speaking soldiers do you think the army has? And you might just guess that most of them are in Europe right now."

"Oh," Doris said.

"And there are hundreds of camps like ours," Martini

added. He turned back to Hildy. "Do you read and write German too?"

She nodded.

"How'd you like a job? At the camp, we hire civilians for office work. I know people, and I can get you in."

Hildy looked suspicious.

"I hear it pays something like two bucks an hour. That's got to be better than pulling corn."

Doris stepped close to Hildy. "Your daddy," Doris whispered.

Hildy's eyes blazed. "Yes. My father," she said. "Private Martini—Jimmy. That's a very interesting idea. I'll think about it."

Martini beamed. "Just go to the front gate on Monday and tell them Jimmy Martini sent you. I'll make sure they're expecting you."

Doris cleared her throat and looked over at Henri and his friend. It was obvious that the young boy wasn't following a thing they were saying. She wasn't so sure about Henri. His eyes sparkled with interest, and when he met her gaze, he winked.

If he spoke English, they could talk. She caught herself, remembering what Martini had said about girls who became fascinated with German prisoners. The thought repelled her. Besides, this Henri wasn't nearly as attractive as she remembered.

Martini was speaking again. "You know, I'm from New Jersey. I wouldn't mind meeting some real live redskins myself. Let's all take a little walk."

"Should you do be doin' that?" Doris said. "I mean, what about your other prisoners?"

"Don't you worry, doll. I've got everything under control." Martini picked up his rifle and gestured grandly that Hildy and Doris should go on ahead in front of him.

As Doris turned back toward the cornfield and the Indians, she noticed the young boy again. He stood rooted in place, still staring at Hildy. Smiling, Henri tugged at his elbow, and the boy stumbled forward.

"Mr. Demsky, I want to thank you for coming in on a Sunday afternoon," Captain Harris said. "I know it's not officially part of your job, but we're so short on translators."

Sam shrugged. "Happy to do it, Captain."

They stood in a large room in the camp HQ building, next to a table with three chairs. Sam guessed that during the formal inquiry, Harris and the other two officers would sit there, looking across a small, open space to the witness chair, and then out the back windows at a stand of pine trees. Those windows were closed, despite the ninety-degree heat, and two fans vainly attempted to move the muggy air around the room.

"You'll sit here," Harris said, indicating a chair at another table placed along one side wall. "Mrs. Lewis will record the minutes." He pointed to another chair at the same table. "In English, of course. Make sure that the witnesses understand everything that's said. It'll be clumsy, but it's important that we do this properly. "

"I understand. A man is dead, after all."

"Precisely."

Sam had worked at the camp for only a week, but he already felt comfortable, even productive. In his tiny office, he sweated over a lesson plan, trying to pull together the directives that had come from Washington and his own understanding of his new job. On his first day, Captain John Harris had stuck his head in, introduced himself, and asked if Sam had everything he needed. Harris was tall, with midwestern good looks and perfectly barbered sandy hair. Unlike the rest of the half-dozen other officers at the camp, he always wore a pistol in a sidearm holster.

Later, Sam had seen Harris walking across the parade ground and noticed that the man limped. Asking around, he found out that Harris had been wounded while serving with Patton in Sicily, and his leg still gave him considerable pain. While Sam assumed that he and Harris would probably never discuss their similar disabilities, he felt a kinship with him.

Mrs. Lewis, Captain Harris's fiftyish, heavyset civilian secretary entered the room. She looked at the closed windows and then glared at Captain Harris, who seemed to shrink slightly under her gaze.

"I'm sorry, Mrs. Lewis," he said. "This must be confidential, of course."

Saying nothing, the woman ponderously edged around the side table and dropped into her seat with a sigh, her cheeks glistening with sweat. She began to frenetically wave her hands in front of her face. Sam noticed that in addition to her pens and notebook, a small Bible lay on the table in front of her.

Sam sat down next to her, nodding in what he hoped would be interpreted as a friendly manner. Mrs. Lewis nodded back.

The room's only door was on the wall opposite Sam, and on each side of it were two more chairs. For the guards. Most of the witnesses would be prisoners.

When two more officers had entered the room and took their seats, Captain Harris stood in front of his chair and looked around. An unarmed enlisted man stepped through the door and then closed it. He didn't sit down.

"Ahem," Harris said. "We might as well get started. As you know, this is a Court of Inquiry into the death of prisoner Sergeant Albert Wilhelm Spinkel."

Harris talked for a minute, explaining that the result of the inquiry would be a report that would establish the cause of death. He said he'd not speculate on what might happen after the inquiry. Sam thought he was being careful not to prejudice the other court members about whether a crime had been committed.

"I will now administer the oath to the translator and recorder," Harris said. "Mr. Demsky, please raise your right hand, place your left hand on the Bible, and repeat after me."

Mrs. Lewis held the Bible for Sam.

He hesitated. While he understood that he had the right to request a civil oath, he didn't want to call attention to himself. As far as he could tell, no one in the camp knew he was half-Jewish. And he'd just as soon keep it that way, at least for now.

Sam raised one hand, placed his other lightly on the Bible, and repeated the oath. He held the Bible for Mrs. Lewis, and it was done. He'd have to tell his mother. She'd have a good laugh.

Captain Harris consulted a sheet of paper. "Corporal, bring in prisoner Edwin Horst," he said.

The corporal at the door opened it, stuck his head outside, said something, and a boy no older than fifteen or sixteen stepped into the room. A guard wearing a sidearm followed him. The corporal pointed at the witness chair, and the boy moved to stand in front of it, holding his GI cloth cap in his hands. He wore an American-style uniform with "PW" painted in yellow on the shirt and pant legs. The corporal and the guard sat in the chairs by the door.

"*Setzen Sie,*" Harris said to the boy, who obeyed and stared at the floor in front of his feet.

Sam realized that Harris must know some German. Mrs. Lewis cleared her throat and Sam said, "He said to sit down."

"Mr. Demsky," Harris said, "please address the entire court when you translate. Also, you need not say, 'he said.'"

"Yes, sir. I understand."

"The translator will swear the prisoner."

Mrs. Lewis slid a piece of paper over to Sam, and he saw that it contained, in German, an oath similar to the one they'd taken. The corporal came forward, picked up the Bible, and held it out to the boy. Sam read the oath.

The boy, Edwin, didn't respond. He kept his eyes on the floor.

"The prisoner will repeat the oath," Harris said.

Sam translated.

Edwin turned and looked over at him. His eyes were wide and glistening.

He's a scared kid, Sam thought, wishing he could say something reassuring. He looked at Harris and shrugged with his palms turned upward, trying to express his concern.

Harris nodded and said, "We'll go off the record for a couple of minutes."

Mrs. Lewis put down her pen.

"Mr. Demsky," Harris continued. "Perhaps you might have a word with the witness. Explain the situation. Try to reassure him."

Sam moved around the table, stood next to Edwin, and bent over, quietly introducing himself. When he put his hand on Edwin's shoulder, the boy recoiled, almost tumbling out of the chair.

"It's all right," Sam said in German, withdrawing his hand. "Look, you're safe here. Nobody is going to hurt you. I promise."

Edwin looked up at Sam. "You're wrong," he said.

"Who are you afraid of? I can talk to Captain Harris. I'm sure he can protect you."

"Tell him I'm not going to say anything. No matter what you do to me. I have that right."

Sam sighed, straightened up, and stepped away from Edwin. He felt Captain Harris's eyes on him, and he turned around to face the head table.

"He says he isn't going to say anything, no matter what. Says it's his right." Sam spoke softly so only the officers could hear. "Captain," he added, "he's just a kid, and he's scared to death."

"Oh, very well," Harris replied. Addressing the room at large, he said, "We're back on the record, and this prisoner is dismissed."

As Edwin stood, he looked at Sam and mumbled something. The guard at the door gestured, and Edwin left the room.

Sam wasn't sure what the boy had said. It sounded like the words "Heilige Geist," which literally translated into "Holy Ghost." What in the world did that mean?

The next witness was a slightly older private named Henri Gelbert, who took the oath and gave his name, rank, and serial number without hesitation. As he sat in the witness chair, looking around the room, his eyes passed over Mrs. Lewis with a flicker of interest, which immediately disappeared.

"Private Gelbert," Harris said in English, "please tell the court what happened on the morning of Friday, September 8, 1944." Sam translated.

"My friend Edwin Horst and I found Sergeant Spinkel in the shower building. He was hanged."

As Sam translated, he noted that Gelbert's grammar was excellent.

One of the other officers asked about the details of the scene, and it seemed to Sam that Henri answered forthrightly.

"Sergeant Spinkel carried a notebook," the officer said. "Do you know anything about it?"

"I have seen it."

"Did you see it on the day in question?"

"No."

The officer indicated with a wave of his hand that he was

finished. Harris looked at the third officer, who shook his head.

"Are you a Nazi?" Harris asked.

"No. I never joined the party."

"Can you tell us why your friend, Edwin Horst, would refuse to testify?"

The prisoner gave a little shrug. "Edwin is young. This war has been terrible for him. He is almost always afraid."

Harris nodded and wrote something.

It seemed to Sam that they were finished with this witness, and he wondered if they'd take a break. With the windows and door closed and with all the people in the room, the air was stifling, his shirt was soaked in sweat, and it stuck to his back. Mrs. Lewis panted and continued to fan her face with one hand, a sour smell wafting across the short space between them. On the other side of the room, the guard stood.

"One more thing, Private Gelbert," Harris said, looking up. "What does 'Heilige Geist' mean to you?"

Sam watched the witness with interest as he translated. Had Harris heard the boy say those words? No, he was certain that was impossible.

Henri swallowed. He shifted in his chair, clearly uncertain what to say.

"*Beantworten Sie die Frage*," Harris said, his eyes boring into the witness. Answer the question.

"Holy Ghost," Henri said. "Theology tells us that the Holy Ghost is not only a strength or an influence, but a person …"

Sam realized that this young man had some education.

"Yes, I understand that," Harris said. "Does it mean anything else to you?"

Sam saw a bead of sweat slide down Henri's cheek.

Henri shook his head. "No," he said.

"Okay," Harris said. "The witness is dismissed."

Henri looked relieved as he stood and walked toward the

door.

"Bring in Staff Sergeant Helmut Gott," Harris added.

The guard opened the door and spoke to someone outside. Another prisoner came in, bumping into Henri, who jumped back and apologized effusively. The new prisoner, a tanned and trim man with a barrel chest, gave Henri a tight smile. He patted Henri's arm reassuringly and then strode to the witness chair. Henri hurried from the room.

Sam forgot his discomfort with the heat. So this was Staff Sergeant Gott, the senior German prisoner and liaison. Mrs. Lewis, who seemed to know everything about everybody, had told Sam that Gott had been captured in North Africa two years ago when he was with Rommel's elite Afrika Korps. Unlike the two previous prisoners, he wore his German uniform, which was clean and pressed. Gott wasn't a big man, perhaps five foot eight, but he had a presence that Sam thought everyone in the room must feel. Sam noticed that the man was completely bald and wondered if he shaved his head every day.

"*Guten Nachmittag, Feldwebel Gott,*" Harris said.

Gott smiled affably and replied in heavily accented English, "Good afternoon, Captain Harris."

It took less than five minutes for Staff Sergeant Gott to give his testimony, all of it in fair English. He'd gone to the shower building shortly after the discovery of Spinkel's body and had nothing to add. When asked if he was a Nazi, he smiled broadly and confirmed that he'd joined the National Socialist Party in 1938. When asked about the words "Heilige Geist," Sam thought the man seemed genuinely puzzled. He said he was unaware of any meaning other than the obvious one.

Captain Harris dismissed the witness.

They did not take a break. Instead, two American guards testified briefly about what they'd found in the shower building, revealing no new information. The camp doctor testified just long enough to submit his written report confirming Spinkel had died of asphyxiation consistent with hanging. Finally, Captain Harris declared the inquiry closed.

A few minutes later, Sam and Harris stood outside the main door of the administration building, watching as a guard escorted the three prisoner witnesses back to the inner gate leading to the barracks.

"How about a drink?" Harris asked.

"Where?" Sam replied. "Nothing in town is open on Sunday."

Harris laughed and slapped his shoulder. "Follow me."

Edwin's mouth felt dry and gritty as he watched a dust devil drift across the assembly area where the Americans held the morning, noon, and evening head counts. A rifle-toting guard had escorted Gott, Henri, and Edwin from the headquarters building to the inner gate of the prisoner compound. Now, just inside, Edwin heard music. He knew that the Americans had a radio in the guard tower, fifteen feet above. This was amazing to him, this lack of discipline in the American army. Without saying a word, the three prisoners started toward the barracks, Gott striding purposely ahead, Edwin and Henri shuffling along behind.

As soon as the guard tower was out of earshot, Gott spun on his heel to face Edwin and Henri. "Attention!" he spat out.

Edwin pulled himself up straight and knew that Henri was doing the same next to him. Gott stood with his fists clenched and jammed onto his hips. He leaned in close, his face inches from Edwin's. Gott's eyes bored into him, and Edwin trembled. He felt a warm spot on his inner thigh and realized that a little urine had seeped into his pants.

"What did you tell them?" Gott asked.

"Nothing, Staff Sergeant," Edwin stammered.

"What do you mean, 'Nothing'?"

"I refused to say anything. I swear. I didn't say my name, and I didn't take their oath."

Gott looked surprised. Then he turned to Henri. "And you?"

"I hardly said anything, Staff Sergeant."

"Did you take the oath? Tell me the truth, because I can find out."

Out of the corner of his eye, Edwin saw Henri swallow.

"Yes, Staff Sergeant. And I answered some questions about how we found Sergeant Spinkel. I saw no harm in that."

"Did they ask about his notebook?"

It seemed to Edwin that Henri hesitated for short moment.

"Yes, Staff Sergeant, but I told them it wasn't there when we found him."

Gott stepped back and dropped his hands to his sides, unclenching his fists. He looked back and forth between them and then finally gave them a mirthless smile. "Perhaps no harm has been done," he said.

Edwin let himself breathe again.

"You boys must be careful with what you say to the Americans. They will ask you about your home, your family. They're just trying to get more information so their damned airplanes can bomb our cities, our Fatherland. There are traitors amongst us, so we must be vigilant. When we finally win this war, when the Führer's new weapons are unleashed, then the faithful will be rewarded. Do you understand?"

"Yes, Staff Sergeant!" Edwin and Henri answered together.

"Very well. Get some dinner." And without waiting for a reply, Gott walked away.

Henri turned to Edwin, concern on his face. "It's over," he said. He tentatively touched Edwin's arm and Edwin began to sob, his breath coming in jagged stabs, and his nose and eyes streaming. Henri attempted to slip his arm around Edwin's

shoulder, but Edwin pulled away and turned his back. They
stood near each other, at the center of the otherwise empty
assembly area, but Edwin felt completely alone, as though he
were lost in a dark wood.

Henri waited.

Finally, Edwin ran his sleeve across his face.

"Come on, let's get cleaned up," Henri said. "And then we
can eat! I wonder what we're having tonight?"

Edwin nodded numbly, and they headed toward their
barracks.

"You know," Henri said as they walked. "It's funny how
both the Americans and Gott are so interested in Spinkel's
notebook." Edwin thought Henri might say something more,
but the two walked in silence.

Inside, they moved down the center aisle, passing the
wooden bunk beds, ten to a side. Like the rest of the camp,
this building still smelled of newly cut pine. The barracks
sergeant enforced regular army discipline, so the floor was
well swept and the beds were made. Near the end of the aisle,
they stopped beside the bunk they shared—Henri sleeping on
top and Edwin on the bottom.

Edwin wanted to change his underwear, but he didn't want
Henri to guess the reason. He tried to think of a way to be
alone for a few minutes.

"So you didn't say a word to them?" Henri asked.

"Not really," Edwin said, shaking his head. "I only spoke
to the translator. His name was Sam something. He tried to
help, but I told him I wouldn't say anything to those
American officers."

"I thought it was better to go along with them," Henri said.
"Not make trouble. Maybe that was a mistake."

"I need to show you something." Edwin sat on his bunk
and pointed up to the underside of Henri's bed.

Henri leaned over, craning his neck around to see. Above

them, four wooden slats spanned the width of the bed and supported Henri's mattress springs.

"When I got back from church this morning, it was there."

Some letters had been scratched into one of the slats. Something sharp had been used, perhaps the tip of a knife.

Reden - sterben! HG

"Talk - die," Henri read. His face paled.

"Maybe it's all right," Edwin said. "You didn't really say anything, right?"

Henri slid down on the floor next to the bed, his eyes still staring at the letters. He shook his head. "Not really. But maybe they won't know that."

"*They*," Edwin repeated. "You mean the Heilige Geist? HG."

Henri nodded.

"What is it?" Edwin asked. "You never told me."

"I don't know much. My sergeant in France told me that in the old German army, sometimes the regular soldiers would take it on themselves to punish one of their own who'd done something wrong. Maybe he steals something or behaves in a way that brings shame to the unit. Then his comrades beat him. When asked who did it, the man will say it was the Heilige Geist."

"I think this was a warning for both of us," Edwin said, pointing at the slat again. "I should've told you."

"I was in the mess hall. You had no chance before we were called by the Americans." Henri smiled wanly. "This is a lesson for me. I should go to church with you instead!"

He got to his feet, lost in thought.

"You go ahead," Edwin said. "I'll see you at dinner."

Henri nodded, turned away. Then he paused and looked back to Edwin. "You know," he said softly. "HG might stand for something else."

"Like what?"

"Helmut Gott."

Sam felt a little self-conscious as he and Harris walked toward the American mess hall where Sam ate his lunches. They both limped, Harris worse than Sam, and he wondered if Harris was aware of this.

Harris seemed not to notice, and he led Sam around to the back of the building where there was a door that Sam hadn't noticed before. A neatly painted sign identified it as the "Officers Club."

"As a civilian employee, you're welcome any time," Harris said, holding the door open for Sam.

The room inside was surprisingly large. There were a half dozen card tables with chairs around an open area that looked like it might be used for dancing. A phonograph played *Ferry Boat Serenade* by the Andrews Sisters. Behind another card table holding glasses and bottles, stood a bored-looking enlisted man. Two young officers, whom Sam had seen around headquarters, played ping-pong and nodded at them as they walked past. An upright piano stood unused against one wall.

"We're going to have a dance this Saturday night," Harris said, "for all of the base personnel, including enlisted men and civilians. Why don't you come?"

Sam appreciated Harris's invitation. His few friends were overseas, and lately he'd been feeling lonely. "I just might do that," he said. "Do I need a date or can I come stag?"

"Up to you. So what'll you have? We've got gin, some decent scotch, and a couple kinds of beer."

Sam took a beer from the enlisted man; Harris had a scotch on the rocks. "Thank you, private," he said. "Put it on my tab."

Sam nodded his thanks.

More people were starting to come in, and Sam and Harris

moved away from the bar. They watched the ping-pong game.

"That Gott fellow is an interesting character," Sam said.

"He is. He's also very efficient. Takes his responsibility seriously and runs a tight ship." Harris took a sip and then added quietly, "Of course, he's a fucking Nazi."

"And proud of it," Sam added.

"I used to think they were all Nazis."

Sam shook his head. "A lot of people think that. They don't understand that the Nazis—the National Socialists—are a political party. Even in Germany today, not everybody joins."

Harris nodded. "In fact," he said, "I'd guess that fewer than ten percent of our prisoners are actually Nazi party members. But they're the hardliners, the true believers. Most of them, like Gott, were captured early in the war when Germany was still winning. They still think the Fatherland will triumph in the end."

Sam shook his head.

"I'm going to tell you something else," Harris continued. "But you've got to promise me you won't breathe a word of it, especially not to your newspaper friends. Okay?"

Sam agreed.

"The prisoners have a framed picture of Hitler that they hang up in their mess hall at night."

"Really?" Sam said. He stared at Harris. "And you allow it?"

Harris shrugged. "It's one of those things. It doesn't do any actual harm."

"Yes, but surely—"

"Look, don't worry about it," Harris said abruptly, an edge in his voice.

Sam caught himself. Remember, this is a military base. And John Harris, as friendly as he might be to a civilian, is in command.

"So Spinkel hanged himself," Sam said, "committed

suicide. No sign of foul play."

Harris nodded. "It won't be official until the board meets tomorrow, but I'm sure that'll be our conclusion. Do you disagree?"

"I guess not." Sam put his empty beer bottle on a nearby table. "A good thing, I suppose. Your relationship with Gott and the other prisoners might be strained, to say the least, if you had to try someone for murder."

Harris smiled broadly. "You got that right, Sam. Let me get you another beer."

Chapter Three

Doris sprawled across Hildy's bed and flipped through a new *Vogue* magazine. She'd first started reading about fashion when she was sixteen, and she couldn't remember a time when it wasn't overshadowed by the war. Everything seemed to be about "make do and mend" or about what women war workers like her were wearing. Every so often she saw mentions of chic, pre-war Paris fashions and wondered if the world would ever return to a time when American women again looked to Europe for the latest styles.

Hildy sat cross-legged next to her, unpicking an old wool sweater in her lap. Every few minutes, Doris put down the magazine and wound the unraveled yarn onto a growing ball. On Hildy's radio, Kay Kyser's band was playing, *Indian Summer*. The radio was tuned to a Canadian station in Windsor because, although it had more static than the Detroit stations, Hildy said she liked the music selection better.

"There's a story here," Doris said, "about sewing up a man's suit to make it a woman's suit."

"Uh huh ..."

"Your daddy got any?" Doris asked. "Maybe you could put together a nice outfit if you go to work at that camp."

Hildy looked up. "You think that Martini guy was on the level?"

"Kind of. I'm pretty sure he don't really have much pull. But I bet they do need lots of translators."

"Papa'd kill me."

Doris didn't reply. She turned the last page on the magazine and tossed it on the floor with the others she'd already finished. Since Hildy's room was on the second floor rather than the attic and it had two large windows, it was much cooler than her own. She looked around and yawned.

The far wall held three wide shelves. The bottom two were jammed with books, magazines, framed photographs, and knickknacks. The top shelf was completely empty.

"So why's that shelf empty?" Doris asked.

Hildy stopped working on the sweater and set it aside. "I'll tell you a secret," she said, leaning closer to Doris. "I used to have lots of dolls. Every year on my birthday, Papa got me a new dolly, and I loved them all."

Doris shrugged. "So?"

"Even when I was sixteen, I played with them. I took them down from that shelf and dressed and undressed them. I made them new clothes. I brushed their hair." Hildy looked down at her hands. "I even talked to them."

"Hildy," Doris replied, "I hope that's not the biggest secret you've got 'cause if it is, then your life is just too damn boring!" She gave a little laugh, but stopped when Hildy scowled.

"You got the second part of that right, anyway," Hildy said. "The boring part."

"Girls! Dinner is ready," Gertrud called from downstairs.

"Coming, Mutti," Hildy shouted in reply. They climbed off the bed and stood together in front of the big mirror over the dressing table. Hildy ran a brush through her hair and then offered it to Doris.

"So what happened to your dolls?" Doris asked as she tugged her wild red hair into place and watched Hildy in the mirror.

"I put them away in the attic the day after Pearl Harbor—the day Hans joined the army." Hildy glanced over at the empty shelf. "You know, maybe it's high time I did something more for the war effort. I'm going to give Mr. Lohmann a call after dinner and tell him I can't pick corn for him tomorrow."

"I saw the funniest thing at the plant a couple days ago," Doris said as she sprinkled salt on her mashed potatoes.

They sat at the dining room table as they had every evening for the past week. The conversation had become more relaxed since that first dinner on the day Doris had arrived.

"Y'all know how I'm a real 'Rosie the Riveter,'" she continued. "I take this aluminum rivet and push it into a hole so it'll hold the wing together. We put in thousands on every B-24."

"That's the 'Liberator' bomber," Karl said. "Four air-cooled radial engines, each with fourteen cylinders."

"That's right, Karl. I usually work on the cowlings, these big sheets around those engines. Well, the wings are so big enough another girl climbs inside. We call her 'the bucker' 'cause she holds the bucking bar up against the rivet. Then I —I'm the riveter, you see—I hammer it from the outside, and it makes a real strong joint."

"Women working in a factory ..." Mrs. Gruden said.

"Let the girl talk," Oskar said, waving his fork. He gave Doris a nod of encouragement.

"Anyways, the wings get real tight out at the tips so that normal people, even a small girl, can't fit. You know what Ford did? They hired midgets to work inside the wing tips!"

"No!" Oskar said.

"Uh-huh. During lunch, they all sit together at one table. It sorta looks like something out of *The Wizard of Oz*. And here's the best part. Ford has this real strict rule. We gotta punch our own timecards. If someone else punches your card, both of you can get fired. Well, on Friday I was in line to punch out and I see one of those midgets at the time card machine. He couldn't reach his card on the rack! Someone had to lift him up so he could get his card and punch it!"

Oskar threw back his head and laughed, and Hildy and Gertrud joined in. Doris grinned. Then she sensed that Karl, sitting across from her, wasn't laughing. Instead, he sat scowling into his plate.

"Did everybody laugh at him, at the midget?" Karl asked quietly.

"No," Doris replied. "I mean, not everyone."

"Did you laugh at him?"

Doris said nothing.

"Just because he's a midget," Karl said, looking directly at her, "that doesn't mean he doesn't have feelings."

"Oh, Karl, it's nothing," Gertrud said. "It's funny, that's all."

Oskar seemed to be pouting. Doris guessed he didn't like having his fun spoiled by someone, especially his son.

"Maybe you're right," Doris said. "I guess I just don't think about midgets like that. Maybe it wasn't such a nice story."

"Nonsense!" Oskar said. "Mrs. Gruden is correct. It's a funny story. And telling us about it did no harm to anyone."

"More *wurstsalat?*" Gertrud asked, pointing at the big serving bowl filled with cold knackwurst and sliced onions.

Doris gratefully helped herself. To her surprise, she found herself enjoying the traditional German dinners that Mrs. Gruden spent most of her afternoons preparing.

"Did I tell you, Karl," Doris said, "that we got anti-aircraft guns guarding the plant?"

"No. Really?" he said. He sat up straight and smiled

triumphantly at his sister. "You see, when I told you about aircraft carriers in Hudson Bay, that wasn't so dumb."

Oskar looked thoughtful "That's odd," he said. "It seems those guns and their crews would be better used near the coast, where—forgive me, Karl—there's a real threat. Tell me, Doris, are the crews from the army or local civil defense?"

Puzzled, Doris replied, "I don't know. I could ask, if you want."

"I'm just curious."

"Papa," Hildy said, "Doris found a magazine article today about how to convert a man's suit into a woman's suit. You know, to save material. Do you have an old one I could have? I was thinking that with me looking for a better job, it'd be good to have a suit."

Oskar shrugged.

"Oskar, that's a gute idea," Gertrud said. "You have two or three nice ones up in the attic."

"I suppose it would be all right," Oskar said, frowning.

"Your father is unhappy because he can't fit into those suits anymore," Gertrud said. "After dinner we'll go take a look." To Oskar she added, "Will you please give me the key?"

Key? Then Doris remembered. At the top of the narrow staircase that led to the third floor, there was a small landing outside her bedroom door. Across it was another door. One day, out of curiosity, she'd tried the knob and found it locked. She figured it must lead to the attic where Oskar Gruden's old suits and Hildy's dolls were stored.

"I'll do it myself," Oskar said to Hildy. "I'll unlock the attic for you."

The following Monday morning, Sam sat in his small, stifling office and read in German:

"What is the good of a free press so long as the

government is in possession of every printing establishment? What is the right of public meeting worth when every single meeting hall belongs to the government?"

Sam thought that this might be something he could use. His first class started the next day and he was still looking for material. He knew that the author, Eugen Richter, had written about freedom and democracy in Germany during the nineteenth century. On Sunday, Sam had used his faculty library privilege to check out Richter's book, *Sozialdemokratische Zukunftsbilder—Pictures of a Social Democratic Future*—from the University of Michigan Graduate Library. Now, as he held the fifty-year-old volume in his hands, a drop of sweat fell from the tip of his nose and landed on the page he was reading.

"Shit," he muttered. He grabbed for his handkerchief and then realized that the sweat had already soaked into the page, leaving a faint but still visible blotch. He set the book down on his desk and wiped his face with his handkerchief. The entire headquarters building was sweltering, and his office didn't have a window.

"Can I talk to you for a moment, Mr. Demsky?" Mrs. Lewis asked from the doorway. He'd left the door propped open, despite the noise and distractions from the outer office.

"Certainly, Mrs. Lewis. In fact, I wanted to ask whether you've had any luck in acquiring a fan for me." Sam wiped his brow again for effect.

"Am I correct in recalling that you have a car, and that you drive out from town every day?" Mrs. Lewis asked, ignoring his question. "And you drive alone?"

"Yes, ma'am."

Mrs. Lewis stepped into the office, squeezing her considerable bulk into the area between the desk and the door. A young woman with dark hair and bold eyes followed, and Sam recognized her immediately. He'd met her at old man

Gruden's house when he'd arranged for his new tires. He jumped to his feet, slamming his chair against the wall behind him.

"This is Miss Gruden," Mrs. Lewis said. "She'll be working with me as a translator and clerk here in the office."

"We've met," Sam said.

"Mr. Demsky," Hildy said, nodding.

"Miss Gruden will ride with you," Mrs. Lewis continued. Staring at him steadily, she added, "There's a war on, you know."

"Of course."

Mrs. Lewis edged toward the door. Hildy backed out to let her pass, and Mrs. Lewis bustled off without another word.

"Come in, please," Sam said. "I'm sorry that I don't have a chair for you."

Hildy stepped back into the office and stuck out her hand. It felt cool but surprisingly rough as Sam shook it.

"I'm sorry to cause you any trouble, Mr. Demsky," Hildy said. She seemed to be batting her eyelashes at him.

"Oh, it's no trouble." Sam felt flustered. "Please call me Sam."

Both still standing, they arranged the time and place where he'd pick her up each morning and drop her off each night. He was surprised when she requested a rendezvous that was some distance from her house, but he didn't ask why.

As Edwin had expected, the class was boring. The instructor stood facing them in front of a movable blackboard, on which he'd written his name, Sam Demsky, and the words *Deutsche Demokratie*. Edwin recognized this Demsky; he was the translator from the hearing. As he and Henri had heard nothing more about Spinkel's death, and there seemed to be no repercussions from Henri's talkativeness, they'd started to relax a little.

It'd been Henri's idea to attend this class. As there was no outside work today, Edwin reluctantly agreed. They'd helped to rearrange the mess hall furniture, stacking the tables on one side and moving the chairs into rows. Edwin wanted to stay in the back of the room, but Henri had insisted they sit up front. For the first few minutes of the class, a guard had stood by the door and watched, but then, obviously bored, he slipped away.

There were about twenty other prisoners in the room, and many of them seemed to be dozing. Henri listened carefully, occasionally writing something on a piece of paper. Demsky had placed a stack of scrap paper and some pencils on the table at the front of the room and invited the prisoners to take notes. Henri and another prisoner named Becker were the only ones doing so. Edwin had seen Becker around the camp. Blond and almost as tall as Henri, Becker reminded Edwin of his brother, Stefan.

Demsky held up a book and said, "Has anyone heard of Eugen Richter?"

No one responded.

"Do you know of this book, *Sozialdemokratische Zukunftsbilder*?"

Nothing.

"When it was first published in Berlin in 1891, it was a sensation. Two hundred and fifty thousand copies were printed and sold in Germany alone. It was translated into a dozen languages and sold all over the world. But none of you have read it. Or even heard of it. Or of Eugen Richter."

Demsky looked around the room. He pointed at Hubert. "You. You're from Berlin, right? Why do you think you've never read this book?"

Hubert stood up and said, "Because it has no pictures?"

Some of the men laughed.

Demsky rolled his eyes and shook his head. "Sit down,

son. The big fellow there. Gelbert, right?" He pointed at Henri. "Why do you think you've never heard of it?"

Henri stood. "Forgive me, Herr Professor, but you see, I have. My father had a copy, and he spoke of Eugen Richter."

"Ah! So why didn't you say anything when I asked?"

Henri shrugged.

"All right, that's fine," Demsky said. "Still, I ask you: why are this book and its author not known to most of the German people today?"

"Because the book is a prophecy, a prophecy that has come true," Henri replied.

Demsky raised his eyebrows. "Go on," he said.

"I've not read it. But my father told me that Richter predicted a new Germany where—"

There was a knock at the door, and a young woman stepped inside. Everyone sat up straight.

Edwin stared. It was her, the girl from the cornfield and the train station! How could she be here in the camp? He was sure that after their two brief encounters last week, he'd never see her again.

Henri leaned over and whispered, "The love of your life, she's come to fetch you."

Edwin scowled and jammed his elbow into Henri's side.

The girl said something in English to Demsky and handed him a note. As he read it, she gazed at him. When he finished, he replied to her in English, apparently thanking her. She left, and Edwin was sure he saw Demsky's hand lightly graze her elbow.

"Did you see that?" Edwin whispered. "He touched her!"

"Easy, my young friend," Henri replied. "I'm sorry, but she doesn't actually live in your little dream world. You can't blame her."

Edwin slouched in his chair and crossed his arms over his chest. "I don't blame her," he said. "I blame *him*."

Demsky resumed his lecture, but Edwin paid no attention. These classes were voluntary, after all. His mind returned to the girl. At Mr. Lohmann's farm, her jet-black hair had been pulled back, but today, it framed her face like a lion's mane. She wore a simple checked dress with a white collar, and Edwin had noticed that it buttoned up the front. He imagined his fingers slowly releasing each button as he kissed her neck . . .

"All right gentlemen, that'll be enough for today," Demsky said from the front of the room. "I hope to see you all next week."

"Let's go," Henri said as he stood up and stretched. "Before they ask us to help put the tables back."

Edwin stood, and they hurried toward the door.

"I'd like a word with you two," Demsky said, pointing at them. "And Corporal Becker, please."

Henri and Edwin stopped; Becker joined them.

"Gentlemen," Demsky said, "Captain Harris has given me permission to start a camp newspaper for the prisoners. Just a couple of mimeographed sheets every week—mainly sports scores, some news, maybe a short feature story." He turned to Henri and Becker. "I saw that you both took notes today."

Henri shrugged. "So?"

"So, how'd you three like to work on the newspaper?"

Edwin glanced at Henri.

"Would there be war news?" Henri asked.

"Yes, some."

"Even when it's not good for the Americans?"

"Yes."

"Ah, I see," Henri said. "This is your famous 'freedom of the press.'"

"That's right," Sam said, smiling. "You've uncovered my secret plan."

Henri laughed.

Demsky turned to Becker. "What do you think?"

"Herr Professor," Becker replied, "if you tell me to work on this newspaper, then that will be my duty."

"No, no," Demsky said. "This is voluntary. Really."

"In that case, I think I prefer to play soccer rather than write about it."

"I understand." Demsky looked at Edwin and said, "You're Edwin Horst, right? We talked at the inquiry."

Edwin nodded.

"What about you?"

Edwin looked at the floor and said nothing.

"My young friend here is shy," Henri said. "I think he wants to know if you are friendly with that young woman whom we just had the pleasure of observing."

"Fräulein Gruden?" Demsky looked surprised. "Why, we just met a few days ago. She works here at the camp now, and she just brought me a message from Captain Harris."

"So you see, Edwin," Henri said, "it's all right."

Edwin remained silent.

Becker suddenly grinned. "I have a question, Herr Professor. Will Miss Gruden be assisting you with the newspaper? Perhaps Edwin here would have a chance to work with her?"

"Why, yes," Demsky said. "I think she might be able to help out."

Edwin swallowed. "I'd like to write about soccer," he said.

Becker laughed and slapped him on the back. "When I score my first goal," he said, "I'll give you an interview."

The basement auditorium of the Ann Arbor Public Library was packed, and at the podium a woman in a wide-brimmed pink hat spoke to the attentive crowd. Sam sat next to his mother who, as a past president of the Ladies Library Association, felt obligated to attend their monthly open meetings. She'd seemed pleased when Sam offered to escort her this time.

"Captain Harris fought bravely in North Africa, and received a serious wound in Sicily while fighting under General George Patton," the woman at the podium continued. "After recovering from his injury, he could've left the army— he'd done his duty. But instead, he stayed on and is now the commanding officer of the Seventy-Third Military Escort Company and of Prisoner-of-War Branch Camp One-Forty-Seven, just north of town. So, ladies and gentlemen, please welcome Captain John Harris."

Sam joined the courteous applause. His mother sniffed and left her white-gloved hands in her lap. As they'd driven to the library, she'd complained that she thought Harris was responsible for the "propaganda" Sam was teaching. Sam couldn't convince her otherwise.

Sam leaned over and whispered, "Come on, Mom. I told you, he's a swell guy."

"Don't say 'swell,' Sam," she said. Then she clapped three times.

The current president of the association, a woman Sam only knew from his mother's caustic gossip, smiled graciously as Captain Harris shook her hand and then took his place behind the podium. He looked out over the audience, a sea of colorful hats with a few men scattered among them like weeds in a flower garden.

"Thank you, Mrs. Howard, for that very generous introduction." Harris turned and looked out over the audience. "I must tell all of you that when I was in Africa, it was the memory of you beautiful American girls that kept us going."

Sam smiled as the women around him tittered. He guessed that the average age of the women in the room must be over fifty. John Harris did make a striking figure. His uniform was perfectly tailored and pressed; his handsome face was both friendly and serious; he seemed to look everyone in the eye with concern and understanding.

"Yes," Harris continued, "I did decide to stay in the US Army, and I'd like to tell you why. You see, I believe that the work my men and I are doing at Camp One-Forty-Seven is of vital importance to the war effort ..."

Harris talked about how German prisoners of war were assisting the local economy, especially the corn harvest. He summarized the Geneva Convention and explained that it forbade the exhibition of prisoners. This meant that there would be no tours of the camp and no photographs of the prisoners for the newspapers. He spoke for about twenty minutes, describing life at the camp and his pride in the men of his command.

Watching Harris talk, Sam was surprised to feel his own sense of pride growing in his chest. He realized that for the first time he was really contributing to the war effort. And for the first time in his life, he was part of a team, a team led by this remarkable man, Captain John Harris.

Sam glanced over at his mother. Would she understand this? She was so hard to read at times. Her face was immobile as she watched Harris talk, but she did applaud without prompting as the speech ended.

"I'm told we have a few more minutes," Harris said. "I'm happy to take some questions."

The room was quiet for a moment. Then a woman near Sam stood up.

"Captain Harris, thank you for your very informative talk. I do have one question. I've heard that you pretty much let the prisoners run things, that you give them free rein. Is that correct?"

"No, ma'am," Harris said, his expression never faltering. "I think you'd find that our prisoners know who's in charge. However, there are two aspects to our policy that might give that impression. First, we use prisoner labor for everything that we possibly can. The prisoners cook; they maintain their barracks and the grounds; they're orderlies in the infirmary. Second, we give the senior noncommissioned officers broad responsibility for organizing the men and maintaining discipline. And these German sergeants are very good at this, I assure you. Please believe me when I say that this system works well. And, most importantly, every time a job is done by a prisoner, one more American soldier is freed up to *fight*."

There was scattered applause, and the woman sat down, smiling.

Another woman rose.

"But what about escape?" the woman asked. "I just can't sleep at night worrying that those awful men might get away and murder us in our beds."

Blanch stirred in her seat. "That Mildred Johnson is an idiot," she whispered to Sam.

"Madam," Harris said, "if there is nothing else I accomplish today, I hope that you'll be reassured and can sleep soundly tonight. You don't have to worry for three reasons. First, my men are highly trained, and we do three head counts every day. Nobody is going to escape. Second, most of our prisoners aren't monsters. They're just boys, far from home. I hope many of you can feel some sympathy for them. And finally, why would they want to escape? How could they possibly get back to Germany from here? I assure you, escape is the last thing they're thinking about."

Sam noticed that his mother nodded slightly. He smiled to himself.

A male voice called out from the back of the room, and everybody craned to see. A man stood up. He wore bib overalls; Sam guessed he was a farmer.

"I hear that those Nazi so-and-sos at your camp are eatin' meat every morning, noon, and night. In my family, we're lucky to have a bit of chicken for Sunday dinner. Sounds like some kind of Fritz Ritz you're runnin' out there."

The woman next to him—probably his wife—sat stone-faced. She reached up to tug at his overalls, but the man shook her off and continued standing.

"Sir, I'm afraid you've been misinformed," Harris said. "The Geneva Convention requires us to provide exactly the same diet for prisoners of war that we provide for our own troops." Harris looked around the room. "I'm guessing many of you here have sons serving in the military right now. I'll bet you get letters complaining of the lousy 'chow.' Am I right?"

A number of people nodded their heads.

"You can take it from me. Our prisoners get no better than your sons, I promise you that."

But the farmer didn't sit down. "Well, Cap'n," he continued, "I reckon that might be a good thing and all. But I still don't see why some foreign piece of paper should force us Americans to treat those … those …"

Sam smiled to himself. If that man was at a Grange meeting with his fellow farmers instead of a room full of his wife's friends, Sam was sure he'd have no trouble expressing himself.

"Let me put it another way," Captain Harris cut in. "We treat our prisoners properly, but not just because of the Geneva Convention or even because it's the Christian thing to do. There's another reason." Harris leaned forward over the podium and dropped his voice slightly, as though he were sharing a secret. "We know by reliable intelligence that our treatment of German prisoners has a direct impact on how our own captured boys are treated by the Germans."

Around the room, many heads nodded.

"From the president on down," Harris continued, "we want to do our best to protect our brave men who are imprisoned in

Germany so that when this war is over in a few more months, they'll come home to us safe and healthy."

Everyone in the room applauded, including the man in the overalls. Even Sam's mother clapped, whispering, "That man wants a political career after the war."

"We could do worse," Sam replied.

A few minutes later, as they sipped weak, sugarless tea, Harris approached them. Again, Sam noticed his limp.

"Sam!" he said. "I'm glad you came."

"Good evening, Captain. This is my mother, Blanch Demsky."

"And I thought she was your date! Mrs. Demsky, I'm very glad to meet you."

Blanch offered her hand, and Harris took it into both of his, bowing from the waist.

"Charmed to meet you, Captain."

Sam glanced at his mother and was surprised to see her blushing.

"Your boy," Harris said, "is doing a fine job for us out at the camp."

"Sam hasn't been a boy for some time now, I think."

"Of course. So what did you think of my little talk?"

"I would say that it was well received," Blanch said.

Harris glowed.

"I couldn't help but notice, Captain Harris," Blanch continued, "that you limp. I assume that's due to the wound you received in, what was it? Oh, Sicily, I believe. Does it cause you much pain?"

The smile on Harris's face hardened. He said nothing for a second and then replied evenly, "No, it's fine, Mrs. Demsky."

Sam spoke up, wanting to change the subject. "I want to thank you, Captain, for letting me start the prisoner newspaper."

Harris shrugged and turned to Blanch. "We're going to let

the prisoners run a little newspaper for themselves," he said. "Sort of an experiment in democracy."

"So I've heard."

"I've chosen two prisoners to work on it," Sam said.

He saw Harris's brow furrow slightly. "Have you informed them yet?"

"Yes, in my class this afternoon."

"Sam, I wish you'd checked with me first. This is one of those things that I like to ..." Harris caught himself. "Well, we can chat about it tomorrow."

"Sure. Sorry if it's a problem."

Harris turned back to Blanch. "Tell your son he needs to socialize with his coworkers." He winked at Sam. They said goodnight, and Harris moved away.

Later, as Sam drove them home in the DeSoto, Blanch said, "Your Captain Harris is an interesting man."

"That's what I told you."

They rode in silence.

"Mom," Sam said after a while, "I've been meaning to tell you something. I've only just figured it out myself. I want you to know why working at the camp is so important to me."

Sam sensed his mother turning to face him.

"Please tell me."

"I have this plan. It's kind of silly, I guess. I'm going to make friends with some of the prisoners. I want to get to know them. Then, at some time in the future, I'm going to tell them I'm Jewish."

"Well, you're not really," she said.

Sam knew almost nothing about Jewish law, but he did know that Jewishness was supposed to pass through the mother.

"Yeah, yeah, I know, but that's not the point. I want to see what happens when I tell them. See how much difference it makes. Maybe I can get some idea about why so many

Germans hate us."

She reached over, grabbed Sam's ear, and gave it a hard twist. "Sam, that's a really imbecilic idea. And it's dangerous."

"Ouch! Okay, Mom. I'll be careful, I promise."

"And remember, it's not just Jews," Blanch said. "And not just the Germans."

"I know."

Sam drove in silence, rubbing his ear.

"What was that bit about socializing with your coworkers?" she asked a few minutes later as they turned onto their street.

"I forgot to tell you. There's a dance at the camp this Saturday night."

"Really? In the camp with the prisoners? How odd."

Sam shrugged. "No prisoners will be there. Just the military people and the civilian staff."

"Are you going?"

"I've never been much of a dancer."

"But still, it'd do you good," Blanch said. "Have you thought about it?"

"As a matter of fact, I have."

"Good. What about taking a date? Do you know of anybody who might go?"

"Yes, I think maybe I do."

Doris stood in the dining room, her back to the table, staring at the Gruden family photographs filling the wall in front of her. Everyone else was out of the house—they'd all left together to visit friends half an hour before. For the first time since she arrived, Doris luxuriated in having the house all to herself. It wasn't the silence—the Gruden family wasn't a noisy bunch—but the idea that nobody was watching her gave her a sense of relief. Every night she had to choose: stay

in her stuffy, tiny room or go downstairs and be with the
family. This Saturday afternoon, for an hour or two, she was
free.

Her *Big Chief* writing tablet lay on the table behind her.
She'd almost finished another letter to Hans and would walk
it down to the post office later. Since she was sending it all
the way to New Guinea, it probably wasn't important to get it
in the mail today, but she really had nothing else to do.
Maybe tonight, while Hildy was cutting a rug at the dance,
she'd flip through the stack of *National Geographic*
magazines she'd seen in a back closet, looking for an article
about New Guinea. She hadn't received a reply from Hans
yet, and she was frankly running out of things to say in her
letters.

Her gaze wandered back to the pictures staring down at
her. That first night they'd given her the willies. Dead people,
she'd thought. Now, she realized that some of the photos
weren't so old. In a wedding picture, she recognized Oskar
and Gertrud. He had no mustache and more hair, of course,
but it was clearly him. He stood stiff and proud, and the
brightness in his eyes gave Doris the impression that he
wanted to grin but had been told by the photographer to look
serious. Beside him, the young and plain Gertrud had no
trouble keeping her face stern.

Next to the wedding picture was a casual family
photograph. Doris immediately picked out the young Oskar in
this picture too. He looked to be only about sixteen years old
and was kneeling in front of an adult couple that Doris
figured were his parents. Next to him knelt another boy,
perhaps a year or two older. Everyone was smiling broadly.

Leaning forward, Doris took a closer look at the teenage
Oskar Gruden. He was dressed in some kind of sports
uniform, a number on his shirt and his muscular legs made
visible by the skimpy shorts he wore. She smiled. He was

kinda cute.

Doris turned around and looked down at the letter she'd written to Hans. Of course! She hurried from the dining room, through the front hallway, and into the living room. There it was. She moved to the fireplace mantle and lifted the framed black and white photo of Hans Gruden. The boy stood stiffly in his army uniform, staring just to the side of the camera. He didn't look exactly like Oskar; his hair was different and he had his momma's flat nose. Then Doris grinned as she realized that he wore the same expression as his father in his wedding picture—Hans was forcing himself to be serious when his real nature was to laugh.

Doris sighed and put the picture back on the mantle. She wished it was hers, or that she had a copy. Maybe a smaller version that she could glance at when, one day, she would finally read a letter from him, all the way from New Guinea.

The house was so quiet. Like a cave. And in a rush, the memory of her time with William came flooding back to her.

He was her second cousin, and he lived with his momma on a farm a few miles on the other side of Brooksville. Last spring, William had taken her to explore a cave whose entrance was aon the farm property. Doris had been seventeen then, and William was just a few months shy of his eighteenth birthday. Wearing tore up old clothes and carrying a single flashlight, they'd shimmied through the tight entrance and clambered over a pile of broken rocks. They worked their way deeper into the cave, and it got colder and darker with each echoing step. William pointed out a single bat, asleep and hanging upside down from the ceiling like a hairy, dark pear. Then he turned off the flashlight. They stood without speaking. Doris's eyes tried to adjust, but they found no light at all. She was amazed that total darkness wasn't really black. Her eyes created shifting patterns of gray around her. "Hold your breath," William whispered, and they did. Silence was all around them. She felt her own heart beating, and she'd swear that she heard William's too. After a few more seconds they both took a breath, and she leaned forward. In the silence of the cave, their lips met.

Over the next three months, they slipped away whenever they could. William borrowed his brother's beat-up Model-A truck, and they headed into the mountains for a picnic, or went to a dance in a nearby town. They didn't say a word to anybody. Doris knew that their families wouldn't accept their love. In church, while the minister led them in the *Lord's Prayer*, she clasped her Bible to her chest, and said a prayer of her own: Dear God, please don't put me with child.

One night, after Doris had gone to bed, there was a pounding at the front door.

"Doris! Come out!"

It was William's voice. Doris grabbed her robe and ran to the front door, where she found her daddy glaring at William.

"Let him in, Daddy, please," Doris said. "He's kin."

Her daddy took a step back, and William pushed into the room.

"It came," he said to Doris, his eyes wide.

She knew what he meant. His draft notice. Its looming arrival had hung over them like a storm cloud, threatening their happiness whenever they tried to figure out what the future might bring.

"We got to get married," William said. He took a step toward Doris, but her daddy stood between them, his face red. He was fit to be tied. Without a word, he left the room, returning a moment later with his pheasant gun, jamming two shells into it. He pressed the barrel up under William's chin.

"Leave my house," he said.

William's eyes found Doris. He started to say something, but her daddy jammed the shotgun harder against his throat.

"Don't say anything to her, you son of a bitch or so help

me, I'll pull this trigger."

William backed away. When he reached the door and as her daddy lowered the shotgun, he turned and took off into the night. Doris felt her momma's arms around her, pulling her back, but she shook them off and dashed for the door. Her daddy blocked her way, but she saw William standing by the Model-A.

"Find a way and come to me!" he'd yelled. "We don't need them!" As her daddy raised the shotgun, William jumped into the truck and sped way.

But she hadn't gone to him. Doris told herself that she couldn't escape her watchful parents, but in her heart, she knew it was the habit of seventeen years of harsh dependency that kept her at home. She finished high school and turned eighteen. She heard that William had been sent to Europe for the invasion of France. She figured he was still there.

Doris looked at the picture of Hans again. Well, her daddy couldn't do anything now. If she wanted to write letters to Hans, wanted to go out on dates with him someday, then nobody could stop her. If only Hans wasn't on the other side of the world.

Maybe Hildy had it right. Tonight she was going to a dance with that nice Sam Demsky. Maybe Sam was 4-F and maybe he did walk funny, but at least he was here. He was also handsome—in his own dark way. And he had a car, a big beautiful car. Doris thought she might make a point of being in the living room when Sam came to pick up Hildy that evening. Maybe she'd put on a little lipstick and make sure her hair looked nice …

Doris caught herself. What was she thinking? Hildy was her friend. Instead, she'd go dig out those magazines when Sam came.

The mantle clock struck three o'clock. Hildy had said they probably wouldn't be back until four. Doris started for the dining room, figuring she might as well finish her letter and run it on down to the post office. But she stopped when she saw the open door to Oskar's study. She'd been in that room only once, on the day she arrived. Curious, she crossed the living room and took a peek inside.

The old desk sat in the middle of the room, covered with neat stacks of paper. In a corner, a small table held a chess set. The walls were lined with shelves, and they were filled with hundreds of books.

She stepped inside and looked at the books nearest the door. After all, Doris told herself, she needed something to read besides Hildy's magazines, didn't she? Most of the books had German titles. She edged around the room, scanning the books, but couldn't find anything that was in English and might be worth reading.

She stepped behind Oskar's desk. Without touching them, she glanced at some of the papers and saw that they were related to his store: sales tax forms, receipts, and the like. She saw a tattered brown book sitting on the corner of the desk and picked it up. The cover read: *DANTE — DIE GÖETTLICHE KOMÖEDIE.* She flipped through a few pages, not surprised that they were in German, and stopped as a picture caught her eye. It showed two robed men in a landscape filled with open tombs, and they just stood there, staring at a third man, lying in one of these tombs, smoke swirling up all around him. Beneath the picture was the single word "Holle," and Doris figured it must be the German word for hell. Least it looked like a picture of hell to her. Why was this book sitting here on his desk and not up on a shelf? Was Oskar in the middle of reading it? Or did he have some strange interest in hell?

Shrugging, Doris put the book back on the desk exactly as she'd found it. She noticed the top right-hand desk drawer wasn't completely closed, sticking out a half inch or so. Doris started to reach for the handle, but a shiver ran though her body, and she pulled her hand away.

This is wrong, she told herself. This is private. If he were to walk in now, I'd be in a whole lot of trouble.

She held her breath and listened. Silence. Like a cave. Reaching out again, Doris pulled the drawer open and almost laughed out loud. Inside she saw a stack of candy bars: two Hershey Bars, four Mars Bars, and a single Milky Way. So Oskar Gruden had a sweet tooth! Doris's mouth watered. If she took one, would he miss it? She lifted a Mars Bar, cradling it gently in her hand. Most candy was rationed, and it'd been months since she'd seen a candy bar. How did Oskar get them? Did Hans send them home like he did Hildy's Juicy Fruit?

There was something else in the drawer. When Doris leaned down to look, she saw a stack of gas ration coupons. She thought back to the night Sam Demsky had come to the house. He'd said something about automobile tires, but Oskar had hushed him right up. Tires, gasoline ration coupons, candy bars. Suddenly Doris understood. Oskar Gruden was dealing in the black market.

She wasn't sure how she felt about this. Part of her wondered if Oskar could get her some nylon stockings. Doris had noticed that Hildy seemed to have so many pairs. It was all against the law, of course. But if she reported Oskar, then she'd certainly have to find another place to live, and that was something she didn't want to do. Doris put the candy bar back in the drawer and decided she'd have to think on this some more.

She should leave. But she didn't move. Instead, she reached down and opened the second drawer. It contained stationery, stamps, and an old fountain pen. Doris closed it and reached for the bottom drawer. This was it, she told herself; she'd look this last drawer and then she'd get on out of there.

The drawer contained a stack of business envelopes, and there was something about them that caught Doris's eye. She lifted one and realized it was identical to the letter she'd seen a couple weeks before lying next to Oskar's dinner plate. She turned it over and found that it had a typewritten mailing address and, as she expected, it was addressed to Oskar Gruden. The return address, also typewritten, was somewhere in Mexico City and the stamp was Mexican. That sure is interesting, Doris thought. The envelope had been slit open, and she peeked inside. It contained another, smaller envelope. Strange. Then she saw its stamp. Her hand flew to her mouth, trying to muffle the cry of surprise that escaped her lips.

The stamp contained a profile portrait of Adolf Hitler, a small black swastika, and "Deutschland 1943."

Somebody in Germany was sending letters to Oskar Gruden and relaying them through Mexico. Doris reckoned that neither Oskar nor the sender wanted the United States Post Office to know anything about it.

She pulled out the letter. It was handwritten in German and went on for several pages. She flipped to the last page and saw it was signed with the single word, "Otto."

Her mind raced. What should she do? Should she tell somebody? The police? The FBI? She'd seen the posters at the plant, urging the workers to be on the lookout for suspicious behavior. This was much worse than dealing in the black market. But what if she was wrong? What if these are just friendly letters from a friend or some kin in Germany? Then Mr. Gruden would be in trouble, and she would be out of a place to live. If only she could read German …

Doris replaced the letter in its two envelopes and put it carefully back into the drawer just as she'd found it. She leaned over to close drawer, but then she noticed something shiny behind the envelopes. She reached into the drawer and pulled it out.

It was a large key.

Maybe this would unlock the door across from her bedroom, the one leading to the attic. And maybe it contained more than Hildy's dolls and Mr. Gruden's old suits. Her stomach tightened. She was alone in the house and might never get another chance.

Taking the key, Doris closed the bottom drawer and pulled the top one out just a bit.

A minute later, she stood on the small landing outside her bedroom. She slid the key into the keyhole of the attic door and turned it. There was a click, and the door pulled inward slightly as the lock released. When Doris turned the doorknob and pushed the door open, hot air blew out of the attic. She stepped inside.

The air smelled of mothballs, as she knew it would. At the far end, a small window, a duplicate of the one in her bedroom, brought bright afternoon sunlight into the otherwise dark space. Doris looked around and saw the inevitable cardboard boxes, luggage, and other odds and ends of a family's normal life. This is real stupid, she thought, and she started to turn toward the door.

Then she saw the dolls. There were some shelves next to the window; the brightness of the sunlight had made them hard to see. She stepped toward them, and the floorboard beneath her gave a loud squeak. Doris froze. Then, even though she knew the house was empty, she moved forward slowly, one step at a time, carefully transferring her weight from one foot to the next.

There were at least a dozen dolls of all different shapes and sizes. At one end of the shelf was a worn and patched Raggedy Ann, probably given to Hildy when she was just a baby. On the opposite end was lovely porcelain doll, wearing a stylish outfit and with luxurious black, brushable hair. Doris realized that, with the exception of the Raggedy Ann, all the dolls had black hair like Hildy's. She imagined Oskar Gruden at the local Kresge's Department Store, or perhaps leafing through a mail-order catalog, trying to find just the right birthday doll for his little girl.

Doris moved to the window and glanced out. She saw the front yard.

To the right of the window stood a scarred wardrobe cabinet. Doris tugged its worn handle and the door swung open easily. The camphor smell of mothballs wafted over her. Hanging on the crossbar inside were several men's suits. Doris remembered Gertrud's comment about Oskar not being able to wear them anymore. Thinking of the trim and athletic man in the dining room photo, she reached in and, with some difficulty, pushed two hangers apart so she could examine one of the suits.

Hanging from a hanger between the suits was a bright red and white piece of material. Doris figured it might be a scarf. She spread it out with her fingers to get a closer look, and her breath caught in her throat.

It was an armband with a black swastika against a white background.

The FBI, she thought. She had to report this. They must believe her! Angrily, she pushed the hanger and armband back into the wardrobe. So he was a Nazi after all.

Downstairs, the doorbell buzzed, and Doris jumped. Oh God, it's them! But why would they use the doorbell? She peeked out the window and, while she couldn't see the front door, she did see a bicycle parked on the front walk. Some kind of delivery?

The doorbell buzzed again.

Doris started to turn from the window, but as she did she caught sight of the Gruden sedan pulling into the driveway. They're back! She had to get downstairs and put the key in the desk!

As she started to turn, she noticed something strange. Instead of pulling into the garage, the car stopped at the head of the driveway, and the Gruden family poured out. Oskar, leaving the car door open, hurried across the lawn toward the front door with Karl, Hildy, and Gertrud following.

A teenage boy wearing a Western Union cap came into view and approached Oskar. A telegram, Doris realized. Then her breath caught. Oh, Lord! Something has happened to Hans.

She turned away from the window and, after hurriedly closing the wardrobe and locking the attic door, she raced down the two flights of stairs, clutching the key tightly. Doris's head was spinning. As she reached the hallway, the front door flew open and Oskar rushed in, his eyes wild, tears streaking down his cheeks. Seeing Doris, he waved the telegram, ran over, threw his arms around her, and whirled her around.

"Hans!" he said, his voice cracking. "Hans is coming home!"

Chapter Four

Edwin couldn't keep his eyes off the mess hall door, expecting to see Fräulein Gruden step through at any moment. He and Henri sat at one of the tables with Sam Demsky on the other side talking about the new camp newspaper. From the nearby kitchen, where the German cooks were preparing the evening meal, the pungent smell of sauerkraut floated in through the connecting door.

"And no more farm work for us, Herr Professor?" Henri asked.

"Please, I'm not a professor, not yet anyway," Sam replied. "Call me Sam. And yes, this is your assignment now. I hope you both enjoy the work. I think you need a change in your luck." He looked at Edwin as he said this. "And I hope we'll become friends."

"No more picking corn," Henri said. "That's a good way to become my friend, right, Edwin?"

They all laughed, even Edwin.

"Your German is very good," Henri said.

"Thank you," Sam replied. "My father was from Germany."

"What a coincidence!" Henri said. "Our fathers too!"

While Henri laughed, Edwin's happiness evaporated, and he stared down at a spot on the pine table in front of him. His own father had died six years before. Tuberculosis. He looked more closely at the dark circle. Someone had spilled soup here. He touched the spot with his finger, and it felt sticky.

"My father died eight years ago," Sam said. "He was sick for a year."

Edwin looked up, surprised, and saw that Sam was watching him. Edwin flushed and looked down again.

"All right," Sam said after a pause, "do either of you know what a mimeograph machine is?"

Edwin and Henri shook their heads.

Sam told them about the camp mimeograph machine and how they'd use a typewriter to make stencils. They could make about two hundred mimeograph copies from one stencil. Since Captain Harris had only allocated two stencils per week for the newspaper, it was critical that they be careful as they prepared them.

"Uh, Sam?" Edwin said, his voice just above a whisper. "Perhaps Fräulein Gruden could help us with the typing of these stencil things?"

"Why, yes. I've been thinking about that. Tell you what. You write up your stories, and we'll go over them, oh, let's say Thursday morning. I'll bring Fräulein Gruden along, and we can work out the details."

Thursday. Just three days away!

"Ah, Edwin," Henri said, "your dream has come true."

"Shut up!" Edwin glared at Henri.

"Sorry, sorry. Of course." Henri looked over at Sam and winked.

"Anyway," Sam said, "let's talk about assignments. Which of you would like to cover sports? I must tell you that Captain Harris believes the main purpose of our little project is to cover all the competitions that you prisoners have organized."

Edwin turned back to Sam. "I would like to report on the soccer games," he said. "Please."

Everyone in the camp was talking about soccer. The previous week, a representative from the YMCA had come to the camp and left German books, some musical instruments, and most importantly, three soccer balls. Corporal Becker, who was in their barracks and in Sam's class, was considered an excellent player.

Sam glanced at Henri, who shrugged, and then nodded. "As I understand it," Sam said, "there are a total of ten or fifteen teams already. Your first job is to find out the details: the names of the teams, the players, the game schedules. I understand that Sergeant Gott is an enthusiast; he can tell you about the league organization."

Edwin swallowed. *Gott!*

"I'll go with you to see him," Henri said quickly.

"Henri, you can cover the non-sports news." Sam reached into his briefcase and pulled out a stack of newspapers. "I know you don't read English, but you might get some use out of these. I'm afraid there aren't many German-language newspapers still being published in America."

Henri grabbed the newspapers and began to scan them. Then, seeming to catch himself, he looked up and glanced back and forth between Edwin and Sam.

"I've got a confession to make," he said. He turned to Edwin. "I've kept a little secret from you. I know some English. It was required at my school, and my father and I sometimes spoke it at home."

"That's excellent," Sam said. Then he added something that must have been in English because Edwin didn't understand.

"Why didn't you tell me?" Edwin asked.

"I'm sorry," Henri said.

Edwin wondered what other secrets Henri had.

"May I ask you a question, Herr Prof—, I mean, Sam?" Henri said. "About America?"

"Why, of course! That's why I'm here, after all." Sam looked a little flustered. "I mean, in addition to instructing you in German history."

"So," Henri said, "there are many Germans in American, am I correct?"

Sam nodded.

"Good. What's happened to them? Edwin's Fräulein Gruden is German, yes? We saw her working in a field like us. Does she live in a detention camp? And yet, we saw her at the train station. You understand my confusion, yes?"

Sam smiled broadly. "Sure. You are correct. There are many thousands of Americans who were born in Germany and many more whose parents were. I assure you, they aren't in any detention camps. Why, I happened to visit Fräulein Gruden's house." When Edwin jerked his head up, Sam added, "to see her father on some business. I think they have a traditional German home in some aspects and aren't restricted or oppressed in any way. And here's proof. We have an election for president coming up in November. German-Americans will be voting, just like everybody else."

"Even American Nazis?" Henri asked. Edwin held his breath. Why was Henri always asking the questions that could get them in trouble?

Sam looked confused.

"Back home," Henri continued, "the newsreels showed a powerful Nazi political movement in the United States. What happened to the American Nazis? Are they in prison?"

"Well, first of all," Sam said, "I don't think there were ever very many Nazis here. They made a few headlines before the war. I read that after Pearl Harbor, the biggest organization—the German American Bund—dissolved itself. That was smart of them. There wasn't much Nazi sympathy in this country before the war and now, well ..."

"You mean they're not in prison?" Henri asked.

"I doubt it. I guess this is a pretty good example of American democracy. Even in wartime, even when you espouse terrible beliefs, the United States defends your right to have and express those beliefs. Or, at least, you won't go to jail for them."

Henri looked skeptical. "And that's also true for the Italians?"

Sam nodded.

"And the Japanese?"

Sam started to say something, but stopped. He seemed to be at a loss for words. Henri, a grim, knowing look on his face, watched him.

"There's something I think we should put in the newspaper," Edwin said.

Sam turned to him.

"We should say something about Sergeant Spinkel."

"You know, I think you're right," Sam said. "We should report any deaths in the camp. Henri, you should write something."

Henri furrowed his brow. "Are you sure that's a good idea?"

Edwin thought of the bed slat with its warning message carved into it.

"But nothing about the way he died," Sam continued. "Just his name, his hometown, that sort of thing."

"Just a sentence or two," Henri said.

Sam nodded. "Is there anything else?"

"So we bring you our stories on Thursday," Henri said.

"And Fräulein Gruden will be there to help?" Edwin asked.

Sam and Henri grinned at each other.

"Yes," Sam said, "I think it's best if she makes the stencils this time, say on Thursday afternoon. You two can help her run the mimeograph machine on Friday and the paper can be distributed for the weekend." Sam grinned. "Pretty exciting, huh?"

Edwin nodded enthusiastically. He'd see her Friday too. This was good!

"And you'll get the official approval on Friday?" Henri asked, looking carefully at Sam.

"No, Henri. I won't," Sam replied. "We'll go to press without any official interference."

Henri shrugged. "You're making a point, of course. About your 'freedom of the press.' We will see."

Sam held the car door open for Hildy in the camp parking lot later that afternoon.

"Are you going to talk to me at all?" he asked. During the ride out to the camp in the early morning, she'd hardly said anything more than a formulaic, "I had a lovely time at the dance on Saturday."

She looked up at him through the car window, opened wide because of the heat, started to say something, and then stopped. Sam sighed, walked around the front of car, and climbed into the driver's seat. As he pushed the starter button, he felt Hildy's hand on his arm.

"I'm sorry," she said. "I've just had so much on my mind."

"Sure, that's okay." He put the car in gear, and they bumped over the rough parking lot toward the road. "Your brother is coming home after all. That's great. When does he get here?"

"He telegraphed from Honolulu. It'll probably be a week or two yet. Anyway, I'm afraid I wasn't much fun Saturday."

"Me neither, I suppose. I guess it was kind of a mistake." Sam held his breath.

"What? Asking me to go out was a mistake?"

"No, no. Sorry. I mean asking you to a dance—with this foot. Kind of stupid, now that I think about it."

"Don't be silly. I danced. Captain Harris was very gallant."

She pronounced it "gaul-*ont*."

It had been a difficult moment for Sam when John Harris asked Hildy to dance. For over twenty years, he'd dealt with being left out of baseball games, foot races, high school dances, and, of course, military service. He thought that it didn't bother him anymore. Then, as he and Hildy sat at a card table in the Officer's Club awkwardly trying to make conversation, Harris had approached. He knew Hildy, of course. And there was nothing wrong with him asking her to dance. In fact, it truly was "gaul-*ont*," as Hildy said. But still, Sam had gulped down his whiskey and then limped over to the bar for another.

"He's married, you know," Sam said.

"Really? That cad!"

He looked over at her and saw that the corners of her eyes were crinkled in amusement. Her lips pursed in an exaggerated pout, and Sam noticed that her lipstick seemed perfect and fresh, as if she'd applied it just before meeting him at the car.

"Anyway, Sam. Next time, take me to a movie, okay?"

Next time! Sam grinned. He felt the urge to take his hand off the gearshift lever and give hers a squeeze, but he resisted. "Yes, ma'am," he said. "I'll do that."

Ahead of them, a farm tractor pulling a wagonload of baled hay lumbered down the gravel road. Bits of straw and dust filled the air in front of them, and Sam eased up on the accelerator. Hildy rolled her window up, and he did the same as he edged the car to the left, trying to see past.

"Seems like we get behind this guy every night," Sam said.

Hildy peered at the farmer, who looked like he was at least seventy. "That's Mr. Hockem. He's one of Papa's best customers. Owns hundreds of acres, and he still drives his own tractor."

Sam gave a quick beep on the horn, tromped down on the

accelerator, and the big DeSoto leaped forward. Hildy quickly rolled down her window and waved as they went past. Mr. Hockem returned the wave.

"Ooooh," Hildy exclaimed, her eyes bright. "I just love your car!"

Sam smiled proudly. "Yeah, me too. Did I tell you that there were only five thousand of them made?"

"I do believe you mentioned it."

"My dad bought it back in '36. I'm afraid he never got a chance to drive it much."

"Why, what happened?"

"He got sick." Sam paused, wondering how much he wanted to tell her. He glanced over at her and saw she was watching him, waiting. "Throat cancer," he added.

"I'm so sorry," Hildy said.

Sam shrugged. "It was a long time ago. Eight years now. Still, I think about him every time I climb in."

Hildy reached over and put her hand on Sam's as it gripped the gearshift. Sam stomped down on the accelerator again and heard the engine roar, and felt its power vibrating up from the transmission, through the long, awkward shift lever, through the big wooden knob, and into his hand. Hildy clamped down hard, and he knew she felt the power of his car. He hoped she felt more than that.

They drove in silence for a while, Sam trying to focus on the road ahead, Hildy gazing out her window. Finally, as they approached the paved road leading south to town, Sam downshifted, and Hildy withdrew her hand. Sam peeked over at her and thought he saw a little smile of satisfaction.

"Uh ... ," he said, trying to think of something to say. "I was wondering why you still want me to drop you off down the street from your house. And why can't I mention the camp to your family? You obviously don't want your father to know we work together. But I've already met him—twice."

"Three times, if you count the fact that he was waiting up for me Saturday."

Sam rolled his eyes. "I don't think he likes me."

"No, it's okay. I know Papa. He's like that with all the boys I date."

All the boys? Well, he wasn't a fool. She must have been popular in high school. Sam remembered his own high school days, ten years earlier. None of the pretty girls wanted anything to do with him. He glanced at Hildy again. Don't screw this up.

"So why the secrecy about working at the camp?" Sam asked.

Hildy said nothing.

"I'm sorry," Sam said. "I guess it's none of my business."

"I told them I got a job working in an insurance office in Ypsilanti; I take the bus. You have to understand. Papa is just a little—well—sensitive. You know, about the war. And the idea of this camp, it really brings it home to him. You understand that, don't you?"

"Sure."

"We came to the States when I was four," Hildy said. "So I don't remember much about Germany; Hans was six and he remembers a lot more."

"Does that mean you're not a citizen?"

"Oh no, we all are. Papa, Mutti—I mean Mother—Karl, and Hans. We were all nationalized a couple years ago. Papa insisted. Lots of German-Americans did it then."

"Right after Pearl Harbor. To show your loyalty."

"Yes."

They drove over the Huron River, which marked the northern boundary of Ann Arbor.

"Karl probably doesn't remember much of Germany," Sam said.

"Yeah. He's the most Americanized of us all."

"He wasn't very friendly when I picked you up. I guess he doesn't think much of 4-Fs." Sam glanced over at Hildy, and she shrugged.

"Does he know? About you working at the camp?"

Hildy shook her head. "Nobody does. Except Doris."

"She seems nice." He'd only seen Doris for a minute when he'd come to the house Saturday night. They'd said hello, and she'd been friendly enough. It occurred to him that he could probably ask her out if he wanted. After all these years, suddenly there was an embarrassment of riches.

"She's a doll," Hildy said. "After growing up with two brothers, it's sure nice having another girl around, especially one my own age."

"I guess that would be true."

"Oh, Sam. Was it hard for you growing up, not having any brothers or sisters?"

"No, it was fine. More attention for me, I guess."

Sam stopped the car at their accustomed spot; Hildy's house was up the block and around the corner. He turned in his seat and faced her.

"A movie on Saturday night?" he asked.

"Sure. I'd love it."

"I'll probably have to spend another ten uncomfortable minutes with your father in the living room, right?"

Hildy laughed. "Part of the package, I'm afraid. Karl might be there too."

Sam reached over and touched the back of her hand. It was warm and dry. "Fair enough," he said. "But, Hildy, I don't want to lie to them about us working together."

She met his gaze. "I know," she said, turning over her hand and giving his a quick squeeze.

Edwin watched Hildy as she carefully wrapped the stencil around the drum of the mimeograph machine. When he and

Henri, escorted by an American guard, had come to the stifling back room of the HQ building, Hildy had been wearing what looked like a man's suit coat. Since the room was small, she convinced the guard to step outside and then took off the coat and carefully draped it over the back of a chair. As they all bent over the mimeograph, Edwin's head was just inches from hers. Hildy's white blouse was open at the collar, and he saw a sheen of perspiration at the base of her throat. He leaned farther forward, trying to peer into those dark and mysterious depths.

Hildy stood up straight, pulling back a black curl that had fallen in front of her eyes and tucking it behind her ear. "That should do it," she said. "You push down this clip so it holds the stencil tight. Make sure there's plenty of fluid in here." She pointed to a tank on the side of the machine, and added, "and stack the paper like this." She adjusted the sheets in the tray.

Edwin and Henri nodded gravely.

"The first few copies are a little scary," she continued. "If things aren't just right, the paper can jam, and you might tear the stencil. Who wants to take the first turn?"

"This calls for a big, strong man," Henri said as he grasped the hand crank. "Move aside, my little friend."

Edwin took a reluctant step back. When Hildy gave him a small smile, he edged a tiny bit closer to her, imagining that their elbows just might touch.

Henri turned the handle, and the first sheet of paper rolled out of the machine and landed in the tray.

Hildy looked at it and then examined the stencil. "Perfect," she said, handing the sheet to Edwin.

The page was slightly damp, and it was covered with crude blue print. Edwin examined it, skimming the short sports pieces he'd written. He grinned at Hildy.

Henri resumed cranking and more sheets began to pile up.

A smell filled the room—a scent that was unfamiliar to Edwin. He lifted the sheet to his nose. It was sweet and strong, reminding him of something medical and, at the same time, of home and his mother's kitchen.

"Don't you just love that smell?" Hildy asked. She plucked a single sheet out of the growing stack and held it to her nose. Her pretty eyes, twinkling at him above the top of the page, transfixed Edwin.

"What does it remind you of?" Edwin asked her, his voice halting.

"Hmmm, I'm not sure." She took another whiff and furrowed her brow. "There's an alcohol smell, of course. But there's something else, something really nice."

"Baking bread?" Edwin asked.

Henri laughed, but stopped when Hildy scowled at him as she put the page back on the stack. "Yes," she said, turning back to Edwin. "Something like that."

"How many copies have I made?" Henri asked.

There was a little glass window on the side of the mimeograph machine and behind it, numbers slowly rolled in and out of view. Edwin glanced at the numbers and said, "Forty-seven. Keep at it, Henri, only another hundred and fifty-three to go."

"This isn't so much fun, I think," Henri said as he cranked away. "So tell me, Fräulein Gruden, how's your red-headed friend?"

"Doris?" Hildy looked surprised. "Oh, that's right. You met her when we were harvesting corn."

"And at the train station when we first arrived," Henri said. "Who would've thought it, eh, Edwin? We come to America and, first thing, we meet two beautiful women and fall in love."

Edwin glared at Henri.

Hildy laughed. "Well, I hope you won't be crushed. I think

Doris has become impatient waiting for you and may have found someone else."

At first, Edwin was relieved they were talking about Henri and this Doris girl. Then he saw that the rotating drum in the machine had slowed, and Henri was staring fixedly at the wall in front of him.

"Only ninety-eight more pages," Edwin said. "Do you want me to take over?"

"No, of course not," Henri replied. With new determination, he put his full energy back into his task, and the pages began to spit out of the machine faster. Rivulets of sweat rolled down Henri's cheeks.

For a while, no one said anything. The only sounds were the steady click of the mimeograph and Henri's increasingly labored breathing. Edwin wanted to glance over at Hildy, but he was afraid. What if she looked at him at the same time; what if their eyes met? Being here with her was all he'd thought about for days. Lying in his bunk late at night, with Henri snoring above him, he remembered the times he'd seen her before, replaying them over and over in his head. It was a good thing Sam had explained that there wasn't anything between him and Hildy. Edwin had decided that he liked Sam, so it was a relief not to be mad at him. And harvesting corn out in that burning field was much less preferable to working on this little newspaper with this beautiful girl. He decided that he needed to say something.

"Uh, that Indian we saw," Edwin said. "He wasn't really red."

Hildy shrugged. "Yeah, that's right. More brown, I guess. His name was George. Henri, you had quite a conversation with him."

"Not really. He just told me where he was from. Some place called Pine Ridge in the state of South Dakoti."

"South Dakota," Hildy said.

"South Dakota," Henri repeated, nodding.

"Back home," Edwin said, "I have some books about Indians. Have you heard of Karl May?"

"Of course!" Hildy said. "Winnetou!"

"And Old Shatterhand," Henri added. "All German children read the books of Karl May. It's how we learn about America."

"My father used to read them to me when I was little," Hildy said. "And to my brothers. Karl ran around wearing a turkey feather, whooping and saying we had to call him Winnetou."

"I have a brother too," Edwin said. "Stefan."

Henri stopped turning the handle. Hildy started to say something but then was silent.

"He's in the army, on the Eastern Front," Edwin continued. "We haven't heard from him in almost two years."

"Oh, God. Two years? What about your mother and father?" Hildy asked. "Are they okay?"

"Papa died when I was nine. Tuberculosis."

"I'm sorry."

"Mother took good care of us," Edwin said. She seemed so strong then, he added to himself.

"And then the war came," Henri said.

"Yes. As soon as Stefan was eighteen, he enlisted." And his mother's strength seemed to drain out of her.

"My big brother Hans did the same," Hildy said.

"So we're much alike," Edwin said. He looked at Hildy's face and was surprised to see her eyes filling with tears.

"Oh, Edwin," she said. "I'm sorry. I feel guilty. My family, well, they're okay. And in a few days, we'll all be together again."

"That's not something to feel guilty about," Henri said. "Isn't that right, Edwin?"

"I think," Edwin said, his voice just above a whisper, "it

was very hard for my mother. And I didn't understand." When the letter had come saying he had been accepted into the army, he had been so excited. He and Axel were going to join together! How stupid he had been.

Edwin was surprised to feel Hildy's hand on his arm. He turned to look at her.

"You know," she said. "I think we've still got our old Karl May books. Would you like to borrow them?"

Surprised, Edwin nodded. "Yes, please."

"And do you have any books about the Indians of South Dakota?" Henri asked. "Someday, when the war is over, perhaps I will visit—"

Suddenly, the door swung open. Staff Sergeant Gott stood in the doorframe, his eyes hard and calculating as he surveyed the small room.

Edwin jumped away from Hildy and came to attention, as did Henri.

Behind Gott stood Sergeant Engels, one of Gott's henchman, his beady eyes darting from one person to the next. They settled on Hildy, and he leered. Edwin frequently saw Engels with Gott, and they made an interesting pair: Gott short and stocky, Engels tall and boney.

Gott stepped over to the mimeograph machine, grabbed a sheet from the stack and began to read. Engels pushed into the tiny room, and Edwin, Henri, and Hildy pressed back against the rear wall.

Edwin could hardly breathe. Out of the corner of his eye, he caught a glimpse of Hildy. She looked uncomfortable and confused, but she didn't seem to be afraid. Edwin steeled himself. Be strong and brave.

Gott turned to them and held up the sheet of paper. "You will not distribute this. I forbid it." He ripped the page in half. "Further, you will show me copies of all future editions and get my permission. Is that clear?"

Edwin and Henri answered together, "Yes, Staff Sergeant!"

"One day this war will be over," Gott continued. "We'll be back home in the Fatherland. What you do here will be remembered. You want your families to be proud of what you do here. You don't want them to suffer because of your actions now. Understand?"

"Yes, Staff Sergeant!"

Hildy stepped forward. "Look," she said, "I'm not sure who you are, but you shouldn't be threatening these boys like that."

Gott turned to her. "You are Fräulein Hildegard Gruden. You work for the camp administration, and you want to keep your job. I know these things. So don't interfere."

Hildy looked startled. "I'll go to Captain Harris," she said. Her lower lip trembled slightly.

"If you do that, Fräulein, then there may be consequences that you do not wish." Gott turned to Engels and pointed at the stack of completed pages in the mimeograph tray. Engels seized them, and then both men marched from the room without another word.

When Gott was out of earshot, Henri whispered, "It's that bit we wrote about Sergeant Spinkel."

Edwin felt his knees twitching. His breath stuttered. He turned to face the wall and rubbed his sleeve across his face.

"He's gone," Hildy said behind him. To Edwin's amazement, he felt her hand patting his shoulder. He clenched his teeth and squeezed his eyes shut, willing himself not to cry. Turning back to her, he nodded.

Henri said quietly, "The fools. They left the stencil."

Doris clutched the overhead strap, bumping into the woman next to her as the bus turned north on State Street. Even with the windows open, the bus was stifling, and the air was thick with the vinegary smell of fifty people who had worked hard all day. Thank goodness it was only a few more minutes to the bus station.

An hour earlier, she and her bucker Sylvia had just started work on their eighth B-24 of the day. They were riveting one of the big curved sheets that made up the engine cowling, and Sylvia was up inside the wing. As she did so often, Sylvia failed to hold her bar tight against sheet, and Doris punched through the thin aluminum, leaving an oversized hole. Doris swore and reached into her pocket for a jumbo rivet that she'd use to repair the damage. Without thinking, she stepped back and brushed her head against a grease-covered fuel line. Even though she wore her big blue bandana, the cosmoline got in her hair and smeared across her face. With the assembly line moving so fast, there'd been no time to clean herself up.

When the whistle finally blew, Doris had hurried toward the ladies locker room, hoping to beat the end-of-shift rush. Homer Jenkins, one of the few male riveters on her shift, fell into step beside her.

"Hi, Doris," he said. "Uh, can I talk to you?"

She'd started to put her hand to her face, trying to hide the grease smear, but decided it was hopeless. Besides, Homer saw plenty of women covered with grease every day. He was a pudgy man, about her height, with a receding hairline. As he had also come up from Kentucky, they occasionally chatted during breaks.

"I've got to catch my bus," Doris said.

"Sure, sure. This'll jus' take a second." Homer looked down at his feet. "Um, I was just wonderin'. Would you like to get something to eat sometime? Maybe see a movie?"

"Why, Homer, that's real sweet of you." Doris wasn't sure what else to say. Homer was at least thirty years old.

"It's okay if you don't want to. I understand."

She didn't say no. She'd put him off, saying she didn't have time to decide right then. Homer Jenkins, from

Owensboro, Kentucky, had seemed satisfied with that. Doris guessed it was a better answer than he'd expected.

During the slow drive along Route 12 from Willow Run, through Ypsilanti, and then pulling into downtown Ann Arbor, Doris had plenty of time to think. All she ever did was go to work and hang around the house with the Grudens. She had a hankering for some fun. When she saw Homer tomorrow, she'd tell him yes.

As the bus drove around behind the bus station and pulled into its parking space, Doris worked her way to the door and stepped off. What a relief! She set out in a fast loping walk, heading north on Main Street, her empty lunch pail swinging widely in time with her pace.

Five minutes later, she was on a quiet residential street, oak trees shading the late August sun, the light breeze wonderful against her forehead and cheeks. She'd walked along this street twice a day for the past four weeks. She knew which houses had dogs and whether they'd bark at her as she went past. She'd also memorized the locations of the service flags hanging in the front windows of seven houses on this street. Each flag had a white center and a broad red border. Five of them contained a single blue star, indicating a member of the family was in the service. Ten blocks ahead, the Grudens displayed theirs in the small window next to the front door.

Doris caught sight of one small house with weeds in its yard and old paint peeling from the eaves. Prominently displayed in a front window was a flag with two blue stars. As she did every day, Doris thought about her Aunt Jeanie and her two sons: Harold and William. Sweet William. Where was he now? She wondered if her aunt had put out a service flag with two stars and figured she probably had. She'd write another letter to Aunt Jeanie that night. Maybe she'd heard from William. And if she had, maybe she'd write back to Doris this time.

Two more houses and then there it was: the unremarkable home that filled Doris with dread. The house was similar to the Grudens, and in the window next to the front door hung a service flag with a single star, this one gold. As the war went on, more and more flags with gold stars appeared around town. At the dinner table, Mr. and Mrs. Gruden often discussed the deaths of people they knew. But they never said a word about the deaths of servicemen. When Doris passed this house, she couldn't help wondering if, one day, she would come to the Gruden house and find a gold star replacing the blue one.

Doris plodded ahead, her shoulders slumped and her feet burning after being on them all day. Some of the girls at the plant talked about going dancing after work, but Doris wasn't sure she believed them. She wondered what kind of dancer Homer was.

Finally, as she turned the corner onto the Gruden's street, she was surprised to see several cars parked in front of the house and people coming and going through the front door. She quickened her pace.

A well-dressed couple, who looked to be about the same age as Mr. and Mrs. Gruden, came out the front door as Doris hurried up the sidewalk. They saw her, frowned, and then the man turned and spoke to someone behind him. It took Doris a second to realize that he was speaking German. As she stepped aside on the porch and let the couple pass, Doris saw that the inside hallway was jammed with people, all talking in a babble of English and German. Many held drinks, and a cloud of cigarette smoke floated above them. Gertrud would have a fit. But Gertrud stood in the entry hall wearing a bright blue dress and waving at the people who had just left. Doris expected disapproval as Gertrud caught sight of her and took in her dirty and disheveled appearance. Then she smiled at Doris.

Confused, Doris pushed through the door, keeping her head down and her eyes focused on the stairway leading upstairs.

"Doris! Hey, look everyone, it's Doris!" Karl's voice rang out above the hubbub. He rushed in from the living room and stood before her, a broad grin on his face. "Come on," he said as he grabbed her hand and tried to pull her into the crowded room.

She held back. Her free hand tried to cover the grease mark on her face.

"What's wrong?" Karl said.

She pulled her hand free and lunged for the stairway, trying to get past some children who were sitting on the bottom step.

"So this must be Doris," said an unfamiliar voice.

She turned. She recognized Hans from his picture. He looked older; his face was deeply tanned, and his eyes were serious. Like Karl, he had his mother's blond hair. As he watched her, he leaned awkwardly against the living room doorway, his army dress uniform hanging loose on his wiry frame. He'd lost weight, she realized, thinking of the photograph on the mantle. But still, he was much the way she'd imagined. Her heart fluttered.

Hans stood up straight and stepped toward her, his hand outstretched. "I'm Hans Gruden," he said.

Doris pulled herself together. She drew her shoulders back, stepped forward, and replied, "Glad to meet you, Hans." She shook his hand. "Your family talks about you all the time," she added, wondering if her hand was dry and clean.

He grinned. "And they've been talking about you."

She wondered what that meant. And then she winced, realizing how she must look. After weeks of thinking about this guy, she finally meets him, and she looked like some dirty hobo. She looked around desperately, trying to figure out what to do, what to say. Karl stood next to Hans, watching; it was impossible to read his expression. Half a dozen other people, none of whom Doris knew, stood nearby, also watching.

"I look awful, I'm sure," Doris said, her hand again at her face. She needed to escape, but wasn't sure how she could leave.

Suddenly someone sidled up beside her. Hildy slipped her arm through Doris's and said, "We girls need to freshen up. We'll be back down in a bit." With that, she firmly pulled Doris around and shooed away the children blocking the staircase.

As they climbed the stairs, Doris heard Hans call out from below, "Hey, Rosie! You look just fine to me."

When Doris descended the staircase an hour later, the crowd had gone home, most likely to their own families and dinners. She'd taken a quick bath, washed her hair, and put on her nicest dress: the white cotton shirtwaist with a slightly revealing neckline. After peeking into the living room and finding it empty, she found the family seated in the dining room, waiting. As Doris entered, Gertrud disappeared into the kitchen, and the Gruden men—Oskar, Hans, and Karl—all stood. Unlike most evening meals, Oskar wore his suit coat. Hans, still in his uniform, stepped around the table and pulled out the chair next to Hildy.

"Miss Calloway," Hans said with a slight bow and a smile.

Doris realized that a sixth chair had been brought in, and she'd no longer be sitting in Hans's place.

"She says it's okay to call her Doris," Karl said.

"I said that to you, Karl," she replied as she sat. "Thank you, Sergeant Gruden."

Karl looked pleased, and Doris winked at him.

"Gertrud!" Oskar called out as Hans took his seat next to Hildy. Gertrud returned from the kitchen, wiping her hands on her apron. She stood next to Oskar and folded her hands against her chest.

"Lassen Sie uns beten ... ," Oskar began and he spoke for several minutes. Doris kept her head down, as she did at every evening meal, and waited. She reckoned she could probably learn German just listening to all these prayers. And that reminded her of the letters she'd found, written in German. She hadn't thought about them all day. Now, as she listened to Oskar pray, as she sat among his family, across the table from his handsome, maybe-hero son, it was hard to think of Oskar Gruden as a Nazi spy.

Finally, the prayer was finished.

"Amen," Doris said.

Oskar looked at her, his eyes intent, as though he were trying to read her mind. Then something seemed to click into place, and his face relaxed.

"My dear," he said as he lifted the napkin-lined basket in front of him, "would you like a roll?"

Mr. Gruden had always been courteous enough, but now he seemed to be making an extra effort. This was very confusing. But pleasant. Doris smiled at him as she took a roll and then passed the basket to Hans.

"So how much leave do you have?" she asked him.

"Four weeks," Hans replied. "It sure seems like a long time, but I hear it goes by pretty quick."

"That means you'll be here for my birthday!" Karl said. "That's swell!"

"Yep," Hans said. "And I've already got your present."

"Wow. I'll bet it's a Jap sword. Hey, did you kill a lot of Japs?" Karl asked. "Is that why they made you a sergeant?"

"Such talk!" Gertrud said as she returned with a steaming platter of potatoes and onions. "I won't have it at my table, Karl! Hans, you too."

Karl and Hans replied in unison, "Yes, Mutti." Karl made a

face.

"Later, Squirt," Hans said. "I don't want to talk about that now, anyway."

"Quite right," Oskar said.

Gertrud set another heaping plate on the table, wiped her brow with a lace handkerchief, and took her seat. "Maybe the war will be over in four weeks," she said. "*Gottwillen.*"

"Don't get your hopes up, Mutti," Hans said. "I'm afraid it could be a while, especially in the Pacific."

"Humph," Oskar said. "This damn war won't be over until that Roosenfeld in Washington puts the damn communists into power in the Fatherland."

Chapter Five

Doris stepped into the stifling kitchen and twirled around for Hildy and Gertrud. She wore her white blouse, the one with a little blue pinstripe, and her tight navy skirt. Her hair was pinned back in what she thought was a current style, and she wore the new lipstick that she and Hildy had picked out that afternoon.

"Whew, it's hot in here," she said.

"Doris, you look lovely!" Hildy said as she wiped her hands on a towel.

Gertrud took the towel from her, folded it carefully, and hung it next to the sink. Then she slowly turned to look, passing her eyes over Doris from head to toe. Gertrud's mouth twitched into a small smile, and the wrinkles at the corners of her eyes deepened.

"Yes," she said. "You look gute. Very nice for Hans."

Doris felt herself blush. She'd hardly spent a minute with Hans since he'd arrived two nights before. He'd been busy with his family and with the few of his friends who weren't away in the service. But tonight at dinner, he'd said that if she had no plans for that evening, maybe they could talk later.

"He's out back with Karl," Hildy said, gesturing toward the door leading to the backyard. "Go on."

Doris took a step toward the door, and then stopped. Biting

her lower lip, she touched her hair. She started to turn, thinking maybe she could find a mirror and check how she looked, just one more time.

Gertrud stepped close, and Doris felt a hand in the small of her back, firmly pushing her toward the door. Taking a breath, Doris opened the screen and went outside.

The back porch ran the full width of the Gruden house. On the far right end, a wooden swing hung empty and still. Half a dozen oak trees shaded the yard from the warm evening sun and, while there was no breeze, the air was cool compared to the kitchen and her room, two stories above. Off to the right was the garage, with Gertrud's rabbit hutches beneath its shady eaves.

Three wide steps led down to the yard, and the two Gruden brothers sat on the bottom step, hunched toward each other. Hans wore civilian clothes, as he had since the night of his homecoming.

"Geez, Hans," Karl said, "I don't get it."

Hans shrugged. "Sorry, kiddo, there just isn't that much to tell. I was on the beach most of the time. All of the action was inland, in the jungle."

"You never saw one Jap?" When Hans shrugged, Karl stood up. "Well, shoot," he said, giving a little kick against the wooden step. Then he looked up and saw Doris. "Gosh," he said, "you look swell!"

"I don't mean to interrupt you boys," Doris said.

Hans stood and looked at her, a shy smile creeping across his face.

He sure is handsome, Doris thought, his sandy hair contrasting with his glowering dark eyes.

"It's okay. I guess," Karl said. Then, as he looked back and forth between Hans and Doris, the life seemed to drain out of him. "But you did bring me a Jap souvenir, right?" he asked, his voice slightly plaintive.

"Sure, I did," Hans said quickly. "For your birthday. Um, tell you what. Let's skip church tomorrow and go fishing."

Karl brightened. "That'd be super. But what about Mutti? She'll have our hides."

"I'll take care of her. I'll wake you up early, and we'll go down to our spot on the Huron."

"Okay," Karl said as he climbed the steps, heading for the kitchen. Doris noticed he kept his distance, cutting a wide circle around her. The screen door slammed as he went inside.

Doris wasn't sure what she should do, and Hans said nothing. He gazed up at her, but she had no idea what he was thinking.

"Would you like to sit on the swing?" she asked.

Hans shrugged, climbed the stairs, and escorted her down the length of the porch. They sat with a couple feet of empty swing between them.

"I wrote you some letters," Doris said. "Did you get 'em?"

"No, sorry. Not yet."

They said nothing for a moment.

"You know," Hans said, "That …" He gestured toward a nearby window. "That's my father's study."

"Well, I reckon we'll just have to keep our conversation decent." Doris thought she saw a hint of a smile.

"Easier for you than me, I'll bet," he said. "I've mainly been with a bunch of GIs for a long time now. The language …"

"You'd be surprised. It gets pretty blue at the plant sometimes."

"I think it's great, you working at Willow Run, building those planes. I've seen them flying over …" He paused. "Anyway, I think it's great."

"Thanks. When I go back to work on Monday, I'll tell people you said that."

Hans twisted himself around so he was facing her, and he

draped his arm over the back of the swing. He watched her face but said nothing.

"I read," Doris said finally, "that New Guinea is the second largest island in the world. Ain't that interesting?"

"I suppose so," Hans replied. "What's the largest?"

"Oh. I don't know."

Again there was silence. Eventually, Hans seemed to decide it was his turn to say something. "Karl has a crush on you," he told her.

"I know. I ain't really sure what to do. He's really a sweet boy."

"Maybe a little intense sometimes," Hans said.

Doris shrugged. "What he needs is a girlfriend his own age."

"Amen to that."

"So what happens when he turns eighteen?" Doris asked.

"You mean with the draft?"

"He thinks he's going to enlist."

"In the air corps," Hans said. "I tried to talk to Papa about it, but all he'll say is that it's taken care of."

"What does that mean?"

"I don't know," he said, shifting in his seat.

Doris wanted to ask him more, but decided not to push him. "So what happens next with you? After your leave is over."

"They're sending me to Europe."

That made sense to Doris. With the Allies getting close to Germany, there must be a huge need for German-speaking American soldiers.

"It used to piss me off, you know," Hans said. "Oops, sorry."

They glanced at the study window, and smiled at each other.

"Anyway," Hans continued, "when the war started, they

sent guys like me to the Pacific. Somebody thought we couldn't be trusted to fight in Africa or Sicily. Now, all of the sudden, they figure we're okay."

"Are you?"

"What do you mean?" He looked at her.

"You were born in Germany, right?" Doris said. "Hildy says you came here in 1929, when she was four. That'd make you six or seven then. You must have some feelings about going back to Germany to fight."

Hans turned and looked out over the yard. "You know," he said, "I got a lot of crap during training about being a Kraut or a Nazi—or worse. Even when I joined my unit, they gave me plenty of flak." He glanced at her. "I didn't let it bother me, though."

"That's good."

He shrugged. "It's funny, everything got better when I made just one little change."

"What?"

"I told everybody to call me 'Hank' instead of 'Hans.' It was smooth sailing after that."

At the other end of the porch, the screen door opened, and Gertrud stepped outside. Keeping her eyes fixed in front of her, she went down the steps and across the lawn toward the rabbit hutches. She carried a metal pail; a wooden handle stuck out of its top and rattled against the rim as she walked.

"Doris," Hans said. He glanced over at his mother and then back at her. "Look, I'm sort of out of practice at this." He stood up, his back to the rabbit hutches. "Want to go see a movie or something?"

"Why, sure!"

"Okay. Let's get out of here right now. Before …" He grabbed Doris's hand and pulled her to her feet.

Inside the house, through the study window, they heard Oskar bellowing, "Karl! Come here!"

"I need to get my purse," Doris said, and they hurried to the back door and through the house to the front hallway. Oskar and Karl stood in the middle of the living room.

"No!" Karl said. "I didn't take them, I swear."

Oskar glanced over at Doris and Hans, and then back to Karl.

"Let's go," Hans said, and Doris picked up her purse from the hall table. As they turned toward the front door, Hildy clomped down the main stairway, her saddle shoes echoing throughout the house. She clutched three slim books tight to her chest. Doris thought she looked both determined and afraid. Hans opened the door, but Doris stopped and watched as Hildy strode into the living room and stood in front of her father.

"Don't blame Karl, Papa. Here." She handed the books to Oskar. "I should've asked."

"You see," Karl said. "I told you."

Oskar glanced down at the books, and then glared at Hildy. "Why?" he asked.

She took a breath. "I met this young German boy. He's only fifteen, and he's very sad. We were talking—"

"Hildegard Beatrice Gruden, where did you met this German boy?" Oskar interrupted, his voice cold.

"At the POW camp. I, well … I started working there last week. They need civilians who speak German. I—"

Doris sensed Hans stiffening beside her.

"You lied to me!" Oskar said, his face turning dark. "You said—"

"I know. I'm sorry. Oh, Papa, please try to understand. I think I'm doing something good, useful. I can help these boys and still not be unpatriotic. You see?"

"Geez, Hildy. That's great!" Karl said. "Papa, she's helping the war effort."

Oskar ignored him.

"You should see them," Hildy continued, her voice pleading. "Most of them are so young. They're far from home. And they're German."

"So the books," Oskar said, "they're for this boy ..."

"His name is Edwin," Hildy said. "He's so scared. He misses his mother back home."

"And you say he's only fifteen?"

Hildy nodded.

The tension seemed to drain from Oskar's body. His shoulders slumped and his face softened. "Fifteen," he repeated.

"I'm sorry, Papa."

Oskar lifted one hand and waved it back and forth weakly. "These," he said, holding out the books, "they're not important. Give them to the boy."

Hildy took them, and then she stepped forward and kissed her father's cheek.

"But," Oskar continued, "you still have much to explain. Hildegard, you will sit down here, and you will tell me all about this camp."

Hans tugged at Doris's arm, and she turned to follow him out the front door. He said nothing as they went down the front walk, and at the street, they turned right, toward downtown Ann Arbor. A breath of air stirred beneath the old oaks, and Doris pulled it deep into her lungs, glad to be out of the house and walking beside this handsome, tall man.

"Did you know?" Hans asked suddenly, turning to her. "About Hildy working at that camp?"

"She's my friend. We talk about things."

He stared at her for a second, his eyes hard. Then his face relaxed, and he shook his head. "I never heard they had camps for prisoners here, back home."

"Hildy said there are hundreds of them all over the country."

"Really?" He shook his head again. "And this one's filled with Germans. Just Germans?"

"I think so."

"She ever say anything about POW camps for Japs?"

"No."

He didn't reply, and they walked in silence for a while. Doris figured it was a lot for him to take in. Imagine, coming back to a world so different, and yet so familiar. He must be all out of kilter. Maybe she could help.

Carefully, casually, she slipped her hand beneath his elbow. It startled him, but then he relaxed and squeezed it against his side. Doris felt hard ribs beneath his shirt and again wondered what the last three years had held for him.

"So," she said. "I have a question. Do I call you 'Hank' or 'Hans'?"

Without looking at her, he said, "Hans. That's my name."

Sam pushed the doorbell button and waited. Please let Hildy be ready on time, he said to himself. The movie started in a half hour, and as the evening was so pleasant, he planned to suggest that they walk downtown.

The door swung open and, as Sam expected, Mr. Gruden stood in the doorway.

"Good evening, sir," Sam said.

Mr. Gruden looked tired. He waved Sam in, closed the door, and walked into the living room. Sam followed, bracing himself for another uncomfortable conversation.

"Please sit," Mr. Gruden said, pointing to the couch. Grunting, he carefully lowered himself into the overstuffed chair across from Sam.

Sam sat down, wondering why Mr. Gruden had not shouted up the stairs to let Hildy know he'd arrived.

"Sam ... ," Mr. Gruden said.

This was the first time Hildy's father had used Sam's given

name. Previously it'd always been "Mr. Demsky."

"I'm afraid that Hildy isn't available this evening," Mr. Gruden continued.

"Is she okay? She's not sick, is she?"

Mr. Gruden shook his head. "It's a family matter. It's my decision."

Sam wondered what he was talking about? Had they found out he was half-Jewish? They were a German family, after all, and the man sitting across from him seemed so conservative. He was probably active in the local German-American community. How could he possibly approve of his daughter dating a man whose father was Jewish?

Mr. Gruden seemed to notice Sam's concern. He leaned forward and said, "It's nothing to do with you, Sam. At least not directly."

"That's good," Sam replied. "I guess."

"Perhaps I owe you a little more explanation." Mr. Gruden leaned back and rubbed his hands across his face. "You see, Hildy just told me that she's working at that prisoner-of-war camp."

"Oh."

"I know you work there too. You've never made any secret of that."

"I had nothing to do with her being hired," Sam said. "I was surprised when I saw her there. I swear."

"I believe you. She said the same thing."

"Thank God," Sam said.

Mr. Gruden nodded. "Now," he said, "I want you to tell me more about this place where you two work."

For the next few minutes, they talked about the camp. Sam emphasized that he saw no danger to Hildy, that the prisoners were well-behaved.

"She mentioned a young boy," Mr. Gruden said. "He's fifteen."

"Edwin."

"Yes."

"He's a sad case, I'm afraid," Sam said. "I suspect he's been badly treated." Sam paused and looked directly at Mr. Gruden. "Very badly, if you know what I mean."

"Oh. I understand."

"But he lights up so when he sees Hildy. He has a huge crush on her."

"Does he know that you're courting my daughter?"

Courting? The word caught Sam by surprise. But perhaps it was appropriate.

"No," he said. "There's no need for him to know."

"That's probably best. Believe it or not, I still remember what it's like to be young and infatuated." Mr. Gruden smiled.

"Is it okay, then?" Sam asked. "Can Hildy keep her job at the camp?"

"Yes, I will allow it," Mr. Gruden said. "I'll share with you a secret, Sam. It's probably a good thing that I give my permission. Hildy is a little headstrong, yes? Life will be more pleasant here if we're not fighting."

"Especially while Hans is home."

"Exactly."

"And," Sam said as he searched for the right words. "Hildy and I can continue to see each other?"

"Yes, but not tonight. Again, I apologize. While Hildy lives under my roof, she must respect my wishes. She lied to her mother and to me."

"I understand," Sam said. He shifted in his seat, thinking that he might as well go.

"Sam, I've meaning to ask you," Mr. Gruden said. "Do you play chess?"

"Not really. My father was an enthusiastic player and tried to teach me. Before he died. It never really took, I'm afraid. I think it was a disappointment for him."

Mr. Gruden didn't reply. He seemed to be staring over Sam's shoulder; the silence stretched out for a time. Sam felt his bad leg start to cramp. Self-consciously, he stretched it out in front of him.

"Being a father isn't easy, of course," Mr. Gruden said finally, rousing himself. "We have such hopes for our children, both our daughters and our sons." He focused on Sam again. "Mr. Sam Demsky, I'm sure your father was very proud of you."

"I guess he took it pretty well," Sam said as he steered the DeSoto into the camp parking lot the following Monday morning. He glanced over at Hildy.

"Yeah, I was a little surprised," Hildy said. "But he did grill me for ages about the camp."

"Me too."

"But he finally gave permission."

"And here we are." Sam stopped the car, switched off the ignition, and turned in his seat. "So I guess it's not a problem about us?"

"Relax, Sam. They like you." She grinned at him.

That did seem to be true. Sam wasn't so sure about Hildy's mother, but Mr. Gruden had seemed genuinely fond of him. After their conversation Saturday night, Mr. Gruden had walked him to the door and then warmly shook his hand. Of course, who knew if Mr. Gruden would feel the same if he found out Sam was half-Jewish.

Sam opened the car door.

"Wait a sec," Hildy said.

He slid back in behind the wheel and glanced at Hildy. He assumed she'd been touching up her makeup using the rearview mirror as she usually did when they arrived at the camp. He was surprised to find her facing him, without any lipstick.

"I like you better that way," he said.

"I know. And it makes it easier to do this." She grabbed his tie and tugged him toward her. For a second, Sam felt self-conscious, wondering if someone might see them. Then he lost track of time and place as he luxuriated in the softness of her lips and the touch of Hildy's tongue against his.

"I just wanted to give you something to think about during the day," Hildy said as they finally separated. She pulled the rearview mirror around and quickly began to apply lipstick, humming a bit as she did so.

A little stunned, Sam watched her. He couldn't believe it. She was beautiful and now, it seemed, she was his girl.

Hildy finished and cocked an eye at him. "How do I look?" she asked.

"Gorgeous. I'm afraid Mrs. Lewis won't approve."

"Good!"

Sam got out and hurried around to open the door for Hildy. As he did, he noticed Captain Harris getting out of his car nearby. As Harris lived in town, rather than at the camp, they often saw each other like this when they arrived each morning.

"Morning, Captain," Sam called out.

"Good morning."

Hildy got out of the car and stood next to Sam.

"Good morning, Hildy," Harris added.

Hildy nodded and smiled.

Sam thought he saw a funny expression pass over Harris's face. Had he seen us necking in the car? Sam wondered. Would he think there was anything wrong with that? Then the memory of Harris asking Hildy to dance on their first date came to his mind, but he dismissed it. Harris was married. And Hildy knew it. Sam told himself to relax.

Together, the three of them walked to the camp's main entrance.

Two guards snapped to attention as they approached, solely for Harris's benefit, Sam was sure. One of them swung open the wooden gate strung with barbed wire, and then both guards saluted. Captain Harris held back, gesturing that Hildy should go through before him.

"Oh, look," she said, "I want to talk to that soldier for a second." She approached one of the guards, and Sam waited for her. Harris continued on, heading for the headquarters building.

"You're Private Martini, aren't you?" Hildy said. "We met when I was working the corn harvest."

With Captain Harris out of sight, the man relaxed, leaning his rifle against the side of the guard shack. "Sure, I remember," he said. "How could I forget? My friends call me Jimmy."

Sam thought this Jimmy was leering at Hildy as he talked. Yes, he was sure.

"Well, Jimmy," Hildy continued, "I just wanted to thank you for helping me get this job."

Martini stepped closer to her. Reaching out, he took her hand and held it in his, all the while keeping his eyes fixed on her face. "Glad to do it. It was a pleasure, you know. Hey, how about you and I go into town sometime? I know how to show a gorgeous girl like you a good time." He continued to hold her hand.

Hildy glanced over her shoulder at Sam.

Sam wondered if she expected him to do something.

"There's this place called Bennie's," Martini continued. "Ya know it? We could have a few drinks and some laughs."

Sam cleared his throat. "Ah, Miss Gruden, I think we need to get to work."

"Hey, butt out, pal. The lady and I are talking."

"Yes, I know, but ..."

Hildy pulled her hand away and stepped back. "Thank you

for your invitation, Private Martini," she said. "But you see, I'm not available at the moment. Good day." She turned away and strode toward the headquarters building.

As Sam fell into step beside her, it felt like Jimmy Martini was staring at his back. He cringed as he heard the sound of a rifle being lifted and its bolt being opened and closed. The door was just ahead, and Sam wanted to dash the last few feet. Instead, he looked at Hildy. He couldn't read her face.

"Sorry," he said.

"Don't be silly. Men try to pick me up all the time," she replied, sounding smug. "I can handle them."

Sam believed her. But still, he should've done more.

Inside the headquarters building, they found Captain Harris in a heated conversation with several other officers.

"I want an explanation … now!" Harris shouted.

Mrs. Lewis hovered nearby, watching. When she saw Sam and Hildy, she hurried over to them. "A prisoner is missing," she whispered. "They discovered it during the morning count. It's our first escape!"

Sam felt a thrill. What a way to start the week. He glanced at Hildy, and she raised her eyebrows. She apparently thought the same thing.

"There's more," Mrs. Lewis continued. "Another prisoner was found—"

"Mrs. Lewis!" Captain Harris shouted, and she hastened to join him.

Hildy gave Sam a quick peck on the cheek, and as she did so, Mrs. Lewis glanced back at them and scowled. Hildy stepped behind her small desk, and Sam headed toward his office, feeling the disapproving eyes of Mrs. Lewis staring at him. It felt as if Private Martini was aiming a rifle at his back.

As he usually did, Sam took off his coat and hung it on a nail on the back of the door. Squeezing between the desk and the wall, he edged his way around to his chair.

A shabby boot stuck out from underneath the desk. Startled, Sam pulled away the chair and found Edwin Horst cowering on the floor. Edwin looked up; his face dirty and streaked with tears. He clutched a piece of paper.

"They killed Henri!" he said.

"What? No, that can't be right." Sam leaned down, trying to get his face close to Edwin's. "Come out of there, son."

"I found him in his bunk. His face was covered with blood. He wasn't breathing."

It seemed that Edwin wasn't going to move.

"I'll be right back, I promise," Sam said and then dashed out to the main office. After a quick conversation with Mrs. Lewis, he returned and bent down close to Edwin again.

"Henri is alive. They found him this morning in his bunk, like you said. He's been beaten, but he's not dead."

Edwin began to cry.

"Listen to me," Sam said. He started to put his hand on Edwin's shoulder but then stopped. "I think you came here, to my office, for a reason. Do you want me to help you?"

Edwin swallowed and stared up at Sam.

"It's going to be all right," Sam continued. "If you come out now, I'll take you to Captain Harris. He probably thinks you've escaped, and that'd look bad for him. He'd have to report it. As it is, this isn't so serious. There may be some kind of punishment, but I'll do what I can."

Edwin didn't move.

"I'll ask if we can go see Henri. Okay?" Sam said, reaching out his hand. "Come on, Edwin. Trust me." He grabbed Edwin's arm and pulled. To his relief, the boy didn't resist and allowed himself to be lifted to his feet.

"What's that?" Sam asked, pointing to the paper Edwin clutched.

The boy handed it to him.

Sam unfolded it. "It's our first edition," he said.

Edwin pointed to the bottom of the page.

Sam read aloud, "Sgt. Albert Wilhelm Spinkel, Third Panzer Division, of Elze, Leinebergland, died Saturday, August 19, 1944. Cause of death: unknown."

"They know Henri wrote it," Edwin said.

Edwin was back in the apple orchard. The wind rustled in the tree branches overhead, and from somewhere nearby he heard the rasp of the horses' heavy breathing and the shuffle of their ironclad hooves in the dirt.

Shivering, he pulled the blanket tight around his shoulders, and wished he had another. But in the middle of July, in France, who could guess that the nights would be chilly? Better that the blankets go to the Eastern Front, to the soldiers fighting the barbarian Russians and the Russian weather. Better they should go to his brother Stefan and his comrades.

Opening his eyes, he saw a yellow quarter-moon and countless colorless pinpricks scattered between the branches of the apple trees. He exhaled, and some of the stars dimmed as his breath swirled in front of his face.

For weeks, they'd been firing the Eighty-Eights, the big anti-aircraft guns, at the advancing American army, firing them like field artillery. Finally this afternoon, the battery had been ordered into reserve, bivouacking in the old apple orchard. As the gun crews unlimbered the horses, Edwin and Axel led them, one by one, to the picket line strung between the gnarled old trees. Axel checked their hooves for stones, while Edwin gave each horse a quick brushing. When it was too dark to see, they each gulped down an army Iron Ration, a small tin of beef and some hard bread. The sergeant came by with a jug he'd liberated from a nearby farmhouse and poured a splash of wine into their mess cups.

Edwin heard the familiar rumbling sound, like distant summer thunder, of enemy artillery on the far side of St. Ló.

No cause for concern, the sergeant had said. Not yet.

When Edwin and Axel were assigned to the 807th Anti-Aircraft Battery, they'd been amazed to find that the guns and caissons were pulled by draft horses. Despite the newsreels and magazine stories about the grand German army, they learned that only a small portion of the artillery was motorized. When they moved the battery to a new location, six horses pulled each gun and four pulled each caisson. And the men walked. The rumor was that only the SS units had trucks.

The horses of their battery were mainly old geldings and mares that had been confiscated from French and Belgian farms. To Edwin's surprise, he got on well with the horses. Axel was less happy; he was a city boy, he said, and he looked down on what he called "farm work." He always worried that one of the horses would step on his foot.

The distant guns rumbled again; they seemed to be getting closer. Edwin shifted his hips, trying to get comfortable. A rock pressed against his side. He forced his eyelids closed for a few seconds, but they popped open. Maybe it was the wine.

Overhead, the apple tree branches were still.

"Axel," Edwin whispered. "You awake?"

When there was no reply, Edwin rolled over and reached out his arm. Axel was gone.

Edwin awoke and found himself on a wooden folding chair next to Henri's hospital bed. There were eight beds in the prisoner's ward, and the other seven were empty. An American guard sat by the door leading to the hallway, his rifle leaning against the wall beside him and a paperback book open in his lap.

Henri groaned.

"Henri?" Edwin whispered. He stood up and leaned over the bed.

Opening his good right eye—the left one was swollen shut
—Henri peered up at Edwin. Henri's jaw was yellow and blue
beneath a one-day stubble.

Edwin picked up Henri's eyeglasses from the bedside table
and gently placed them on Henri's head.

"It's not so bad," Edwin said. "The doctor—"

"I know, he told me." Henri grimaced as he talked. "I'm
thirsty."

Edwin grabbed the water glass from the table and helped
Henri take a few painful sips.

"You want to know what happened," Henri said as he
leaned back. "Everybody wants to know what happened." He
started to chuckle. "Ouch," he said, rubbing his ribs.

"So?" Edwin whispered.

The guard at the door looked up for a second and then
returned to his book.

"What have you heard about the paper?" Henri asked. "Did
we have a successful first edition?"

Edwin smiled. "Oh, yes," he said. "The whole camp is
talking about it. Before I found … uh, before I found you,
everybody I saw wanted to know how often we'd publish.
Henri, it's wonderful."

"Did they like my news stories?"

"Yes. Of course."

"But they liked your sports stories better, right?"

Edwin didn't reply.

"That's all right."

There was a noise in the hallway, and the guard put down
his book and climbed to his feet. He sat down again when
Sam Demsky entered the room and hurried to Henri's bed.

"I'm fine," Henri said before Sam could speak. "The
doctor says I can go back to the barracks in a day or so."

"That's good," Sam replied. "I've been worried about you.
And we need to get back to work. Don't we, Edwin? We have

to get this week's edition out."

Edwin looked at Sam for a second and then nodded.

Sam turned back to Henri. "So," he said. "Who—"

"Who did this? Everybody wants to know."

Sam pulled out the crumpled copy of the paper Edwin had given him. He pointed to the brief statement about Sergeant Spinkel. "Edwin seems to think this might have something to do with it."

Henri glanced at the paper and then at Edwin. Before he could answer, the guard jumped to his feet, grabbed his rifle, and stood at attention.

Captain Harris and Staff Sergeant Gott entered the room. When Harris saw Sam and Edwin, he paused. He exchanged a brief look with Gott and then stepped briskly to the foot of Henri's bed.

Edwin stood at attention, and Henri seemed to lie more rigidly.

"Prisoner Gelbert," Harris said in passable German, "the doctor tells me you're well enough to talk. I want you to tell me who did this. That's an order."

Henri glanced around, first looking at Sam, then Edwin, and then at Gott. "I don't know, sir. I was sleeping in my bunk. Someone put a blanket or something over my head and started to hit me."

"Then who do you guess might've done it?" Harris continued.

Henri shrugged and then winced.

Edwin's mouth was dry, and he tried to swallow. He looked at Sam. "The newspaper ..." he said, his voice cracking.

Sam held up the paper.

"I think," Edwin continued, "Maybe—"

"Silence!" Gott said. "You will not speak unless you are asked a question." He paused for a moment, then turned to Harris. "But the boy may have a point. Perhaps these 'news' stories in Herr Demsky's little newspaper have enflamed the patriotic passions of some of the men. Certainly, the stories claiming Allied victories over the Fatherland can only cause trouble."

"But they're the truth," Sam said. Henri nodded in agreement.

"And how do we know that?" Gott put his hands on the railing at the foot of the bed. He leaned over and glared at Henri. "You have only what the Americans tell you, right?" Gott turned to Harris. "Captain, this so-called newspaper is a bad idea."

"Wait a minute!" Sam said urgently. He waved the crumpled paper under Gott's nose. "You don't like it because you know how popular it is, and you've got no control over it."

Gott stared at Sam, his fists clenching and unclenching at the metal bed railing, his face dark and menacing. Edwin felt his throat tighten; it was hard to breathe.

"Easy, Sam," Captain Harris said. "Don't make things worse."

Gott managed to get control of himself. He took his hands from the railing and flexed his fingers. His face relaxed. Turning to Captain Harris, he came to attention, saluted, and said, "Herr Captain, as the designated prisoner liaison, I officially request that you suspend the publication of the camp newspaper."

"Captain," Sam said, "please don't do this."

Harris hesitated.

"Besides," Gott added, "a prisoner newspaper needs prisoners to work on it." He glanced back and forth between Henri and Edwin. "Perhaps these men *now* better understand their duty."

Harris looked at Henri. "What do you think?" he asked. "Will you work on this newspaper if I agree to let it continue?"

"Yes, sir!" Henri said.

Harris turned to Edwin. "What about you?"

Edwin's mouth opened slightly, but he couldn't speak, his chest seemingly girded with iron bands. He felt Gott's cold eyes boring into him. He looked down, away from Gott, concentrating on the brown fabric of Henri's blanket. Henri's hand touched his, and Edwin looked at him. Slightly, almost imperceptibly, Henri shook his head.

Edwin guessed that Henri was telling him it was all right to back out, to be afraid of Gott. But Edwin didn't want to be afraid any more. Edwin looked across at Sam, who was watching expectantly.

"I like writing about soccer," Edwin said, his voice almost a whisper.

"All right then," Harris said. "I approve another edition of the camp newspaper."

Sam smiled, and the bands around Edwin's chest seemed to loosen.

"With one condition," Harris continued. "Mr. Demsky, you'll submit a complete draft to me prior to printing the copies. I want to look it over." He turned to Gott. "Will that be acceptable to you, Staff Sergeant?"

Gott's expression changed to a tight smile. "Yes, Herr Captain," he said. "That will be quite acceptable."

"John," Sam said, "this is censorship. What kind of message does this give to the prisoners? We're trying to teach them something about democracy."

"Mr. Demsky," Harris replied. "I remind you that this is a military base, and I am in command." He turned on his heel and walked from the room, the guard saluting stiffly. Gott quickly followed him, and Edwin thought that the guard was still saluting as Gott walked past.

Sam stood beside Henri's bed, his head down, and his

hands stuffed into his pockets.

"My dear professor," Henri said, "please don't be so sad. I will tell you the truth. This freedom of the press idea has always made me a little uneasy."

Doris came down the narrow stairs from her bedroom and paused on the second floor, glancing at her watch. Earlier, Gertrud had told her that Karl's birthday dinner would start promptly at six o'clock, so Doris had fifteen minutes to kill.

Hans's door was closed. The door to Hildy's bedroom, on the other side of the bathroom, was cracked open, so Doris crossed over to it.

"Hildy?" she said.

"Come in!"

Doris went in and saw Hildy sitting at her dressing table.

"You look nice," Hildy said, glancing over her shoulder. She turned back to the mirror and resumed brushing her hair. "Forty-five, forty-six," she whispered in time with her strokes. Doris remembered that Hildy always brushed exactly one hundred times, and as near as Doris could tell, she did it two or three times every day.

Doris glanced down at her white blouse and pale blue skirt. "I've plumb run out of clothes. Hans's already seen me in this, twice."

"Don't worry about it. I don't think men really care that much about what we wear. Fifty-four."

Doris pushed aside a stack of movie magazines and sat on Hildy's bed. "So Sam's coming to dinner," she said.

"He's so brave," Hildy said, looking at Doris in the mirror. "I hope everybody is nice to him, especially Karl."

"I remember my first dinner here."

"Gosh, so much has happened in a month. Who'd have guessed when we first met that we'd both have boyfriends now? Sixty-five."

"I ain't so sure. I don't think Hans is really …" So far, Hans had taken her out on two dates: last Saturday and then last night. Both times they went to the movies, and last night they'd hardly talked.

Hildy stopped brushing and turned around. "I wish you'd met Hans before he went away. Back in high school, he was so much fun. He was just the best big brother you could have." Hildy looked down at the brush in her lap, pulling hairs from it and winding them around her fingers. "He's different now. It's this damn war, of course. But he's still Hans; he still talks to me. And Doris, he likes you, okay?"

"That's real sweet of you to say."

"In fact, I'd have to say that all the men in this family are just about in love with you."

"What? How do you figure that?" asked Doris.

"There's Karl, of course. Han's is getting close, like I said. I think even Papa has a little crush on you."

Doris stared at Hildy, not knowing what to think.

"Of course, some day you'll be gone and things will go back to normal," Hildy said, turning back to the mirror and lifting the hairbrush.

"What do you mean—" Doris stopped as the doorbell rang downstairs.

"That's Sam. Doris, be a dear. Since you're ready, would you go down and keep him company? Tell him I'll be just a couple minutes."

"Uh, sure."

"Seventy-one, seventy-two …"

Doris stood behind her chair and looked around the dining room. It was crowded. Earlier that afternoon, she'd helped Gertrud add a leaf to the table and had dragged in the extra chair for Sam from the living room. On the big sideboard sat the Geburtstagorten cake. Hildy had explained that it had nineteen candles, one for each year of Karl's life and one more for luck. Gertrud had risen before sunrise to bake the cake, and she now stood gazing at the assembled family and Doris and Sam. Only Karl was missing.

"It's a real pretty cake, Mrs. Gruden," Doris said.

There were murmurs of agreement as everyone stood waiting.

"Make a wish, girl," Gertrud said. "The smoke will take it up to heaven."

"But it's not my birthday," Doris said.

Gertrud gave her a thin smile that made Doris feel like a slow child.

"It's a German tradition," Hildy said. "We all do it. Of course, Karl will still blow out the candles."

Doris nodded, dutifully closed her eyes, and wished that Hans would talk to her more.

When she opened her eyes, she watched the smoke rising from the thick candles to the ceiling, where it seemed to spread out like a sheer blanket. Doris looked across the table at Hans, trying to catch his eye, but his head was down. He seemed to be staring at his plate.

Karl stepped into the room. He was neatly dressed in a white shirt and gray pleated trousers, his hair neatly combed, but his face was dark.

"Here is our birthday boy!" Gertrud said. "Karl, tonight you sit by Papa."

As Karl edged his way past Hans, Doris could tell there was some sort of tension between them. Standing behind the chair at his father's right hand, Karl looked around defiantly.

At the head of the table, Oskar waited and, as usual, he was watching everyone. Doris was used to all this by now, but she wondered how Sam would bear up under the scrutiny.

"Sit," Gertrud said and everyone sat, except for her. Sam leaped back up and started to pull out her chair.

"I said, *sit*, Mr. Demsky," Gertrud said, waving him away.

"Sorry," he replied as he took his seat again. "Please, call me Sam."

"We shall see." Gertrud clasped her hands across her chest and waited, as Doris had seen her do many times before. Doris folded her own hands and lowered her head, still watching with almost closed eyelids.

"Lassen Sie uns beten … ," Oskar began.

Doris was used to Oskar's long dinner prayers. She recognized a few German words now and could guess at some of their meanings. As usual, she heard her own name, and he made mention of everyone in the family. There were other words that she thought might be names, but she wasn't sure. She was a bit surprised when Oskar said, "Sam Demsky," and Sam apparently was too, because he shifted a little in his chair.

Oskar finished, and Gertrud disappeared into the kitchen, reappearing a moment later with a steaming platter. Hasenpfeffer. Earlier that day, Doris had watched from her bedroom window as Gertrud walked across the backyard to the hutches that stood against the side of the garage. For the first time in a week, Doris had closed her window.

"That smells wonderful, Mrs. Gruden," Sam said. "What is it?"

"Rabbit," Karl said. "Cooked in *bacon*." He watched Sam carefully.

"Ah, hasenpfeffer," Sam said. "I haven't had it since I was in Cologne."

Karl hunched down in his chair.

"And does your mother make hasenpfeffer for you, Mr. Demsky?" Gertrud asked.

"Ah, sadly, no."

Gertrud made two more trips to the kitchen, bringing out a bowl of mashed potatoes and another filled with carrots and onions. "Eat, eat," she said as she took her seat.

There was no talking while they helped themselves and passed the food around. Doris stared directly at Hans. Finally, he looked up and gave her a grim little smile. He glanced around the table and rolled his eyes slightly, so only she could see.

Well, Doris thought, thank the Lord for that.

He must find this sort of family gathering tiring. She wondered why—what was going on with him anyway? Of course being back from the war was hard for him. Or was it something else, something about Karl? Oh, what the hell. Under the table she reached out with her foot until she felt her toe touch Hans's leg. She gave it a rub as she smiled coyly at him.

Next to her, Oskar suddenly jerked up in his chair. He stared at Doris, his eyes blinking rapidly behind his glasses.

Doris jerked her foot back. *Oh, God!* She felt her face grow hot.

Oskar continued to stare. Doris saw Hans looking at them both, trying to figure out what was going on.

"So, Mr. Gruden," Sam said from the other end of the table. "How's business?"

"What?" Oskar glanced back and forth between Doris and Hans. Finally, the crease between his eyebrows relaxed. With one last glance at Doris, he forced himself to smile and turned to address Sam. "Fine," he said. "Business is very good, in fact."

Doris closed her eyes and took a deep breath. How embarrassing. She wondered what Hans would think of this, afraid to look at him. Something touched her leg, and her eyes sprang open. Hans was watching her. He nodded slightly, and Doris felt his toe slide up and down her shin. Carefully, Doris slid her leg forward an inch, and Hans smiled.

"It's an odd thing, isn't it?" Sam said. "Here we're in the

middle of a war, business is good, and there's a shortage of so many things: tires, gasoline, meat—"

"Not in this house," Karl said.

"Thanks to your mother's ingenuity," Sam said, pointing at the platter of hasenpfeffer. There were nods of agreement around the table.

"Hans," Gertrud said. "Did you and Doris have a gute time last night?"

"Uh, sure," Hans replied. "We saw a swell Gene Autry picture."

Doris waited for him to say something more—something about her—but Hans didn't say another word. She turned to Karl and said, "Your brother ain't much of a talker, is he?"

"Shows what you know," Karl replied. "Back when he was in high school, we had loads of girls come to the house. Seems like he sure knew how to sweet-talk them. Right, Hildy?"

"He did have a few girlfriends," Hildy replied.

"Just can it, you two," Hans said. Hildy stuck out her tongue, and Karl snickered.

Doris noticed that Hans had pulled back his foot, and he was looking down at his plate again.

Later, after everyone had finished eating, Oskar looked down the table at Gertrud. She nodded to him, and he stood up. "Today, as you all know, is Karl's eighteenth birthday," he said.

Hildy clapped her hands and everyone joined in.

Oskar beamed. "Karl, please stand."

Karl reluctantly got to his feet.

Oskar began to sing, "*Hoch soll er leben ...*"

Doris didn't know the song, but everyone else, even Sam, joined in. She smiled at Karl, nodding her head in time with the singing, and was glad when it was over.

"Happy Birthday, Karl!" she said. The others shouted,

"*Alles Gute zum Geburtstag!*" as Karl blew out the candles.

"Speech! Speech!" Hildy cried.

The room became quiet, and Oskar sat down, smiling broadly.

"Thanks, I guess," Karl said, almost in a whisper.

"You can do better than that," Oskar said.

Karl stared straight ahead, at the pictures on the wall behind Doris. "I do have something to say," he said. "It's an announcement, I guess."

Oskar stopped smiling and looked at Gertrud. She shrugged.

"I've decided to join the Army Air Corps."

The room was silent for a moment. The candle smoke swirled above their heads.

"Oh, Karl," Hildy whispered.

Oskar stood up again, his face flushed. He leaned in close to Karl and said, "Have you signed the papers?"

"No. Tomorrow morning."

"You will not do this. I won't have it!" Oskar clenched and unclenched his hands at his sides. "It's, well, unnecessary. I've made arrangements."

"You can't stop me. I'm eighteen."

Oskar raised his right arm, his hand a tight fist. Karl tried to step back, but he bumped up against the sideboard.

"Stop him!" Hildy cried. "Hans, do something!"

"Don't, Papa," Hans said. He started to reach for his father's arm, but then held back.

Oskar leaned closer, and Karl cowered before him. Oskar grabbed the front of Karl's shirt and shook him. On the sideboard the figurines rattled, and one crashed to the floor.

"Oskar, no!" Gertrud shouted, her voice shrill and commanding. Everyone froze.

Oskar let go and staggered back a step, his face draining of color. Putting a shaking hand on the table to steady himself, he dropped into his chair.

"Look," Hildy said. "Maybe it won't matter. Everybody says the war is almost over. Isn't that right, Sam?"

"I don't know. Nobody really knows," Sam said, clearing his throat. "The papers do say that Germany is finished. They'll probably surrender by Christmas."

"What!" Oskar said. "You speak of the Fatherland like that? In my house!"

"Mr. Gruden, I'm sorry. It's just that—"

"Quiet, all of you!" Hans stood up. "Nobody here knows what they're talking about," he said. "Have you forgotten about the Japs?" He turned to his brother. "Karl, don't do it."

Keeping his distance from Oskar, Karl edged closer to the table. His hands grasped the back of his chair and looked at Hans. "But you said—"

"Listen," Hans said. "The Japs aren't finished. Nowhere near it. You still could get killed—"

"Nein!" Gertrud cried.

"—or wounded." Hans glanced down at the table, and then with what seemed like a force of will, he stared into his brother's eyes. "And sometimes," he said, "you do things that other people can never understand." His voice trailed away.

"You mean like my birthday present?" Karl asked, his voice bitter.

"Shut up!" Hans shouted at him. "Look, just don't do it. That's all."

Watching Hans, Hildy's face showed concern and confusion. Then she turned to Karl and said, "Listen to him. Please."

"Hildy, I thought you would understand," Karl said. "You too, Hans. We're grownups now. They can't tell us what to do."

"Papa," Hildy said, "what did you mean when you said you'd made arrangements? Karl, listen to Papa."

"You've got a friend on the draft board, right?" Karl said.

"It's best," Oskar replied.

"You think nobody will know? How much did you pay?"

"You will go to university next fall," Oskar said. "Until then, you work in the store. Just like we planned."

"You planned!" Karl yelled. He lifted the chair in front of him an inch and slammed it down. Glasses and silverware rattled. "Just like you planned for me to get a damned deferment, right? What is it? A 4-F?"

Oskar said nothing.

"Great. Great! You want me to be a, a fucking 4-F, right? Just like this guy." Karl pointed at Sam. "Just like this guy who's screwing Hildy!"

"No!" Hildy and Sam shouted together. Oskar stared at them, his mouth open.

Karl turned to Hildy. "You think nobody knows that you sneak out at night and don't come home until dawn. I know! I heard you twice."

"Karl!" Hildy said, her eyes wide. "That's not possible; it's not true."

"Leave us now, Karl," Gertrud said as she stood up. "You will go to your room and wait for your father."

Karl swallowed. "No, Mutti," he said with a shaky voice. "You can't make me to do that. Not anymore." He stumbled from the room, and Doris heard the front door slam.

"Come, Oskar," Gertrud said, and he followed her silently into the kitchen.

Doris glanced around the room, thinking that she needed to get out of there. Maybe she should go up to her bedroom and stay there until she figured out what to do. Maybe she needed to find another place to live.

She stood up. Hans also stood. He glanced at Hildy and then turned to Sam, his face rigid. "Is it true?" he asked.

"What?" Sam looked confused. "No! Of course it's not

true." He stared at Hildy, who wouldn't look back at him.

"Come on, Hans," Doris said. "Let's leave them be." She stepped around the table and tugged at his arm. Without a word, he followed her out into the front hall and across to the living room.

They sat on the couch, saying nothing. In the dining room, the voices of Sam and Hildy grew louder and increasingly angry. Hans got up and turned on the radio. As he fiddled with the dial, Doris heard the front door slam again, and Hildy ran up the staircase, sobbing.

Hans found the station he wanted and turned up the volume.

Chapter Six

Edwin stood next to the hospital bed and watched as Henri carefully swung out his long legs and tentatively touched them to the floor.

"You must be happy to get out of here," Edwin said. He wrinkled his nose at the smell of disinfectant and urine coming from a nearby bedpan. A gaunt prisoner coughed almost continuously just a few feet away.

"I suppose," Henri replied. Bending over and pulling on his cloth slippers, he asked, "Has anybody bothered you?"

"No. It's been all right."

Henri reached out his hand, and Edwin helped him to his feet.

"I suppose it's for the best," Henri said.

Edwin wondered what he meant as he picked up a bag containing Henri's few personal items.

"Where's our escort?" Henri asked, looking around.

"When I came over here, the guard at the inner gate said it was permissible to come without one."

Henri frowned.

"You're worried they'll attack you again?" Edwin asked.

"No, not really," Henri said. "They were just giving me a message." He smiled wryly at Edwin. "I hope it's very clear to them that this message has been received."

"Who was it? Don't you know?"

"Come on," Henri said, glancing at the man in the next bed.

At the door, the American guard scribbled a few words on a pass form and handed it to Henri. He barely glanced at Edwin's pass. They walked down the infirmary hallway, through the front door, and stepped outside onto the perimeter road that ran just inside the main fence. On the other side of the barbed wire, a dark oak wood stood only a hundred meters away.

"Ah," Henri said, taking a deep breath. "It *is* good to be out of that room."

The air was crisp and a light breeze swirled leaves around them. They both gazed at the nearby trees as they headed toward the barracks and the inner fence.

"If we could just get to those trees …" Henri said.

Edwin had heard some of the other prisoners half-heartedly talk about escape. He glanced at the woods. "Would you really go if you had the chance?" he asked.

"Of course."

"Why? So you can fight for the Fatherland again?"

A jeep came up behind them, and they stepped off the road to let it pass.

"No, because we're not safe here," Henri said.

"Who was it? You can tell me now."

Henri glanced around and whispered, "Remember the message carved into the bed slat after we testified about poor Sergeant Spinkel?"

"Of course," Edwin replied. They'd turned the slat over so Edwin didn't have to stare up at it from his bunk. "You think it was some men calling themselves the Heilige Geist like you told me about?"

"It makes sense."

"I bet Sergeant Gott knows something," Edwin said.

"Probably. Do you want to go ask him?"

Edwin shuddered at the thought and shook his head.

At the inner gate leading to the barracks, prisoners stood in line waiting to have their passes checked. When Henri showed no hesitation in joining the line, Edwin realized that he must feel safer with other prisoners around. The soldiers of the Heilige Geist had attacked Henri when he was in the barracks alone.

Edwin thought about the nearby woods. If he had to go through those trees in the dark, could he do it? Would it be safer if there were a full moon? If they somehow got through the barbed wire, maybe the Heilige Geist couldn't reach them, but then what would they do?

As he turned to ask Henri, he caught sight of two people walking toward the headquarters building. It was Sam and Hildy! They weren't far, and Edwin raised his hand and was about to shout hello when he noticed they were deep in conversation. Hildy moved one hand back and forth and poked the air in front of her as she walked. Sam kept his hands in his pockets and listened intently, occasionally nodding or shaking his head. His face was grim.

"Uh, oh," Henri said, next to Edwin. "That looks like trouble for our friend Sam."

Together they watched as Sam and Hildy stopped and faced each other. Edwin saw that Hildy was crying. Sam pulled out a handkerchief, and she took it. Sam's face softened. He touched her cheek and bent forward. He said something, and Hildy threw her arms around him.

"Ah," Henri said. "All is well."

"He told me there was nothing between them," Edwin said. "He lied!" His face was hot. He wanted to run over to and yank them apart. He hardly noticed Henri's hand on his shoulder.

Sam and Hildy pulled away from each other. Hildy stood

on her tiptoes and gave Sam a quick kiss on the cheek. Then they both seemed to become aware of their surroundings again and glanced about, looking embarrassed. They saw Edwin and Henri, and both waved as they resumed walking.

Henri waved back.

Edwin stared after them and whispered, "She kissed him."

"Yes, my young friend. She kissed him. What a terrible thing for a girl to do."

"Hey!" It was the guard at the gate. Edwin and Henri obediently stepped forward and held out their passes. Inside the gate, they crossed the wide assembly area toward the dozens of identical barracks. Edwin started to lead the way between two of them when he sensed that Henri wasn't following him. Turning, he saw Henri standing still, the sun of the open assembly area still on him while he peered into the relative darkness between the buildings.

"Come on," Edwin said. "There are plenty of people around."

Henri still hesitated.

Another prisoner came up behind Henri, also crossing from the gate. Henri jumped aside and seemed ready to run.

"Henri! Welcome back," Corporal Becker said. "How are you feeling?" He shook Henri's hand vigorously.

"Fine," Henri said, looking relieved and grimacing a little.

Becker clapped him on the back, and together they joined Edwin.

A minute later they were inside their barrack. Saying goodbye to Becker, Edwin and Henri continued down the central aisle. "Ah, home at last," Henri said as they stopped at the bunk they shared. Groaning, he folded his tall frame into Edwin's lower bed and sat, with Edwin standing beside him, silent, still gripping Henri's bag. Henri looked around, took a breath, and seemed to relax. "Put that down," he said pointing to the bag. "And sit."

Edwin did as he was told.

"Now listen," Henri continued, "I know Fräulein Gruden likes you very much. I saw it when we worked together on the newspaper."

Edwin looked at him with hope.

"But you do understand," Henri continued, "that she's at least three years older than you."

Edwin scowled. "But Sam is really old. He must be almost thirty. Hildy is closer to my age than his."

"That's true. But you're not a complete fool, right?" Henri said. "You must understand that you have no chance with this girl. She's American. You're a prisoner."

"You don't understand. None of that matters."

Henri gazed at Edwin for a moment. Then he reached out and patted Edwin's hand. "Of course. You are correct. In love, none of that matters. Please, when I try to give you advice about love, you must pay no attention."

When Edwin didn't answer, Henri sighed and stood up. Groaning, he climbed up to his own bunk. Then with a loud gasp, he immediately jumped back down, landing with a thump next to Edwin, his face pale.

"What's wrong?" Edwin asked. He stood up next to Henri.

Henri reached up and pulled back the coarse brown blanket from his bed. There, sitting against the white of the sheet underneath, was a pile of small, bloody bones.

Edwin stared at the bones. A smell, both acrid and sweet, rose from them. "What does it mean?" he asked, tasting something sour in the back of his throat.

"It's obvious. It means the Heilige Geist is not done with me."

Edwin looked at his friend, whose eyes were big with fear. Henri seemed to sway as he stood. "Sit down," Edwin said, pushing Henri back onto the lower bunk. Edwin sat beside him. "They're probably just chicken bones," he added, his voice shaky.

"So why did they leave them for me and not you?" Henri asked.

Edwin tried to think about that. He was ashamed to realize that he felt relieved. "They know you talked about Spinkel at the hearing, right?" he said.

"That was perhaps the stupidest thing I've ever done in my life." Henri put his head in his hands. "You were smart to keep quiet."

"I was just scared. Besides, I saw the warning before the hearing." He glanced up at the bed slat with its hidden message. "And you didn't."

"They must know that I really said nothing," Henri said. "They have their ways of getting information from the Americans. I said nothing!"

"Yes," Edwin said. He started to touch Henri's arm, but then pulled away.

Henri looked at Edwin, his face grave. "Of course, it must be the notebook."

"What?"

"I haven't told anyone this. When they beat me, they kept asking about the notebook. I told them I didn't know. I told them it was gone when we found him."

Edwin was quiet for a moment. He thought of Spinkel, hanging beneath the dripping pipes in the shower building, his black tongue protruding and a pool of urine on the plywood floor beneath him. Edwin shuddered.

"I'll go to Gott," he said quietly. "I'll tell him we know nothing about that notebook."

Henri turned and looked at him. Despite Henri's distress, Edwin thought he saw the hint of a smile. "You would talk to Gott?" he asked. "For me?"

Edwin swallowed. "Yes," he said solemnly.

Henri nodded. "Good for you, my friend. I am truly proud

of you. But perhaps it won't be necessary."

"What do you mean?"

"The time for you to know will come. Soon, I hope."

Sam sat in the otherwise empty mess hall, as across the table Henri poured over the newspapers Sam had brought in: copies of the previous week's *Ann Arbor News*, the *Detroit Free Press*, even the Sunday edition of the *Chicago Tribune*. In the nearby kitchen, Sam heard jokes and laughter as the prisoner-cooks prepared dinner, and occasionally he caught the vinegary scent of sauerkraut drifting through the connecting doorway.

Henri had told Sam that Edwin wouldn't be joining them today.

The ride from town with Hildy that morning had been silent and angry with neither of them wanting to discuss the uproar at the family dinner the previous Saturday night. Then, just as they entered the camp, Hildy had started to talk. She tried to explain Karl's accusation about her sneaking out of the house at night. She said that maybe Karl had heard Hans going out for some reason. Or Hans and Doris together. Or Karl had made it up. After all, he was angry with Hildy for not supporting him against their father. She said she'd talk to Karl and get him to explain.

It turned out that it was easy for Sam to believe her. It just made no sense that she'd be sneaking out at night to be with someone else. Hildy wasn't like that. Outside the administration building, he told her this, and they'd shared a brief kiss.

"Oh!" Henri said.

Sam looked up to see Henri staring at the *Free Press* front page. "What?" Sam asked.

"Rommel died."

"Yeah, so I heard," Sam said. "I thought we should include

it in this edition. It's important German news."

"But what about Gott?" Henri asked. "He and some of the others served under Rommel in the Afrika Korps."

"It seems they'd want to know."

Henri shook his head as he pulled another paper toward him. "There was a big German surrender at Aachen," he said, examining the headline.

"Yes, I saw that too. You know, I visited Aachen once—before the war, of course."

"Hitler calls it the home of the First Reich," Henri said absently, holding his wobbly eyeglasses with two fingers as he read. It struck Sam that Henri could be one of his students, examining an old Germanic text, discussing the coronation of Charlemagne.

"Because it was the center of the Holy Roman Empire," Sam said. "Beautiful cathedral."

"Five thousand men surrendered," Henri said as he leaned back. "This will be difficult for many of the men to accept. It won't be just Gott who's unhappy with this news."

"But it's the truth. The men should know the truth."

"Herr Professor," Henri said, taking off his glasses and rubbing his eyes. "I am thinking that perhaps it's not necessary that I be the one to bring them this truth."

"What? What're you saying?"

"This newspaper work is a voluntary assignment, is it not?" Henri asked.

"Sure, of course. But ... you'd rather go back to working in the fields?"

"No, Herr Professor. I must assure you that I much prefer sitting here with you in the dining hall."

"But ..." Then Sam stopped. Earlier, when Henri entered the mess hall, he'd limped, and he'd groaned as he eased himself into his chair. This man is injured, fearful for his very life, Sam said to himself. Somebody beat Henri, possibly for working on this newspaper.

"What about Edwin?" Sam asked.

"I don't think he's coming back either."

"Why? Is he afraid too?"

Henri shrugged. "That's part of it," he said.

Sam realized that his newspaper project was falling apart. Maybe he should give up. It seemed that everybody would be happier ... and nobody else would get hurt.

"I've one small favor to ask," Henri continued. "Please, may I have this newspaper?" He pointed to the *Chicago Tribune*.

"Sure. Why not?" Sam replied, sighing in resignation. "Take them all if you want."

The housing office at the Willow Run plant was just four walls and a corrugated roof tucked up against the outside of the main assembly building. As Doris stood in line, she heard the constant *rat-a-tat-tat* of the air-powered rivet guns through a nearby door. There were two people ahead of her.

She worried that she was going to miss her bus and be late for dinner. Of course, she was just about fed up with eating dinner with the Gruden family. After all, that's why she was standing in this line.

The line moved forward. The shift had been uneventful; Doris and Sylvia kept up with the assembly line and used only three jumbo rivets during the entire day. Sylvia had finally gotten the knack of her job, working her bucking bar on the other side of the big aluminum sheets synchronized with Doris's riveter. They talked more now, and Doris was tempted to tell Sylvia about the recent events in the Gruden house. Many of the girls chattered away all day about the most intimate parts of their lives, but Doris couldn't bring herself to do this.

The housing office's wooden counter spanned the width of

the room and behind it stood a desk, some file cabinets, and a harried-looking woman. "Next!" she called out.

The man in front of Doris stepped forward; she was next in line.

The shoulders of the man slumped. "Three months? You've got to be kidding!" he said. "I got a wife and a baby. We're living in a damn tent, and it's getting cold at night!"

Three months! The housing situation was worse than when she'd first come up from Kentucky. Then it had only taken two days to be placed with the Grudens.

"Next!"

Doris went to the counter. She told the clerk her name and her current address.

"So you've got a place with a family in Ann Arbor, right?" the clerk asked.

"Yes, ma'am," Doris said, "but it ain't working out so well."

"Well, make it work. There's a war on, you know."

"But—"

The clerk crumpled up the form she'd been writing on and tossed it into the overflowing wastebasket at her feet. "Next!"

As Doris turned away, she saw Homer Jenkins watching her.

"Hi, Doris," he called out. "How ya doin'?"

She walked over to him, glad that she'd changed clothes in the ladies locker room and brushed her hair.

"I'm doing jus' fine, Homer," she said. "You?"

He shrugged. "Fair to middling. You lookin' for a new place to stay?" he asked, his eyes glancing toward the woman behind the counter.

"Maybe."

"You see, I'm living with my sister and a cousin," he said. "We got us a place in Ypsilanti."

Together, they walked out of the housing office and toward

the main employee gate.

"It ain't fancy or nothin'," Homer continued. "But I figure we could fit in one more body, so to speak. And we could use some help with the rent."

Doris looked at him as they walked. Homer had slicked back his hair, and his clothes were clean. He wasn't a handsome man, but he wasn't ugly either. She reckoned his sister must be a decent enough cook, because he didn't have that lean, hungry look of many war workers up from the South. With so few eligible men around, most girls would consider him a good catch.

"Want to show me?" she asked.

"Sure. We got time to catch my regular bus, so's you can see what it's like." He was smiling broadly. "If you want, you can stay for dinner. Sis'll have something ready. Nothin' …" He frowned a bit.

"Fancy?" Doris said. "Homer, that sounds jus' fine to me."

It was almost nine when Doris finally got home that night, and the house was quiet. She crept up the front steps, hoping they wouldn't creak and give her away, because she just wanted to sneak up to her room and go to bed. As she slipped through the door and crossed the front hall, she saw that a single lamp was on in the living room. Keeping her head down, she tiptoed to the stairway. She was on the second step when she heard a voice.

"Doris? Is that you?"

It was Karl. Deciding to ignore him, Doris climbed another step, and the tread gave a loud squeak.

"Doris?"

There was a sad, lonely quality to his voice. Her shoulders drooping, Doris turned and went back down the stairs and into the living room.

He sat on the couch; the lamp behind him left his face in

shadows.

"Hildy's really riled up about what you said," she told him.

"I know."

"So why'd you do it? Why'd you say those awful things about her? And Sam?"

"They're true."

"I don't believe it for one minute. I'd know if she was sneakin' out to, uh, be with him. She'd tell me."

"You think so? Look, all I know is that my bedroom is next to hers, and I hear her leave and come back. She did it last night too."

Why was he saying such crazy things? She knew he was mad at Hildy because she hadn't stood up to Oskar for him. For some reason, he had never liked Sam, of course. But why this awful story?

She sat down beside him on the couch. For once, he didn't react to her being so close.

"What's going on?" she asked.

"I didn't sign the papers. The enlistment papers. The guy there was pretty mad."

"Why? Is it because it because of what Hans said about the Japs? Or about dying or gettin' wounded? I mean—"

"No! I'm no coward."

"Why sure, I know that. Is it something else Hans said?" she asked. "You seemed kind of peeved at him."

"Oh, that was something else. His birthday present ..." Karl shook his head. "It's not him, not really."

Doris waited.

Without looking at her, he went on, "You see, I thought the army was what I wanted. To get away from here, away from *them*. But now it isn't going to happen. I'm stuck here for the rest of my life."

"You'll go to college. Your father said so."

"Yeah, right here. At Michigan, right here in Ann Arbor.

I'll live at home. It's all arranged."

Doris leaned back and rolled her eyes. "You could do worse, you know. Goin' to college and all. I wish I had your opportunity."

"I know. You're right. Papa and Mutti are right. Like they always are."

"So why didn't you sign the papers? If you want to get away, you can just sign 'em and go."

Karl leaned forward and put his face in his hands. Hesitantly, Doris reached out and touched his shoulder. It trembled beneath her fingers. His head still down, he leaned toward her, and she reached over, stretching her arm across his skinny back, and pulled him close. They stayed like this for a while. Then Karl turned his face to hers, his eyes filled with tears and his cheeks wet. He leaned closer, staring up at her, his lips pursed and trembling slightly.

Whoa! Doris put her hand firmly on his shoulder and held him back.

"Karl," she said. "You're a sweet boy, and I like you a lot. I hope you know that. But not that way."

He froze. His eyes seemed to glaze over, and then he turned away from her and stared at the other end of the couch. Doris put her hands in her lap.

"You know," she said, "I reckon just about everybody who ever joined up was scared. It makes sense. And it don't really have anything to do with the fighting stuff. I mean, it's hard to do something so new and strange like that. I was really scared when I got on that bus to come up north. I was leavin' behind everything I knew, my kin, my friends. All I had was a flyer that some stranger gave me coming out of church. 'War workers needed in Michigan,' it said. My folks didn't want me to come, but I did it."

"It's not the same," Karl said, his voice tentative.

"Sure, I know that. I'm just saying that it's okay to be a

little, uh, hesitant. It's kind of natural."

Karl turned back around and looked at her. "So you think I should sign those papers?"

"Sure, if that's what you want," Doris said, shrugging.

"When I come home on leave, in my uniform, will you go out to dinner with me?"

Doris laughed. "Why I'd be right proud to. As friends though, right?"

Karl sighed and nodded. He reached into his pocket, pulled out a wadded-up handkerchief and wiped his face. As he put the handkerchief away, he smiled crookedly, his eyes bright.

"I'm going to be a fighter pilot," he said.

"I think that's swell," Doris said.

They talked for a while longer. Karl asked why she was so late, and she told him about going over to Homer's place and eating dinner with him and his sister and cousin. He seemed a little uncomfortable with this, but she reassured him that it was good for her to have friends at the plant, and he agreed. Doris didn't tell him that she'd been invited to live with them.

As Doris sat on the couch listening, her eyes strayed to the door leading into Oskar's study. She remembered the last time she'd been in that room, returning the attic key to Oskar's desk, the day the telegram had arrived saying Hans was coming home. It was the day she found those letters from Germany—and the armband in the attic.

"I was wondering," she said to Karl, "how old were you when y'all came to America?"

"Three, I think."

"So you don't remember much about Germany."

Karl shook his head. "I remember being on the boat."

"It must have been strange for your family when Hitler took over."

"I guess," Karl said. "I was still pretty young when that happened. I don't remember hardly anything."

"What do you remember?"

Karl glanced around uneasily. He looked just like he did that first night after Doris had arrived, when he'd played that record, when he seemed afraid that his father might pop up from behind the couch and catch him.

"I remember seeing swastikas," he whispered.

"You mean in the newsreels?"

"No," Karl replied. "Here, in this house."

Sam sat in the dark, untidy living room of the house he shared with his mother, a half-empty glass of beer getting warm on the coffee table. Across from him, Blanch sprawled across the threadbare couch holding her glass of scotch, the bottle sitting on the floor within easy reach. She wore her pottery work clothes, and Sam saw a smudge of dried clay on her cheek. In the corner, the big Zenith quietly played live dance music from a Detroit hotel, its bright dial providing the only light in the room.

Sam shifted in his chair and noticed his glass on the coffee table. He picked it up and took a sip.

"How are things out at the camp?" his mother asked.

"Pretty awful," Sam replied. "The classes are okay, I guess. Most of my students don't care much about what I'm saying, but a few do."

"And your little newspaper?"

Sam shook his head. "Dead, I think. The boys who worked on the first edition have quit, and I can't get anyone else to volunteer. That bastard Gott must really be crowing."

"So he's won?"

Sam glared at her. For the thousandth time he decided he needed to get his own place to live.

"I don't think of it like that," he said.

"What does that nice Captain Harris think?"

"Look, Mom. This is my business, okay?" Besides, he'd

hardly seen Harris lately. It seemed like Harris was avoiding him.

"I'm just asking," she said. "He just seemed so pleasant and helpful when you introduced us that evening."

Sam shook his head, thinking that she had a little crush on John Harris.

"Is something else bothering you, dear?" she asked. "How are things with that German girl?"

"Hildy."

"Yes, of course. Hildy."

"We had a little disagreement when I was over there the other night. There was a big hubbub about her brother Karl— he's the younger one—and whether he was going to enlist. For some reason, he got mad at both Hildy and me. Said some nasty things."

Blanch leaned forward. "Oh?"

Sam looked across at his mother. Don't do it, he told himself. Don't tell her about Karl saying Hildy was sneaking out at night. Why did Karl say that? Hildy said he wanted to get back at her for not supporting him against their father. And Karl was not fond of Sam. But why would he say that particular thing?

Sam wished his father were still alive. Michael Demsky, formerly Mikhail Demeshilo, had died of throat cancer when Sam was eighteen. A year before, they'd bought the DeSoto, and the two of them had loved that car together, spending Sunday afternoons washing and polishing it, and then taking his mother on long drives along the Huron river, west to the towns of Dexter and Chelsea and beyond. Sometimes his mother and father sat in back, and he played the role of chauffeur while they laughed and haughtily commanded that he drive them for ice cream at the Washtenaw Dairy on the south side of Ann Arbor.

He remembered asking his father about girls back then,

when his father was sick but could still talk, and he remembered getting kindly if slightly befuddled answers. It'd be nice to talk to him about Hildy now.

"Sam?" Blanch said.

"It wasn't really anything. Besides Hildy and I talked, and it's okay."

"You know, I think it's time I met this girl."

"No, Mom. Please."

"And why not? Here's what we're going to do. I'll make a reservation at the Lighthouse for dinner—let's see—Thursday evening. You'll invite Hildy, of course. And ..." She grinned at Sam. "And you'll also invite Captain Harris!"

"Listen, that's not—"

The telephone rang in the hallway. Sam pulled himself to his feet and went to answer it.

"Hi, Sam. This is Doris Calloway."

"Oh. Hello."

"That was right strange the other night, wasn't it?" Doris said.

"Yeah, it sure was."

"Who is it?" Blanch called from the living room.

Sam put his hand over the mouthpiece and shouted back to her, "It's for me." A second later, he heard the radio switch off.

"I know it's late," Doris said. "Can you do me a little favor?"

"What's that?"

"I can't talk about it now. Can we get together sometime? It's just some translating, but it's kind of, ah, sensitive."

"Sensitive? Sounds like government secrets. Who are you, the first girl agent for the FBI?" Sam chuckled.

Doris said nothing for moment, and then said, "No, course not. It's just kind of a personal thing."

"Well, sure. I guess that'd be okay. I could come over to

the house."

"No, that's not good. Karl's still here."

"Okay, how about here?" Sam said. "Say seven o'clock tomorrow night?" His mother would be at her bridge club. Doris agreed, and he gave her the address. After they said goodbye, Sam stuck his head through the door leading to the living room. "I'm going to bed, Mom," he said.

"Who was that?" Blanch asked. "A girl?"

"She's a friend of Hildy's. I don't really know her."

"Oh. Well, you know, I was thinking about your newspaper problem. Why don't *you* write the next edition? You don't really need those boys to help, do you?"

"But the whole idea was to get the POWs involved. To make it their paper."

"I know. But right now, you just have to keep it alive. If you do, I bet you get some help again on the next edition."

"But ..." Sam stopped and thought about it. Hildy could help.

He walked into the living room and turned the radio on again. Then he leaned over and kissed his mother on the forehead.

Doris lay awake in her bed, the faint sound of classical music drifting up from the living room two floors below. Mr. Gruden was listening to his phonograph records.

It wasn't hot so she hadn't turned on the fan—Hans's fan. Karl had taken it from Hans's room and given to her that first night. She figured she should probably give it back, but it hardly seemed to matter. The Indian summer had finally passed and besides, she was probably going to move out soon. She'd told Homer that she'd give him an answer tomorrow. It didn't mean she had to end things with Hans, at least she hoped not. Maybe if they no longer lived in the same house, this crazy house, maybe he'd be more romantic.

Maybe not.

The music stopped, and a moment later, she heard the heavy tread of Mr. Gruden on the stairs leading to the second floor. The toilet flushed, and soon afterward a door—undoubtedly the door to his and Mrs. Gruden's bedroom—clicked shut.

Doris waited. The old house creaked. Occasionally, she heard the squeak and rustle of the rabbits in their hutches below her window. And still she waited.

Finally, certain that everyone in the house was asleep, Doris slid out of bed, pulled on her robe, and tiptoed from her room—her bare feet testing each stair tread in front of her as she descended to the main floor. It took only a moment to slip into Oskar's study, pull open the bottom drawer, and find the bundle of envelopes just as she expected. She'd practiced it all mentally as she lay in bed. She pulled two envelopes from the center and tucked them inside her robe.

Back in her room, she was afraid to turn on her light. Groping, she opened the bottom drawer of her dresser and slipped the letters under her carefully folded brassieres and underpants. Tomorrow, she'd take them to Sam, and finally figure out the truth about Oskar Gruden.

As she lay back down on her bed, she fought to control her breathing and her racing heart, trying to listen to the house, needing to be sure that all was quiet. Eventually, there was no sound; not even from the rabbits. Doris rolled over and faced the wall, her eyes closing, and the fuzzy grayness of sleep began to enfold her. For some reason, Sam Demsky drifted back into her thoughts …

Downstairs, a door opened and closed. Doris's eyes opened wide, and she held her breath. The door sounded heavy. The front door? Relax, she told herself. Whatever's going on, it's nothing to do with me. She heard steps on the stairway, and then a bedroom door opened and closed.

Was it Hildy? Could Karl have been right about Hildy sneaking out to see Sam? Or maybe it was Karl. That's right, it was probably him. Maybe he made up that story about Hildy to cover his own nightly outings. Maybe he has a girlfriend after all. Doris smiled and rolled over again. Good for him.

Then another possibility slipped into her thoughts. Maybe it was Hans.

Edwin's hands hurt. He lay on the lower bunk, staring up at the bed slats and the bottom of Henri's mattress springs. They'd spent the day working at Max Lohmann's farm, and as he flexed his fingers, he grimaced in pain. The corn crop was in, but Lohmann had contracted for prisoners to help bring in one last mowing of hay.

At first, Edwin had walked behind the baler with Henri, Hubert, and another boy. As each bale emerged from the chute, two of them grabbed it and tossed it onto the trailing wagon where two other prisoners wrestled it into position. It was backbreaking work, and Edwin felt guilty because he had so much trouble doing his share.

Then Edwin's luck changed. The hay baler had two automatic twine knotters and just before noon, one of them began to break down, its knots coming loose and the bales falling apart as they were pulled from the chute. Each time this happened, Max Lohmann stopped the tractor and waited as the prisoners gathered the loose hay and carried it forward to scatter in front of the baler. Lohmann was no fool. The third time it happened, he installed Edwin on top of the twine box and as each bale emerged, Edwin leaned over, inspected the knots, and retied them if necessary.

Now back in the barrack, inside the barbed wire, Edwin opened and closed his hands, dreading the next few hours, the night, and the coming days. Would the Heilige Geist come for

Henri again? Would they come for Edwin? He wished he was still perched on Max Lohmann's baling machine, hunched over and working without gloves on the moving bales, his feet just inches from the plates that crushed the hay into shape. While he tied the knots, he felt safe.

Edwin heard whistling and looked up. Corporal Becker, still wearing the cutoff uniform trousers that he'd made for playing soccer, sauntered down the central aisle between the bunks. He looked at Edwin and grinned.

"Got a letter for you," he said.

As Edwin scrambled out of his bunk and jumped to his feet, Becker pulled an envelope from the small stack that he carried and handed it to him. Edwin stared at the envelope, and his heart seemed to stop as he saw the stamp. It was from home! Then he noticed something else: the envelope had already been slit open. He glared at Becker.

"That's the way they all are when I pick them up," Becker said, holding out the rest of the envelopes for Edwin to see. "We suffer many indignities as prisoners, right? Having our mail opened is just one. But don't let it spoil a good thing: you got a letter from home!"

Edwin nodded and smiled sheepishly.

"Now read your letter," Becker said, pushing Edwin back down onto his bunk. "I've got these others to deliver." He turned away. Once again, Edwin was struck by how much Becker reminded him of his brother, Stefan.

"Becker!" Edwin called out. "How about you? Did you get a letter?"

The taller boy stopped and looked back over his shoulder. "No," he said, shaking his head.

"Sorry," Edwin said. "Maybe tomorrow."

Becker gave a little shrug and continued down the aisle between the bunks.

Edwin lay back on his bed, the envelope on his chest. He

yanked out two sheets of cheap writing paper covered with tight script.

"My dearest Edwin," it began. His mother wrote that she'd been relieved to get the postcard from the Red Cross telling her that he was a prisoner and wasn't injured. She clearly saw his capture by the Americans as a positive thing. She still hadn't heard anything from Stefan. As Edwin read, he heard the words on the page in his mother's voice. And while the quality of her handwriting didn't change in any obvious way as she wrote about Stefan, in his head, her voice quavered.

She talked about their neighbors and the shortages of everything. Near the end, she wrote that she had very good news. She didn't use any names, apparently afraid that someone might read her letter—and in fact, they had—but Edwin understood. The woman in the apartment below, Axel's mother, had told her that Axel was hiding in France and was safe. Somehow he had gotten word to her.

Edwin didn't know what to think. He was glad to know that the SS had not captured Axel. But when Axel slipped out of that apple orchard in the middle of the night, just before the Americans overran their bivouac, why did he leave his best friend behind?

His mother closed by saying that she loved and missed him, and that she hoped this foolish war would be over soon, so she'd have both of her beautiful boys back in her arms.

Edwin's eyes filled with tears. He'd never felt so far from home. His mother needed him. Six years before, she'd had a house full of family: a husband and two sons. Now, she was alone.

Henri walked up the aisle, and without a word to Edwin, he started to climb up to his bunk.

Edwin quickly wiped his hand across his face. He was tired of crying in front of Henri. "I got a letter," he said. "It's from my mother."

Henri paused, one foot hanging in mid-air. Then, he slowly descended and leaned down so he could see Edwin. His face was expressionless, and he said nothing.

"She's all by herself," Edwin continued. "I've got to get home somehow."

Henri shook his head.

"What does that mean?" Edwin asked.

"We're never going home. We're going to die here in this stinking camp."

"No! Don't say that."

"Just like poor Sergeant Spinkel," Henri added.

"But he chose to die. You and I won't do that. Right?"

Henri said nothing and stared at the floor.

Edwin stood up next to him. "Look, I think Spinkel hanged himself because he was all alone. But you and I, we're friends. We've got each other!" He grabbed Henri's arm tightly and shook it. "Right?"

Henri reluctantly met Edwin's eyes. He shrugged.

Edwin's mind raced. "Escape," he said. "What about escape?"

Henri shook his head. "I've been trying to figure out a plan," he said, taking a deep breath. "It's very difficult."

"But not impossible?"

"It all depends on Martini," Henri said.

"Martini?"

"Perhaps you've noticed that our friend Martini has a certain casual approach to his duties," Henri said.

"Yes," Edwin said. He saw a flash of enthusiasm in Henri's eyes.

"I need to think about this some more," Henri continued. "I will tell you about it at the right time."

"That's good, Henri," Edwin said. "I trust you."

"You put a burden on me," Henri replied.

"Just take me with you."

Chapter Seven

Doris pushed the doorbell button and listened to the distant buzz inside Sam's house. She'd arrived after a twenty-minute walk from the Gruden's, and glancing at her watch, she was pleased that it was seven o'clock on the nose.

No answer. She turned and looked up and down the street. This neighborhood was a lot like the Gruden's, tree-lined and pleasant, but maybe a little shabbier. The sidewalk in front of the house was cracked, and the Demsky front yard hadn't been mowed recently.

Doris had cleaned up and changed after her shift at the plant. Now, tucking her calf-length skirt under her, she sat on the top step of the wooden porch, her purse holding the two letters clutched to her chest.

A car came down the street, its horn beeping. Sam leaned out of the driver's window and waved as he drove the big DeSoto onto the gravel driveway.

"Sorry," he said as he got out and crossed the lawn to her, his right leg dragging slightly. "I got held up at the camp."

"Oh, that's okay. I ain't been waiting long," Doris said, standing up and holding out her hand as he reached the top step. He shook it awkwardly.

"That's sure some nice car," Doris said.

Sam grinned and then turned to open the unlocked front

door.

It was dark inside. The curtains were drawn, blocking the fall twilight. Sam crossed the living room, turned on a lamp, and Doris gazed around in amazement. All the surfaces—the tabletops, the shelves, the top of the big radio in the corner—all were covered with small, almost identical vases.

"Mom's a potter," Sam said. "Come in here, and I'll show you." He led her across the hallway and turned on the kitchen light. "You ever seen one of these?" He pointed at what looked like a small, round table sitting where a kitchen table would normally be. "You sit here and turn it with your foot. Try it."

Doris reluctantly sat down, thinking about the letters in her purse. She found the iron wheel near the floor and gave it a push. The flat upper wheel slowly started to turn. She gave a couple more kicks and the stained surface spun faster.

"I've heard of these, but I never saw one before," she said as she turned back to look at Sam. "I reckon she likes making those little pots." Three of them sat on top of the refrigerator.

"Yeah. They do kind of pile up. She seems happy when she's working at the wheel. Since my father died ..."

Neither of them said anything for a second.

"Karl enlisted this morning," Doris said. "He leaves in three weeks. The family is all riled up, of course." She looked at Sam and cocked her head. "You know, Hildy wasn't home yet when I left. Was she with you?"

"Sure, she rides with me."

"And you were at the camp?"

"Yeah, sure," Sam replied. Then he squinted and looked at her. "Why, what are you implying?"

She smiled. "I'm just saying that it makes sense to me if you try to figure out times when you two can be alone."

Sam blushed. Doris thought it made his dark, olive complexion even more handsome.

"We were working together on the camp newspaper. It's for the prisoners."

"Oh. Well, that's good. I guess."

Sam asked if she'd like something to drink, and Doris said she'd like a glass of water. She watched as Sam poured her a glass from a bottle in the Frigidaire and got himself a glass of beer. He led the way back to the living room, and they sat on the couch.

"So you and Hildy patched things up?" Doris asked.

Sam nodded. "Yeah. We talked. It was hard for me to understand why Karl would say such an awful thing."

"I've gotten to know Karl. He ain't a happy boy."

"Maybe the army will be just what he needs."

"It'll get him out of that crazy house, anyhow." Doris shook her head. "There's just so much, you know, *drama*." Too much like home, she added to herself.

"Are you going to stay?"

Doris took a sip of her water. "I'm trying to decide. I got a friend at work who offered to let me stay with him."

Sam's eyebrows went up almost imperceptibly.

"Him and his sister and a cousin. Sam, don't look at me like that."

"Sorry."

Doris sighed. "If I move, maybe it'll get better for Hans and me, not being in the same house together, I mean."

"With his parents."

"Yeah. You know, I reckon Hans was glad to enlist. That it wasn't just patriotism."

Sam smiled. "You mean, secretly he felt like Pearl Harbor was a good thing? Got him out of the house. Like Karl."

"I don't know. He doesn't really talk so much."

Sam said nothing.

"Look, I've got these letters—" Doris reached for her purse.

"Wait, Doris. Can you help me? I want to believe Hildy about there not being another guy. About her sneaking out to meet someone. Just tell me what you know."

Doris leaned forward. "Sam," she said, "When Karl said what he said, I thought it might be true—that she was sneakin' out to see you. But I'm pretty sure that you two ain't …well, not yet anyway. Here's the thing. There's a bunch of reasons for him to say something like that. Maybe he made it all up because he's mad at Hildy and doesn't like you. Maybe he heard someone else go out."

"Really? Like you?"

"No, no. Or maybe he's the one sneakin' out, and he's trying to cover it up. I don't know."

"But you don't think …" Sam struggled for a second. "You don't think there might be someone else?"

Doris leaned back. "Nope. Sam, you're the one. You're all she talks about."

He smiled. "That's good to hear." He took a sip of his beer and stared straight ahead. Stretching out his right leg, he put his foot on the coffee table, and Doris wondered if it pained him.

"So," he said finally. "You mentioned some translating. German, I assume?"

Doris nodded, opened her purse, but then paused.

Sam looked at her expectantly.

"Maybe this ain't right," Doris said. "Maybe it's a mistake."

"Why don't you just tell me what this is all about."

Before she knew it, the words came tumbling out. She told Sam about her suspicions: Oskar's asking about the anti-aircraft defenses at Willow Run, the letters, and the swastika armband. And finally, she told him what Karl had said—that he remembered seeing men wearing swastikas in the house.

"Those are the letters?" Sam said, pointing at her open

purse.

Doris nodded.

"Hand them over," Sam said. "Look, I think you're right to be worried. You've got to understand; now I'm involved. You're talking about my girlfriend's father, her family. I need to know the truth now too." He reached out his hand, his face stern and insistent.

Doris gave him the letters, and a sense of relief washed over her, knowing that now she no longer had to bear this burden alone. Sam wouldn't want to falsely accuse at Oskar any more than she did.

Sam looked at the outer and inner envelopes. "These are interesting," he said. "Mailed through Mexico City."

Doris nodded.

He pulled a letter from its inner envelope and leaned back on the couch to read. Doris sipped her water and watched.

The front door opened.

Startled, Doris looked up and saw a small woman wearing white gloves and a big hat. "Sam," the woman said, "you've left the car …oh, excuse me."

Sam jerked his foot off the coffee table. "Hello, Mother. You're home early."

"Why, yes I am." She glanced back and forth between Sam and Doris. "So, this must be Hildy. I'm delighted to finally meet you, dear."

"No, Mom," Sam said as he stood up. "This is Doris Calloway. She's a friend of Hildy's. She rooms with the Grudens."

"Oh, I am sorry," Blanch said as she held out her white-gloved hand. "That must be dreadful for you."

"Doris, this is my mother, Blanch Demsky."

Doris stood. As she shook hands, she was suddenly conscious of how raw and rough her own hands were from working at the plant. "Glad to meet you, Mrs. Demsky," she said.

"So, what're you kids up to?"

"Mom, can I get you a drink?"

"Why, yes. That'd be lovely, dear. I'll just sit and chat with Doris."

Sam gave Doris a quick, apologetic look and then disappeared into the kitchen, leaving the two letters on the coffee table.

"I embarrass him," Blanch said as she pulled the pins out of her hat and took it off. "It's one of my little pleasures." She sat down.

"Yes, ma'am." Doris looked down at the letters and then back at Blanch.

"So," Blanch said. "I hear that the oldest Gruden boy is home on leave. Is that true?"

Later, Sam drove Doris home.

"I'm sorry about her," he said. "She can be a little overbearing at times."

"Nah, she's okay, maybe just a little sad."

"Yeah. Anyway, she liked you."

"Do you think? All I did was ask her about that pottery wheel."

"That's all it takes." Sam turned the car onto North Main. "She does what's expected of her. She goes to her meetings and teas. I think if she let herself, she'd stay home all day and work at that wheel."

"And make another hundred identical little pots," Doris said.

"Probably."

"She gave me one, you know." Doris opened her purse and showed him the vase wrapped in newspaper.

"Wow. She really does like you."

Doris closed her purse. "About the letters…"

"I'd hardly gotten started reading when Mom walked in."
Sam slowed the car to a stop.

Doris noticed that they'd parked around the corner from
the Gruden house.

"I used to let Hildy out here," he added.

Doris nodded.

"It probably wouldn't be a good thing for anyone to see me
dropping you off," he continued.

Doris wondered if he was talking about Mr. Gruden or
Hildy or Karl? Probably all three.

"I should go," Doris said. "Sam, thanks. This was real
nice." Then she grimaced. That sounded like the end of a
date.

Sam gave her an odd look, and then jumped out of the car
and came around to open her door. Doris climbed out, stood
beside him, and he said, "I'll read through those letters when I
get home, I promise."

Sam felt like an idiot as he drove to the camp the next
morning with Hildy dozing in the seat next to him. Why had
he left those damn letters sitting out on the coffee table while
he drove Doris home? When he'd returned to the house, they
weren't there, and his mother had gone to bed. And, as was
usually the case, she was still in bed when he'd left for work
that morning. Fortunately, Blanch Demsky couldn't read
German. Sam wondered if any of her friends could.

Sam turned the car onto the gravel road leading into the
camp and as it bounced over the ruts and potholes, Hildy
perked up and looked around. She'd been quiet since he'd
picked her up in front of the house.

"It was fun last night," Sam said. "Working together on the
paper."

"Not exactly dinner and dancing," Hildy said. "You really
don't know much about what girls like to do on a date."

"I guess. Well, I'll take you out to dinner anytime." Sam paused. "I'm not so sure about the dancing."

"Oh, Sam. I was kidding, okay?"

Sam took a breath. "Do you miss it? The dancing?"

"Who says I don't dance?"

What did that mean? Had she been going out with someone else after all, someone who dances?

"Sam, don't look so sad."

"Look, Hildy," Sam said. "I'm not seeing anyone else, nobody but you." Even as he said it, he wondered about seeing Doris last night. Did that count? Surely not.

"Well, I'm glad to know I've got you all to myself."

"And ..." Sam prompted.

"And you want me to tell you the same thing," she said. "Right?"

Sam was afraid to reply.

"You big dope," Hildy said. "Why would I go out with anyone else? I've got this handsome, educated man, with this big beautiful car. Men are so scarce, you know, it'd be unpatriotic to take more than my fair share!"

Sam wanted to shout, "Yippie!" but instead he grinned at her and said, "Thanks."

"You're quite welcome."

He turned the car into the camp parking lot, pulled into a space, and stared across the top of the steering wheel. He still couldn't believe that Hildy, this beautiful girl, was all his. But there was still one more thing he needed to know.

"There's something I've been meaning to tell you," he said. "It's about my father."

"You're going to tell me he was Jewish, right?" Hildy said. Her eyes were serious.

"But how—"

"Mrs. Lewis told me last week. She knows everything."

Sam shook his head. How did Mrs. Lewis know? He stared

at Hildy. "How do you feel about it?"

"Sam, dear. Not all Germans are Nazis. You understand that, right?"

He nodded. "But still, I've always assumed that many Germans, most even, had some negative feelings about Jews. I mean, what about your father? If he knew, how could he be comfortable with his daughter dating someone like me?"

"He knows," Hildy said.

Sam stared at her. "Really?" This was all so hard to take in. Hildy knows. Mr. Gruden knows. Mrs. Lewis. Who else?

She shrugged. "I'm a little surprised too. We were talking about you last night, and somehow it came up. It's not a problem for him."

"Wow … I mean, that's wonderful! What a relief," Sam said. He paused. "Wait, what about your mother?"

Hildy opened the car door and climbed out without answering.

The two sheets of paper in Sam's hand still smelled slightly of mimeograph fluid. When he and Hildy had worked on the new edition, she had told him about Edwin's description of the smell: like baking bread. Not an obvious choice, but apt somehow. He held the sheets to his nose as he knocked on Captain Harris's door.

"Come."

Sam stepped inside. Harris sat at his desk, his disassembled Colt pistol spread out on the desktop before him. Sam had often seen him wearing the pistol in a sidearm holster. A half-empty cup of coffee sat on the desk at Harris's elbow, next to an open pack of cigarettes and a full ashtray. Behind him, the room's single window was propped open, and Sam heard the sounds of prison camp life: a truck rumbling by, a German sergeant shouting out drill commands, cheers from the nearby athletic field.

"John, I've got the next edition of the camp newspaper. You wanted to see it."

"You know anything about firearms?" Harris asked.

"Not a thing," Sam replied as he approached the desk and looked down. The pistol was in a dozen pieces, all neatly arranged on the desk blotter, along with a stack of small white pieces of cloth, and an olive drab can with a screw-top labeled: "OIL, LUBRICATING."

"The M1911 Colt single-action, semi-automatic is the finest military pistol in the world," Harris said, not looking up. He poked a long, narrow brush into the pistol barrel and scrubbed vigorously.

"Uh, looks complicated," Sam said.

"Not really. Of course, when you strip and clean the same weapon once a week for three years, you get pretty efficient at it."

"You wanted to see the next camp newspaper," Sam repeated, holding out the pages.

"Just put it in my in-box," Harris replied.

Sam looked at the overflowing wooden box on the corner of the desk and wondered why Harris was wasting time cleaning his pistol when he clearly had plenty of real work to do. He guessed he just didn't understand the military way of doing things.

Harris followed Sam's eyes, glanced at the in-box, and then put down the pistol barrel and brush with a sigh. "Okay. Let's take a look," he said, rolling his eyes slightly as he reached for the sheets.

Sam handed them over and dropped into one of the chairs in front of the desk. He watched as Harris took a sip from his coffee cup and scanned the first page, his brow furrowed.

Sam guessed that he probably didn't read German very well. And he looked tired.

"Not much sports news," Harris said.

"I lost my sports reporter. I hope to get him back."

Harris flipped to the second sheet. He frowned.

"Sam, I don't know about these news items."

"About Rommel?"

"And the German surrender at Aachen."

"The prisoners should know," Sam said.

Harris continued to frown. He leaned back and pulled a cigarette out of the pack lying on the desk. "Did Miss Gruden help you with this? She was only supposed to help you with the first edition." He lit the cigarette. "She has other duties."

"She stayed late with me last night. On her own time."

Harris's eyes squinted at Sam through the cigarette smoke, and when Sam met his gaze, he glanced away, shifting in his seat. "Be that as it may," he said, "our hardliners are going to claim that these reports are fake. That we made up the stories to dispirit them. Staff Sergeant Gott served under Rommel, you know."

"In North Africa. Look, John, this is the news. It's true—you and I know that. The men have a right to know."

Harris bristled. "The Geneva Convention doesn't require me to distribute this." He waved the sheet at Sam. "Don't talk to me about these prisoners having rights like Amer—"

BANG!

Both Sam and Harris jumped. *What the hell?*

BANG! BANG!

A truck backfiring? Sam leaped to his feet, and as he started to walk around the desk toward the open window, he saw that Harris had dropped to the floor. Harris reached up, his hand shaking, and dragged Sam down next to him.

"Get away from that window, you fool!" Harris said. "That's an M-1, and it was close." He glanced up at the top of his desk, clearly unhappy that his pistol was useless.

As Sam knelt down, he saw that Harris's eyes were wide and the pupils big; the man was terrified. Maybe it was shellshock, something from when he was in action overseas and was wounded.

As he crouched on the floor next to Harris, Sam became aware of a pungent smell. What was it? Did it have something to do with the cleaning of Harris's pistol? Then, to Sam's consternation, he recognized it. It was the smell of mothballs.

Edwin watched Becker dribble the ball down the soccer field, feinting left and then passing to Hubert on his right. The ball struck Hubert on his thigh and bounced out of bounds.

There was no work in the fields today, and Edwin was happy he could come out and watch the soccer games. It was almost like reporting on the games for the newspaper again. The local farmers had finished making their late hay harvests, and there was a rumor that the prisoners might be moved to another camp, somewhere south where there was more work. Henri had stayed in the barracks, sleeping.

BANG!

The sound of a gunshot rolled across the soccer field and echoed against the nearby trees, smudging and softening the original, sharp report. Startled, Edwin looked around.

BANG! BANG!

The only time any of the prisoners heard gunshots was when the guards practiced at the improvised rifle range they'd built in a nearby field. These were different. They seemed to come from the prisoner compound.

Most of the players had also heard them and were staring, like Edwin, back toward the camp. Becker, intent on the game, easily intercepted a pass and took the ball toward the other team's goal. He scored as the goalkeeper stood motionless.

One by one, all the players froze and stared. The three guards, who had been sitting next to each other smoking and ignoring the game, climbed to their feet. Each man lifted his rifle and held it nervously across his chest.

"What was that?" Hubert asked, walking up to Edwin. "You think we'll keep playing?"

Edwin ignored him.

The guards were talking. It seemed to Edwin that they didn't know what to do. Out on the field, Becker, the captain of his team, began to move toward the compound. One by one, his teammates and the other prisoners joined him. They didn't hurry. They didn't run. Following Becker's example, they moved slowly and carefully, instinctively knowing that the guards might react to anything else. And the guards didn't try to stop them. Instead, they trailed along with the prisoners —everybody, including Edwin, heading toward the source of the gunshots.

The thirty or so prisoners from the soccer field streamed through the back gate of the inner fence, twelve feet tall and strung with barbed wire, that surrounded the barracks. Edwin was one of the last, and he noticed that the guards stayed outside. He heard the click of the big padlock that secured the gate every night.

Inside, except for the sound of shuffling feet, the camp was silent. The prisoners, still led by Becker, picked their way between the closely packed barracks, instinctively moving toward the front gate and the assembly area where the counts were done every morning, noon, and evening.

Edwin wondered where Henri was.

As Edwin emerged from between two buildings, he saw a crowd filling the assembly area. Unlike during the counts, when everyone stood at attention in ranks, the prisoners were jammed together, creating a wall of backs as they faced the front entrance. They stood motionless, watching something. Edwin scanned them, looking for Henri's head sticking above the crowd, but couldn't find him.

He pushed forward and because he was small and didn't

block anyone's view, the other prisoners let him slide in front of them. Within the crowd, he heard whispers.

"Was anyone hit?"

"No, they were just warning shots."

Edwin reached the front of the crowd. There was an open area between the prisoners and the front gate, and in this space, Staff Sergeant Gott stood with his fists jammed on his hips and his feet spread wide. Edwin saw that this gate was also locked.

"Return him to us," Gott shouted. "I demand it!"

Outside the front gate, two guards aimed their rifles directly at Gott. Between them, kneeling on the ground, cowering and trembling, was Henri.

Edwin stared, his mouth dropping open. What were they going to do to him? Why was he there?

He whispered to the man next to him, asking what had happened.

"That traitor ran to the Americans. He ran through the open gate, screaming like a little girl. We almost caught him."

They were chasing Henri? Startled, Edwin looked up and recognized the man: it was Engels, the sergeant who had been with Gott that day at the mimeograph machine. As Edwin tried to edge away, he realized that many of the men near him were in Gott's faction of hardcore Nazis. Edwin desperately wanted to slip through the crowd and then run, but he knew he couldn't abandon Henri.

There was a shout in English from the direction of the administration building, and the soldiers lowered their rifles. Edwin saw that one of the guards was Martini, and the tip of his rifle barrel was shaking.

Captain Harris, leading a small group of people including Sam, approached the guards. Edwin momentarily felt relief. Surely Captain Harris wouldn't let things get out of hand, and Henri should be safe. And he wouldn't be surrendered to

Gott.

As Harris talked with Martini, Henri looked back and forth between Harris, Martini, and Gott. Henri's face quivered in terror. Edwin started to raise his arms to wave, wanting to show Henri he was there. But he stopped, afraid of what might happen if the men around him, Gott's men, realized that Henri was his friend.

"Staff Sergeant Gott!" Captain Harris shouted in rough German. "What is your complaint against this man?"

"He's been spreading lies about the Fatherland, Herr Captain," Gott replied.

Edwin heard mutters from the men around him. "Traitor," they snarled. "Liar."

"What lies?" Harris asked.

"I won't repeat them, Herr Captain."

For the first time, Henri said something, and Harris listened. Sam stepped forward and, as Henri spoke, Sam reached down and pulled him to his feet.

Harris said something in English, and Martini unlocked the gate. Harris pushed it open, came to the position of attention, and then marched forward to stand in front of Gott. He waited, and after a second, Gott saluted. Harris returned the salute and, despite the stern military aspect of these actions, Edwin relaxed a bit.

"Staff Sergeant Gott," Harris said, "I regret to inform you that there are reliable reports that Field Marshal Rommel has died."

Edwin couldn't see Gott's face, but the muscles in the back of his neck seemed to tighten and bulge as Harris spoke. There were mutterings of disbelief from the men around Edwin.

"Further," Harris continued, "there has been a major surrender of German forces at Aachen."

"Herr Captain," Gott said, "with respect, but why should

we believe you? These things aren't possible. Your government tells these lies to break our spirit."

"I've seen the newspapers myself."

"American newspapers! Right? Why should we believe them?"

Sam stepped through the gate and stood next to Harris. He looked at Gott, but he spoke loudly enough for everyone to hear.

"Sergeant Gott, I had the great pleasure of traveling through Germany, long before the war, of course. Those of your men who have been in my classes know of my respect for German history and for German culture. Am I right?"

Nobody said anything.

"I've been fortunate to visit Aachen, the city of Charlemagne," Sam continued. "I've stood beside his shrine in the beautiful cathedral."

The men listened. Edwin thought there was a grudging sense of acknowledgement around him. It seemed that Gott's neck muscles were relaxing, maybe just a bit.

"Soldiers of Germany," Sam continued, his voice louder, "I've examined the newspapers and listened to the radio. Yes, these are all American sources of news. But I must tell you that I believe them. I'm sorry for the unhappiness that this news causes you."

Gott stared intently at Sam, who took a breath and looked directly back at Gott.

"This news," Sam said, louder even than before, "will be published in the next edition of the camp newspaper." He pulled a sheet of paper from his coat and waved it over his head. "It will be distributed this afternoon."

Captain Harris glanced at Sam for a second and then nodded in agreement.

"That traitor," Gott said, pointing at Henri, "wrote those lies for your idiot paper."

"No!" Sam said. "This man quit the newspaper. He quit because he didn't want to be responsible for bringing you this unfortunate news. Those of you who have seen Henri working in the fields lately know the truth of this."

Edwin took a breath. Around him, he heard the shuffling of feet in the dust.

Captain Harris pulled himself up straight and spoke formally to Gott. "I will return this man to your authority, Staff Sergeant Gott." Like Sam, he spoke loud enough for the prisoners to hear. "I trust you understand that he's not a traitor. I will hold you personally responsible for his safety."

Gott turned and looked at Sam. Then he glanced over at Henri, and Edwin saw that Gott's face was hard and calculating.

"Very well, Herr Captain," Gott said. He saluted, turned on his heel and addressed the crowd of prisoners. "This man is not to be harmed. That is my order!" He strode forward, the men parting before him, with Sergeant Engels and some others falling in behind. The other prisoners quickly dispersed into the barracks, except for Becker, who came up to stand beside Edwin. Together they waited.

Captain Harris spoke to Martini, who then used his rifle butt to push Henri forward into the compound. As Martini locked the gate, Harris, Sam, and the others turned and walked back toward the headquarters building.

Henri stood alone. His eyes darted about, passing over Edwin and Becker without acknowledgement. Then he turned and hammered on the pinewood gate.

"For God's sake!" Henri screamed. "Let me out!"

The house seemed quiet as Doris climbed the front steps and opened the door. Today's shift had been typical, just like dozens that had come before, and like many more to follow. While she was tired and dirty, she was satisfied with the day.

She had fifty-two dollars and forty-three cents in her pocket —a week's pay. Amazing. She'd give ten to Gertrud for room and board, send twenty home to Momma, put another fifteen in the bank, and she'd still have seven dollars and change in spending money for the next week. But what would she spend it on? The stores were almost empty.

As she set her purse on the hall table, she noticed two letters. The top one was addressed to her, and as she snatched it up, she saw the return address. It was from Aunt Jeanie, William's mother. Doris tore open the envelope, pulled out a page of stationery, and was surprised to see it held a single sentence.

William says to tell you nothing.

Doris struggled to understand. William wanted nothing to do with her. He was still angry that she hadn't left home to join him, to marry him. But what did he expect? If she had, what would she have done after he went into the army? If only she could explain, maybe he'd understand. She looked down at the page again; it was clear that William's mother wasn't going to help.

Stuffing the letter into a pocket, she picked up the other envelope. Its shape was familiar, and then she noticed the return address: Mexico City. She dropped it and jerked her hand back as if the envelope were a red-hot rivet. It was another letter from Germany. That night, Mr. Gruden would read it. And sometime soon, he would add it to the bundle in his desk drawer. Maybe he'd notice that two of the letters were missing. She glanced over her shoulder at the front door. Would Sam be home now? Should she rush it to his house and get the letters? No, just wait and figure this out first.

Doris started across the front hall, heading for the main stairway. Then her nose twitched. Did she smell cigarette smoke?

"Hello?" she called out, looking around.

Nobody answered for a moment. Then she heard Hildy reply, "I'm in here."

Doris walked into the living room and saw Hildy sitting casually on the couch. Around her, Doris saw the faint, but unmistakable traces of smoke. Hildy wore her green dress. Her hair was done up, and she'd obviously applied her makeup carefully. She looked sophisticated, like someone out of a movie.

Hildy looked up and said, "There's a letter for you."

"I saw it," Doris replied. "Don't you look nice."

"Thanks. Sam is taking me out to dinner. At the Lighthouse."

"Ooh, that's supposed to be a real fancy place. What's the occasion?"

"I think he's just being sweet."

Doris felt a twinge. Why couldn't Hans do something like that? "Where is everybody?" she asked.

"Mutti and Papa are out for the evening. Hans is around somewhere. I don't know where Karl is. I haven't seen him much lately."

"Poor Karl. I hope he's havin' some fun while he can."

Hildy shrugged.

"Well, have a nice time," Doris said. "Say hello to Sam for me."

"Sure."

Doris climbed the main staircase to the second floor and then the narrow, winding stairs to her room. She quickly undressed and pulled on her robe, now desperate for a bath and to wash her hair.

As she returned to the second floor and crossed to the bathroom, she noticed that the door to Han's room was closed. She wondered if he was in there.

Doris spent the next hour in the bathroom, and it felt like she'd died and gone to heaven. Nobody came to the door.

Gertrud didn't knock, insistently asking whether Doris was using too much hot water. There were no angry male stomps down the stairs to the other bathroom. After a long and leisurely bath, during which she added hot water three times, Doris washed her hair in the sink. She scrubbed her face with some sweet-smelling soap she'd found at the Ben Franklin Five and Dime. After she rinsed, she leaned forward, wiped a clear area on the mirror and examined her face. Doris had never worn much makeup, and now, her face scrubbed clean and flushed from the steam and heat of the bathroom, her red hair peeking out from the white towel, framing her face with its sprinkle of faint freckles, now as she ran her fingers over her cheeks and nose and lips, Doris frowned.

An image of that soldier named Martini popped into her head. She remembered the day at Lohmann's farm, when Martini had looked up to find Hildy and Doris standing in front of him. He'd looked back and forth between the two of them, finally settling on Hildy. The same thing had happened with that German boy at the train station, and again the night when Sam came to the door. Hildy was her friend, but Doris reckoned that Hildy would always be the one that men looked at. And she knew that Hildy loved it.

Doris leaned in closer to the mirror and stared into her own blue eyes. Blue, with a touch of green. Her momma had green eyes. And her momma was the only person in the world who had ever noticed the green tint. Even William had said they were the prettiest blue eyes he'd ever seen.

Sighing, she wrapped her old robe around her and opened the door. As she stepped out into the hallway, she bumped into Hans.

"Sorry," he said. He took a step back and stared at her.

Doris blushed and pulled the robe tighter around her. "Hi," she said. "You had any supper yet? I could fix us something."

Hans didn't answer. She saw, she felt, his eyes traveling up and down her body, taking in her bare feet, pausing at the point where the robe crossed above her breasts, and then moving back to her face. He reached out and touched her cheek with the tips of his fingers. He traced the outline of her jaw. It felt good—the touch of this man she hardly knew. She leaned forward ever so slightly. His hand slid down to her neck and caressed it. Heat seemed to radiate from the tips of his fingers, and it joined with the warmth that still lingered from her bath. Please don't stop, she begged silently. Please don't pull away.

Hans didn't pull away. Instead, he cupped her face in both hands, stepped close, and gently touched his lips to hers.

Thank God, a kiss at last! She responded, opening her lips and lifting herself on her toes. His tongue touched hers.

Heat flashed along the surface of her skin, starting at her lips, moving across her face, and down her neck. Hans wrapped his arms around her, pulling her tight against him. He was aroused; she felt it. He gently ran his hands down her spine, and beneath the robe, her body vibrated at his touch.

Doris pulled away, but he pulled her back tight against him. She put both hands on his chest and pushed firmly. Confusion flashed across Hans's face, maybe anger. He started to speak, but Doris pressed a finger to his lips. Without taking her eyes from his, she slid sideways, through the door to his room, her fingers working at the knot to her bathrobe.

He watched her, his mouth slightly open, and she heard the whisper of his breath. She took a step back, and he followed her. The knot came loose, and she slipped the robe from her shoulders. As it fell to the floor at her feet, he closed the door.

Afterwards, they lay together on his bed, the room so stuffy that the only contact between them was her hand held lightly in his.

"You done this before?" he asked.

"You mean, was I a virgin?"

"I guess."

"There was this boy back home ..." She paused, embarrassed, thinking of William. "That okay?"

"What? Oh, sure."

"Just the one. I mean, I don't want you thinking I'm some kind of loose woman."

"It's okay. It kind of takes off some of the pressure, if you know what I mean."

Doris smiled. Sweet boy.

"What about you?" she said. "I reckon you army fellas get plenty of chances."

"Not really."

They said nothing for a while. Doris stared at the ceiling. Model airplanes made of balsa wood and lacquered tissue hung by threads, slowly revolving. "I got me a friend at the plant who has a place and said I could move in," she said, telling herself not to let on that it was a man. "Maybe it'd be better if I weren't here all the time."

"Better how?"

"Just more natural. You could come over and pick me up. You could give me a kiss goodnight without thinking who in your family might be watchin'."

"And what if I wanted to do more than that?"

"I reckon my friend would understand." She knew this was a lie. Homer would understand no such thing.

"I guess that'd be okay."

Doris sat up, swung her feet onto the floor, and stood. Her robe lay near the door, and she crossed over to it and slid it on, its soft caress against her skin reminding her of that moment when he'd pulled her to him.

Wandering around the room, she was aware that he was watching her. Hans was twenty-one years old and an experienced soldier, but the room was still what you'd expected for a high school boy: the airplane models, some books, a University of Michigan pennant on one wall, and a framed picture of a track team on a battered wooden desk.

"Hildy says you were right popular in high school," she said.

"It seems like a thousand years ago."

"Before the war."

"Yeah." He pulled himself up and leaned back against the headboard, the sheet draped across his waist.

Doris touched the wingtip of a hanging model, a small one that she guessed was a fighter plane. There wasn't a speck of dust on it. "Your momma's quite a housekeeper," she said, turning and scanning the rest of the room.

"You have no idea," Hans replied, smiling.

At that moment, Doris reckoned he might've been the most handsome boy she'd ever seen. She smiled back at him, looking over her shoulder.

She noticed an olive-green cloth bag on the floor next to his dresser.

"This bag is filthy dirty," she said. "You musta had it in the jungle with you, dragging it through the mud. Right?"

Hans leaned forward. "Yeah, that's my duffle bag."

Without looking at him, she bent over and reached for it. "Like I said, it's dirty. Let me wash it." She picked up the bag, noticing that there was something in it. "I'd just like to do something nice for—"

Suddenly, he was beside her, grabbing her wrist so tightly that she cried out. The bag dropped to the floor with a clunk. "Leave it be!" he said. He was breathing hard. "It's none of your business!"

Doris stumbled back against the dresser, stunned. What had just happened? One moment she was warm and contented, wanting to do something nice for this man she'd just made love to, something domesticated. Now, she felt a stab of fear as she looked into his blazing eyes.

He released her wrist. "Sorry," he said. His face softened and his shoulders slumped. "I'm so sorry."

"It's this damn war, ain't it?" she asked. She pulled him into her arms, and as she pressed her face against his naked shoulder, she felt him put his arms around her and hold her tight.

The house was quiet.

"It's okay, baby," she whispered. "Let me help you."

Chapter Eight

The prisoner canteen was nothing more than a table set up at the back of the mess hall three days a week. Sergeant Engels and another of Gott's henchmen ran it, and everybody said that the prices were so high because they skimmed off an extra profit. The canteen carried cigarettes, a few American magazines, Bibles in German and English, some shaving supplies, and other toiletries. And some days, there was candy.

As Edwin stood in line, he gripped the wrinkled script that served as currency in the camp. He had one dollar and sixty cents. When the prisoners worked, they received eighty cents a day in script. They could spend it at the canteen or accumulate it, and the U.S. government was supposed to redeem the script in cash when they were finally released. Nobody believed this, and so the canteen was always busy.

Fifteen-year-old Edwin kept his eyes on the big glass jar sitting on the counter. Judging by the picture on the label, it had once held pickles, but now it contained something else: lemon drops, his favorite candy.

Six years before, when he was only nine, his father had bought him candy. It was one of the best memories Edwin had: walking after church, Stefan on one side of his father and Edwin on the other, holding hands. His mother had gone on home to continue preparations for Sunday dinner while the three of them strolled around the nearby park. Stefan pulled away to run ahead, wanting to see the swans in the small lake, but Edwin was content, his hand soft and small in the firm grasp of his tall and handsome father.

The candy shop was crowded. As they stood in line, his father made both boys swear not to tell their mother. Stefan selected a hard chocolate bar. And Edwin picked the lemon drops.

Later, as they walked back to their apartment, his father began to cough.

Today, in the camp canteen, there was only a handful of lemon drops in the bottom of the jar, and Edwin was desperate to get to the front of the line before they were gone.

Henri had not been in his bunk when Edwin had awakened that morning. From the next row over, Hubert said he thought Henri had gone out early on a work detail. Edwin had felt a moment of panic. Why hadn't Henri said anything to him? Since the corn and hay harvest was finished and there wasn't much work now, the men were allowed to volunteer or stay back in the camp. Why would Henri volunteer to work in some local farmer's fields? Maybe he felt safer away from camp. But why didn't he take Edwin with him?

"*Sabah al-hayri*," said a voice behind Edwin. Even as he wondered what the words meant, Edwin shuddered.

"That means 'good morning,'" Staff Sergeant Gott said.

Swallowing, Edwin turned.

Gott stood next to Edwin, and it was clear that he wanted everyone to know that he wasn't standing in the line. Although his stance was relaxed and casual, his bright blue-gray eyes seemed to drill into Edwin.

"Arabic is a difficult language, you know."

Edwin nodded.

"Say it," Gott said. "Sabah al-hayri."

Edwin tried, stumbling over the unfamiliar syllables.
"Again."

This time, Edwin seemed to say it correctly.

"And it means?" Gott asked.

"Good morning," Edwin replied, his voice shaking.

"Good! See, you are starting to learn Arabic. Not so hard for a smart German boy like you, right?"

"Yes, Staff Sergeant."

"I was in North Africa, you know. I had the great honor to serve under Field Marshal Rommel."

"Uh, Staff Sergeant," Edwin said, looking at the floor. "I have something I need to tell you."

"Look at me, son," Gott said. "Look at me when you talk to me."

"Yes, Sergeant." Edwin forced himself to look at Gott's face. It was clean-shaven, his eyebrows were light in color and with his bald head, Edwin was reminded of a skull. Swallowing again, he forced himself to continue, "It's about my friend, Henri Gelbert. You see, the notebook was gone when we found Sergeant Spinkel. I was there too. Spinkel was dead, and we found him. That's all there is to it. You see?"

"Yes. And why are you telling me this?"

"Henri, well, he's worried that you might somehow think that he had that notebook."

Gott raised an eyebrow. "And why should I believe him? Or you?"

Edwin didn't know what to say. How could he make Gott believe him? "I have no reason to lie," he said finally.

"Of course you do! You wish to protect your friend. You see, I understand. I admire your loyalty. But remember, you have a higher loyalty, to the Fatherland. Do you understand?"

Edwin nodded.

Gott moved closer. "Your mother is alone. She wants both

her sons to come home someday. Do you love your mother? Of course you do. So, be a good boy, a good son. Don't protect this communist, no-soldier slob. When the time comes, you will show your true loyalty. I am certain of it."

Edwin was horrified as he realized that Gott had read his mother's letter.

Gott placed his hand on Edwin's shoulder. "*Ma'assalama*," he said. "You know what that means?"

Edwin shook his head. Gott leaned forward, and Edwin tried to step back. Gott tightened his grip, pulling Edwin close, clamping down on his shoulder so tightly that Edwin wanted to cry out.

"I'll tell you what it means. Come closer."

Edwin let himself be pulled toward Gott, who moved his mouth next to Edwin's ear. "It means," he whispered. There was silence for a second. Then Edwin felt the gentle touch of Gott's lips against his cheek.

Edwin jerked back, and Gott released his grip. Edwin looked around frantically, wondering if anybody had seen. Surely the other prisoners in line, the men on either side of him, must have. But the they all seemed unconcerned. Either they were deliberately not paying attention, or they assumed that Gott had simply whispered something in Edwin's ear.

Gott watched Edwin, a tight, grim smile on his lips. Then, with exaggerated casualness, he turned away and strode to the canteen table, moving past the other men in line. Without a word, Gott pointed at the pickle jar, and Engels wrapped all the remaining lemon drops in a scrap of newspaper. He handed the bundle to Gott, who opened it, took out a single piece, and popped it into his mouth. He sauntered toward the door, passing the men in line. As he passed Edwin, he winked.

Sam stared across the linen-covered table at his mother as

she calmly sipped her second gin and tonic. It was only six o'clock, and the Lighthouse Restaurant wasn't yet busy.

Sam wondered if she had the letters with her. She hadn't mentioned them when she'd called the camp an hour ago, telling him to meet her for dinner. The Lighthouse was Blanch's favorite restaurant, and she dined there at least once a week—once a month or so with Sam. He hadn't mentioned that he'd brought Hildy there just the night before.

"So dear, did you have a good day?" Blanch asked.

"Mom, we didn't get a chance to talk last night." Sam told himself to be careful, to slow down and not push her. "Actually, there was an incident yesterday. You remember I told you about the two prisoners who helped with the newspaper?"

"The young boy and the one with the French name."

"Yes, Edwin and Henri. Anyway, Henri tried to push his way out through the inner compound gate yesterday. The guards stopped him, of course."

"That doesn't sound like a method of escape that's likely to succeed."

"The awful thing is that he was being chased by a mob," Sam said. "It seems he told some other prisoners about Rommel's death and some other news. The Afrika Korps hardliners accused him of being a traitor."

"The Nazis, you mean?"

Sam nodded.

"And what happened?"

Sam told her about Harris attempting to negotiate with Gott and his own role in resolving the problem.

"Good for you, Sam. You see? Your little newspaper is doing some good."

"Yeah, well something tells me that neither Henri nor Edwin will ever work on it again. And I can't say I blame them. It's caused them nothing but trouble."

The waiter came to take their order, mentioning that steak was on the menu. Sam suspected that a local farmer was butchering his cows and selling the meat directly to restaurants, avoiding the meat ration restriction. He ordered a steak.

"So," Sam said after the waiter left, "I think you found some letters the other night."

Blanch leaned back in her chair and gazed at him. Her eyes narrowed. "I should've gone to the FBI," she said.

"Jesus, Mom! Why would you do that?"

"You know very well why. That Oskar Gruden is a Nazi, no better than those animals at the camp who chased that poor boy."

"But how do you know that? You can't read German. You don't know what's in those letters." What if she'd shown them to someone? "Right?" he said.

"I know more about Oskar Gruden than you might think."

"What do you mean?"

"Oh, never mind that now," she said, smiling and seeming to enjoy her secret. Then she pulled the letters from her purse and laid them on the table in front of Sam.

Sam guessed that she didn't know what was in them. And she was anxious for him to read them now.

"Of course," Blanch continued, "I couldn't help but notice the envelopes. Routing the letters through Mexico City. That's pretty damning."

"Yeah," Sam said. "That's what made Doris suspicious. Me too."

"That girl has a good head on her shoulders."

Sam pulled all the pages from both sets of envelopes, unfolded them, and saw that they were dated October 12 and November 24, 1943. About a year old. He turned to the last page of each and found that someone named Otto had signed them both. Spreading the October letter out on the table next to his plate, Sam began to read.

Within seconds, he knew the letter was harmless. His shoulders relaxed. It contained family news. Apparently, Otto was Oskar's brother, who seemed to have returned to Germany from the United States some time before the war started. Otto asked about Karl, Hildy, and especially about Hans. He talked at length about conditions in Germany and mentioned that there was still no news of Dieter. Sam guessed that Dieter was Otto's son, and he was in the German military.

"Well, what does it say?" Blanch asked.

"Just wait a second."

She pouted and waved at the waiter, pointing to her empty glass.

Sam put down the first letter and glanced at the second, certain it'd contain more of the same. He hesitated, embarrassed to be poking into the private lives of these people. What was he doing? He had no right to do this. As he started to refold the letter, he noticed the opening sentence.

Gute Nachrichten. Ich habe sie gefunden. Good news. I have found her.

Sam read on. Otto wrote that he'd finally located a woman named Lena Bauer, whom he referred to as Oskar's "accuser." It wasn't clear what this accusation was about, but it must have been serious, and it appeared to have happened many years before—before the Grudens immigrated to America. Maybe this incident was the reason they'd come, because Oskar was in trouble back home. Sam kept reading.

Otto went on to say that this woman had married and lived in a nearby town. He'd gone to see her. She was no longer pretty, and she'd grown fat. In return for one thousand reichsmarks, she promised that she'd go to the police and withdraw her complaint. And then, Oskar and his family could finally come home! After the war, of course.

The remainder of the letter was much like the first, family

news.

Frowning, Sam carefully folded the pages and returned them to their envelopes. So a woman in Germany had accused Oskar Gruden of something. Hildy had said they came to America when she was four years old, so it must have happened at least fifteen years ago. Oskar would've been in his thirties, maybe his late twenties.

"Sam! I want you to read them to me," Blanch said, interrupting his thoughts.

"They're mainly personal," he said, shaking his head. "Oskar Gruden may be an unrepentant Nazi, but there's no clue of that in these letters. I will tell you that they're from his bother in Germany and they contain family news. That's all."

"But that's not fair. Ah! So this Otto, who signed the letters, must be his brother, right? Is he married? Where in Germany?"

Sam hardly listened as he tucked the letters into the inner pocket of his suit coat. A pretty young woman, this Lena Bauer, had accused the young Oskar Gruden of something very serious. He had a sinking feeling. Standing up and tossing his napkin onto the table, he said, "I'm sorry, Mom. I've got to go."

"Why? What's wrong?"

"I've got to take these letters back."

"But why now? Can't you stay and eat your steak? What's the hurry?"

Sam leaned over and gave her a quick peck on the cheek.

"It's Doris," he said. "I think she could be in danger."

Ten minutes later at the Gruden house, Karl answered the door. He seemed startled to see Sam and quickly said, "Hildy's not here." As he started to push the door closed, Sam blocked it with his foot.

"I know you don't like me, Karl," Sam said. "I want you to

know that that the awful thing you said about Hildy and me, well, it's not true. Okay?"

"I know," Karl said, without looking at Sam.

"Oh," Sam said. "Then why …"

Karl said nothing for a moment, and then he said, "I guess maybe you better come in."

Sam followed him into the living room, where Doris sat on the couch. Karl moved to stand in front of the Victrola.

"Are you okay?" Sam asked Doris, thinking of Lena Bauer.

She looked puzzled. "Yes, but … oh, Sam," she said, almost whispering. She looked at him with soft, sad eyes.

He glanced back and forth between Doris and Karl. "What's going on? Is Hildy okay?"

Karl turned and lifted the Victrola lid. Then he closed it.

"Come sit down," Doris said, patting the couch next to her. "Hildy's, well, she's fine."

Sam sat. He was surprised when Doris put her hand on his arm.

"Sam, there ain't no good way of telling you this," she said. "A man came to the door a bit ago. We were all here, the whole family and me."

"He was drunk!" Karl said, turning around to look at Sam. "And acting crazy!"

"That's right," Doris continued. "And he wanted Hildy to go with him."

"What?" Sam shook his head. "I don't get it. Some drunk shows up to bother Hildy and you and Hans don't throw him out?"

"I wanted to," Karl said. "But …"

"But," Doris continued. "The man said something. He said he was tired of sneaking around." Her grip on Sam's arm tightened. "Sam, Hildy knew him. She's been seeing him."

Sam tried to swallow. He shook his head. No, this didn't make any sense. Hildy had been so sweet, so reassuring.

"He's the one!" Karl said. "I told you she was sneaking out at night. Nobody believed me, but I was right!"

This couldn't be true. If Hildy was out at night, then they were probably—his mind refused to follow the thought. "I don't believe it," he said.

Doris nodded. "I reckon it's hard, Sam. Mr. Gruden was fit to be tied. It was just awful. He kicked 'em both out. The man had a wedding ring, you see."

"Hans went after them," Karl said.

The memory of Hildy nodding off in the car as they drove to work flashed through Sam's mind. *Damn.* Tears welled up in his eyes.

"I was wondering why she started smoking," Doris said. "I think it was him."

Sam stared at her. "Hildy doesn't smoke."

"She does now."

"Yeah," Karl said. "I've seen her too."

Who was this girl they were talking about? It couldn't be Hildy; it was some other girl, someone he didn't even know.

The front door opened, and Hans walked into the living room, his face grim. "Where are Papa and Mutti?" he asked.

"Upstairs," Karl said.

"What're you doing here?" Hans said to Sam.

Sam didn't know what to say.

Doris stood and crossed over to stand at Hans's side. "We told him what happened," she said.

Hans stared at Sam, and then his eyes softened. "Uh, look, I'm sorry …"

It felt to Sam as if the room was flooding with pity, awful suffocating pity. He stood up and staggered toward the door.

"Wait," Doris said, following him. "There's something else."

Sam paused at the front door, and dimly it occurred to him that she must mean the letters. Wearily, he reached inside his suit coat.

"You know him," Doris said.

Sam's hand froze.

"I hate to tell you this, Sam, I surely do. But you gotta know. He works at the camp."

Martini! Of course. He smoked. Sam didn't know he was married, but then why would he? He should've done something that morning he talked to Hildy. I'll kill that bastard, Sam swore to himself.

"Sam," Doris said, "it's—"

She stopped as Sam pushed the door open and stumbled out. He almost bumped into Hildy, who was coming up the porch steps. He jumped back and stared at her, groping for words. Then, he noticed the man beside her.

Captain John Harris.

Doris watched in dismay as Sam pushed past Hildy and Harris, hurried down the sidewalk with his right leg dragging, climbed into his car, and sped away.

"What do you want?" Hans said to Harris, his voice cold and threatening. "Karl, go upstairs and get Papa."

Karl turned to obey.

"Karl! Stop, please," Hildy said. "Wait a second." When Karl hesitated, she said to Hans, "I just need to pick up some things. Some clothes. Doris, please help me. Come upstairs with me. Please."

"Don't do it," Hans said. "This isn't your business."

Doris figured he was right. Hildy might be her friend—at least Doris thought she was—but she'd better be careful. "Where will you go?" she asked Hildy.

Hildy said nothing, and then she glanced back at Harris, who stood a half step behind her. He seemed to be shaking; his eyes were wild.

"And how can you make a living?" Doris said. "You can't

go back to the camp, even if Sam is forced to quit." She glared at Harris. "Not when folks find out."

"Look," Harris said, swaying a bit from side to side. "Maybe it's best for everybody if we just keep this quiet."

Hildy turned to him, her eyes blinking rapidly. She swallowed. "You said ..."

"Yeah, yeah, I know," Harris said. He lifted a hand—Doris thought that it twitched—and started to put it on Hildy's shoulder. He then stopped as Hans took a step toward him. Harris's eyes flitted around, searching for support from somebody, but there was none to be had. Turning back to Hildy, he pointed inside the house. "Hildy, you've *got* to get the ..." He hesitated. "You know ..."

"Hildegard!" Oskar Gruden's voice boomed from the top of the stairway, and Hildy jumped back, shuddering.

Doris turned and saw Oskar ponderously coming down the stairs, the treads creaking with each step, his clothes rumpled, his hair disheveled and his face dark with rage. Gertrud followed, her expression blank. They stopped at the landing, half a dozen steps from the bottom, and stared down at the young people gathered at their front door.

"Hildegard, you will go to your room immediately!" Oskar shouted.

Hildy looked up at her parents like a rabbit hiding from a hawk circling overhead. She turned to Doris. "Please," she said. "I just need a few things. You're my friend."

"Stay out of this," Hans said.

Doris didn't move.

Hildy turned to Harris. "What should I do?" she asked.

"We need to get ..." His eyes darted around.

Doris reckoned he had sobered up a bit, but he was fidgety and still breathing hard.

"Look, I'm sorry," Harris said. "This's all a big mistake. I shouldn't have come here." He backed out onto the porch, his eyes averted. "I'm sorry," he repeated as he reached the top of the porch steps, almost stumbling down onto the lawn. He steadied himself, turned, and hurried away.

Hildy stood for a moment with her mouth half open, tears running down her cheeks. Her shoulders slumped, and she leaned back against the doorframe. Doris rushed to her side, wrapped an arm around her, and pulled her close.

"He left," Hildy whispered. "He just left."

"Come on," Doris said. She guided Hildy across the front hall and up the stairs. Doris was aware that Hans and Karl had slipped out the front door, and she figured that Captain John Harris should probably head for the hills. She pulled the weeping Hildy closer.

At the landing, Oskar and Gertrud stepped back so Doris and Hildy could pass. Doris glanced at Oskar's face and was surprised to see tears glinting in his eyes. As mad as he was, he couldn't stand to see his daughter suffering so much. Her gaze passed over to Gertrud's face. Her eyes were hard and her mouth was a thin, grim line.

The DeSoto careened around the curve, its rear wheels sliding in the gravel as Sam jerked the steering wheel back and forth, struggling to bring the big car under some semblance of control. The road turned and twisted as it followed the south bank of the Huron River, but there was a straight stretch ahead. He jammed the accelerator to the floor.

That two-faced bitch!

He gripped the steering wheel, twisting it beneath his white knuckles. How could she do this? How could she sneak around behind his back? How could she screw John Harris?

As he approached the next curve, Sam let up on the accelerator, and as he moved his bad right foot to the brake, it caught momentarily on the back of the pedal. When the DeSoto entered the curve too fast, Sam slammed down on the brake with both feet. The car spun around, throwing gravel everywhere. Panicking, Sam realized there was no guardrail between the road and riverbank, and as the car slid backwards, he felt one of the rear wheels slip off the shoulder. The car came to a sudden halt, partially off the road and facing the wrong way, the engine stalled and dust swirling around it.

Dazed, Sam stared straight ahead through the dirty windshield, seeing nothing, his heart pounding, and the steering wheel slippery with sweat beneath his hands. He took a breath.

As the dust began to clear, Sam regained his wits and realized he needed to move the car. Fortunately, it started right up, and he edged forward onto the right side of the road, facing back toward town. But that was the last place he wanted to go.

About fifty feet ahead, the county had built a small parking area in a wide spot between the road and the river. Used primarily by fishermen, it was empty now, so Sam eased the car forward and pulled in. He shut off the engine, slouched down, and threw back his head so it rested on the top of the seat.

Why did she do this? What did she see in John Harris?

Sam's right leg ached, and he kneaded his thigh as he thought.

He hoped it wasn't the stupid dancing. It was such a trivial thing. This damn leg. She did tell him she was bored with her life; she said it even after they started seeing each other. He guessed maybe he simply wasn't exciting enough for her. Sneaking out at night, having a secret lover—that must have been pretty exciting. Not to mention the sex. Sam rolled his head back and forth on the seat back. He should have moved faster.

On their fourth date, they'd sat in the car in front of her

house kissing, and when he touched her breast, she pushed his hand away. A minute later, he touched her again, and this time she let him. She then put her hand on his chest, unbuttoned a shirt button, and slipped it inside against his bare skin. Sam didn't know what to do. There was a street lamp, and the front porch light was on.

A few minutes later, when he'd walked her to the front door, she'd laughed and called him "such a nice guy." Now it was clear to him that she meant that he was boring.

Sam sat up and looked around. In front of him, through the windshield, he saw the Huron River drifting past in the gathering dusk. On the far side, a lone fisherman, an elderly man wearing hip waders, worked his way upstream. Heading for some favorite spot, Sam guessed.

He should've brought Hildy out here that night. He should've started the engine, driven to this very spot, and they would have climbed into the big back seat. If he had been smart enough, brave enough to do that, he knew she'd be his girl today. If he had not been such a nice guy.

The old fisherman came abreast of the car, saw it, and waved. Sam ignored him.

He'd thought John Harris was his friend. All this time, for weeks now, he'd been friendly in the office during the day, while at night the two of them had been shacked up at Harris's apartment in town.

He closed his eyes. He understood the "heartache" cliché for the first time in his life as he felt something cold and hard stabbing into his chest. This just wasn't worth it. From now on, he wouldn't be so stupid. He'd never let this happen to him again.

And what about his job? Could he go back to the camp and continue to work for Harris? Would Hildy be there? They couldn't all work in the same office. Right? Should he resign? Would the university take him back? The newspaper? He'd find something, of course; there were plenty of jobs with so many men in the service.

Sam opened his eyes and stared ahead. He eventually focused on the gas ration sticker pasted on the inside of his windshield. On the back side, facing him, were printed the words, "Is this trip really necessary?"

He decided he'd go to work tomorrow, to the camp, just like a regular day. He'd teach his Tuesday morning class on German history; do his paperwork. He'd somehow find two more prisoners to work on the newspaper. And he'd march right into Harris's office and ask him to approve his choices, just like he was supposed to do. He'd see what happened. If Harris tried to fire him, he could threaten to go public about his affair. In fact, Sam realized, he didn't need to get permission for the newspaper—or for any other goddamn thing! Harris was married and wanted a future in politics; he couldn't afford a scandal. Sam had that bastard by the balls.

The fisherman stood still, mosquitoes flitting around him as the sun slid deeper into the trees and shadows crept across the Huron River. His line drifted with the current.

Sam again wondered if Hildy would come to the office tomorrow. He smiled grimly. She wouldn't be riding with him, that's for sure. He pressed the starter button and the DeSoto's engine roared.

Then he turned off the ignition, and silence closed in around him again.

Hildy, he whispered. One thing I just don't get. Why did you keep going out with me? Why did you string me along?

It was dark, but Doris hadn't turned on the porch light. She sat on the wooden swing, gazing across the backyard, barely able to make out the rabbit hutches leaning against the side of the garage. It was so quiet that she heard the rabbits moving around inside and crunching on the collard greens, carrots, and endive that Gertrud fed them.

She figured she should go to bed. She had to work tomorrow.

But the prospect of climbing those two flights of stairs, the possibility of an encounter with Oskar or Gertrud on the second floor, it was just too much. She'd sit for a bit longer. Of course, she'd get more and more tired, and then she'd be even less likely to head upstairs. Maybe she was stuck here for the rest of her life.

She wished Hans would come home.

As she leaned against the back of the swing, it creaked, and Doris glanced up at the nearby window. Oskar's study. She needed to get those letters from Sam and put them back where she found them before it was too late. What a stupid thing to do.

Doris remembered the look in Oskar's eyes as she and Hildy had passed him on the staircase. A few weeks ago, he'd lifted Doris up and whirled her around when he'd announced that Hans was coming home on leave. Could such a man really be a Nazi?

The screen door squeaked as it opened.

"Hans?" Doris called out.

"No, sorry," Oskar said, stepping outside. He stood near the door, at the other end of the broad back porch, and squinted at her.

She shifted in her seat on the swing. It creaked again. She didn't know what to say.

"The house is so quiet," Oskar said. "I've been sitting in my study."

Doris nodded but said nothing. She watched his dark profile as he turned to look out over his small backyard. He stooped a bit. The rabbits, perhaps sensing that someone had come out of the house, were suddenly still. Oskar stared out at them. Finally, he turned away and pulled open the screen door. His feet shuffled on the wooden planks, and his shoulders drooped.

"Would you like to sit a spell?" Doris said.

Oskar turned and gave a hint of a smile. "Yes, thank you," he said. "That would be pleasant."

Doris stood, guessing he wanted to be alone.

"No, no, Miss Calloway. Please stay. We can talk a little."

He waited while she sat back down, and then carefully lowered himself onto the swing beside her. Looking over at him, it felt oddly familiar as Doris realized that she and Hans had sat together like this during his first week home. It seemed so long ago.

"So how's your family back in Kentucky?" Oskar asked.

Doris shrugged. "They're okay, I guess."

"That's good. You have brothers and sisters, yes?"

Doris shook her head. "No, sir."

"This house," Oskar said, "used to be so noisy. Three children, their friends. It seemed I was always yelling at them to turn down the radio or the phonograph."

Doris smiled. "I bet. I've got a mess of uncles and aunts and cousins. It's kind a like that at Christmas."

"I thought with Hans home, it would be the same," Oskar said, looking at his hands, folded in his lap.

"Did you talk to Karl?" Doris asked gently.

"He won't speak with me. He leaves in two weeks. Hans leaves next week."

Doris sighed. She'd known this, but she'd been trying to forget. What would happen? Would he just disappear from her life? Like William.

"And Hildy still might move out," Oskar continued.

"And then the house will be real quiet," Doris said. "But I reckon she's got to go some day."

"I know. Her mother wants her to marry, of course. I think maybe it'd be good for her to live by herself for a while.

Close, but not too close, you see."

"I'm surprised."

"What? That I am so progressive?" Oskar gave her a weak smile and shrugged. "Probably, I am just selfish. I know if I try to hold Hildy too tight, I may lose her forever." His smile faded.

Doris started to lift her right hand to reach across and give Oskar a reassuring pat. Then she stopped and put her hand back in her lap. "I was looking at the pictures in the dining room," she said. "There's this one of you in a track uniform. You sure do look a lot like Hans."

Oskar chuckled and waved his hand. "That was many, many years ago. Back home, of course. I ran the thousand-meter race for my gymnasium, my high school."

Doris remembered the track team photograph in Hans's room. "Hans was six when y'all came to America, right?" she said.

Oskar nodded.

"He seems pretty American."

"I suppose. Less than Hildy and Karl, of course. I think he remembers more about Germany." Oskar paused and looked at Doris. "He misses Germany. Or at least the Germany he remembers."

"And now he's got to go there and fight," she replied. And see what terrible things have happened, Doris thought, and are going to happen. He'd already gone through so much for his adopted country, and it ate him up inside. She reckoned that's why he so angry sometimes, like that afternoon with the duffle bag.

"Yes," Oskar was saying. "It will be very different from fighting the Japanese."

"It must be hard for you too," she said. "I mean, him going to back to Germany like this."

Oskar looked at her for a moment, and then he nodded and

said, "Fighting the Fatherland. Yes, it's very difficult—for me and his mother."

Doris stared across at his dark profile. This strange man. He was loyal to Germany, her country's enemy. He didn't want his son to fight there. And he admitted it.

"Mr. Gruden, do you still have family back in Germany? That must be—"

The porch light flared on, the screen door banged open, and Karl and Hans stepped outside. Doris leaped to her feet and next to her, groaning a little under his breath, Oskar pulled himself up. His sons turned toward them, both boys smiling broadly.

"Where have you been?" Oskar asked, his voice gruff as he walked toward them, Doris following.

"We had a little talk with that Harris guy," Hans replied.

"Yeah!" Karl added, rubbing his knuckles.

"Don't tell me you beat him up!" Doris said.

Hans seemed to notice Doris for the first time. "You're defending him?" he said.

"No, no. Of course not," Doris said quickly. "But he's a captain in the army. He could—"

Hans grinned at her and said, "He's married. It's pretty clear that if this gets back to his wife, it's going to cause big problems for him. I think we came to an understanding. Right, Karl? He's not going to see Hildy anymore, and he's not going to give us any trouble."

Hans seemed pleased with the way things had worked out, and with himself. Doris glanced at Karl, who continued to rub his knuckles. She thought that maybe this was for the best. But what about poor Sam? Would he lose his job? And Hildy? Suddenly it was all too much; she was wore out. She tried to catch Hans's eye, but he was watching his father. She figured she could talk to him tomorrow. Her bed beckoned to her, and she inched toward the kitchen door.

Oskar stood in front of his sons, looking back and forth between them. His face was unreadable.

Karl and Hans stood silently, waiting.

Oskar finally smiled. Looking at Doris, he said, "These are gute boys, eh?" He stepped forward awkwardly and then stopped, seemingly unsure what to do. Finally he stuck out his hand, and Hans shook it vigorously. "Gute boys," Oskar repeated. He turned to Karl, arm extended. Karl took his hand and started shaking it. Then Oskar put his other hand on Karl's shoulder and, after a moment of hesitation, he pulled his youngest son close in a clumsy hug. Karl wrapped his arms around his father and buried his face in the older man's shoulder.

Doris felt a tear welling up in the corner of her eye, and she quickly wiped it away. How could this man be a Nazi?

Chapter Nine

Adolf Hitler would soon be looking down on him. Edwin stared at the empty space on the far side of the mess hall, barely able to make out the nail where the portrait would hang later that night, after the American guards had left.

Two hours before, he'd taken a chair from one of the tables and placed it against the back wall. Sitting in it now, he knew he wasn't safe, but this seemed as close as he could get, especially until Henri returned.

The mess hall was empty, but the prisoner cooks were busy in the adjacent kitchen. As one of them sang an old Bavarian song, a silly ballad about lost love, Edwin listened and thought of Hildy. With all the trouble now, probably he'd never see her again. If only they hadn't found Spinkel in the shower building. If only Henri had not talked to the Americans. If only he and Henri had not come under the scrutiny of Staff Sergeant Helmut Gott. Then, maybe there would be a way to talk with her again. He remembered the smell of the paper coming out of the mimeograph machine. He'd told Hildy that it reminded him of baking bread, and her pretty eyes had smiled at him.

Edwin wondered if he should go back to the barracks. Henri might be waiting. He must have come back from his work detail by now. Edwin did not move.

The singing stopped, and he glanced at the door leading to the kitchen. One of the cooks came out. He looked like most of the prisoners, young and dressed in his old German army uniform, and Edwin guessed he was the one who had been singing. Now his lips were pursed in a silent whistle as he carried a metal box full of forks and spoons, set it on a table, and then glanced at Edwin. His face turned hard. He stared at Edwin for a moment and then returned to the kitchen.

Where was Henri? As the question passed through Edwin's mind for the hundredth time, Henri walked through the door, followed by Martini.

Edwin jumped up and started toward them. Then he noticed that Henri and Martini had their heads together in an intense, whispered conversation. As Edwin watched, Henri took something from his pocket and slipped it to Martini, who quickly tucked it into his own pocket. He nodded to Henri and left.

Henri started to follow, but then he noticed Edwin. A shadow passed over his face for a second, but then he smiled and strode over.

"So, what are you doing here?" he said, gesturing at the chair. "Sitting back here by yourself."

"Where have you been? Why are you going out on work details when you don't have to? Why are you leaving me here alone all day?"

"Slow down, slow down, my friend." Henri glanced around the empty room. He gently pushed Edwin back down into the chair and then pulled another over from a nearby table. He sat. "This is a good place to talk," he said.

Edwin stared at him.

"I have some news," Henri continued quietly. "Look." He pulled an envelope from his pocket. "I'm afraid I've kept another little secret from you, my young friend. From that first day when we met on the train, I've wondered if I should tell you." He showed Edwin the envelope. "My father has a sister, my Aunt Marthe, who lives in Chicago. That's a large city only a few hundred kilometers from here. I've written to her, and today I received this letter back."

Edwin struggled to understand what Henri was saying. He looked at the envelope and saw that it was addressed to Max Lohmann—the farmer they'd worked for.

"Yes, you see I am not using the camp post office," Henri said, smiling. "Max has been very helpful, mailing my letter and receiving this one for me. He wants to help."

"Help you do what?" Edwin lowered his voice. "Escape?"

Henri nodded. "Dear Aunt Marthe has sent money. Max will provide clothes. Sometime soon, that snake Martini will look the other way when I slip off the truck coming back from working in the fields. In return for two hundred American dollars."

"What about me? You promised you'd take me."

Henri tucked the envelope into his pocket. "I know," he said. "I've been thinking about this a great deal." He stood up and scanned the room. Then he turned back to Edwin. "You speak almost no English," he said. "How can you pass for an American?"

"I won't say anything. I'll stay with you."

Henri began pacing back and forth.

"I look young," Edwin continued. "Nobody will guess I'm an escaped prisoner."

"My friend, there is something you don't understand about me, a difference between us. You want to return home, to your dear mother. You think you can find a way back to Germany. But Edwin, I don't want to go back. I will climb onto a freight train heading for Chicago. It passes right by Max's farm. There, my aunt will help me. Chicago has millions of people, many thousands of Germans. I will disappear. And I will stay in America, even after the war."

Edwin leaned forward, his elbows on his knees and his hands covering his face. He squeezed his fingers over his eyes until flashes danced through the darkness, and his eyeballs ached. The light shifted and shivered. A crescent moon came and went. The wind rattled bare branches over his head.

Edwin snapped his eyes open. "I also have a secret," he said.

Henri sat down in his chair next to Edwin.

"The night before the Americans captured me," Edwin said. "I woke up and Axel was gone."

"Your friend deserted."

Edwin nodded.

"And he left you behind," Henri continued. "I see. And I am very sorry. But you understand that I am not this Axel, yes? I'm telling you now what I'm going to do. It's not a surprise."

Edwin glared at him. "So it's all right to abandon me if you tell me first? Is that what you're saying?"

Henri's mouth opened to answer, but he said nothing.

"You think you're so smart," Edwin continued, "that you know everything. But you don't. No one knows this. The next morning, the Americans overran our bivouac. We didn't see them coming, and there was no fighting. That was good. We became prisoners. They put us inside a metal fence. They gave us food and water; we ate better than we had for days. I thought it wouldn't be so bad." He stopped.

"Go on," Henri said gently.

Edwin continued, his voice flat. "That night, three of them came. They had wine."

"The Americans?"

"They took me into a dark wood. They … they … it went on for a long time. I remember the moon shining through the branches of the trees."

"The monsters." Henri stood up, his face red. "The fucking

monsters."

Edwin saw tears in Henri's eyes. Edwin tried to wipe his own tears, but his cheeks were dry.

"Gott," Edwin said. "He kissed me."

Henri sat down again as Edwin described what had happened in the canteen. When Edwin finished, Henri said, "And if I leave you here, by yourself ..." Henri stared at the floor.

Edwin waited, watching Henri, afraid to breathe.

Finally, Henri spoke quietly. "You will go with me," he said still gazing at the floor. "We'll escape to Chicago together. We'll get jobs, you'll learn English, and someday you will go to school." He looked up at Edwin. "Maybe me too, eh? Soon, when the war is over, you will take a big ocean liner back to Germany to be with your mother. You'll look back and see me standing on the dock, waving goodbye. A good plan, yes?"

Edwin swallowed and nodded.

Henri reached over to put his arm across Edwin's shoulder.

Edwin jerked away.

As Sam stepped through the front door of the HQ building, he saw Mrs. Lewis sitting at her desk with her face in her hands. Behind her, the door to Captain Harris's office was closed.

"Is everything okay, Mrs. Lewis?" he asked.

She looked up and, as she focused on Sam, she pulled a lace handkerchief from her sleeve and dabbed at her eyes. Sam wasn't sure how old she was, maybe in her late fifties. She'd worked in the University of Michigan records office for many years, he knew, and she ran the HQ office with stern efficiency. It was disconcerting to see her upset.

"The camp is being shut down," she said.

"No!" Sam said. He'd heard rumors, of course. The

prisoners had mostly been idle now that the fall harvest was finished. But it was still hard to imagine.

"The prisoners and soldiers will move south," she continued. "The civilians, you and me and the others, will be let go."

For the second day in a row, Sam's world suddenly shifted around him. It seemed that all his worries—working with Harris, driving to work without Hildy, his classes, the newspaper—none of them mattered anymore. And, he needed a job.

"I'm sorry," Sam said. "Is it going to be hard for you to find another position?"

She dabbed her eyes and shrugged. "There are plenty of jobs. Even for old ladies like me."

Sam knew this was true. And it wouldn't be so bad for him either—he'd been thinking of leaving anyway, of course, and was pretty sure he wouldn't be out of work for long. That was important; his father's small pension wasn't enough to support his mother.

"You'll go back to the university?" Mrs. Lewis asked.

"I doubt they'll have a lecturer position open," he said. "Certainly not until the winter term starts. I can probably do some reporting for the *News*. Like you say, there's plenty of work, but it sure is inconvenient."

"I felt like I was really helping the war effort," Mrs. Lewis said. "That's what I'll miss."

Sam nodded and moved to stand next to her.

"How long do we have?" he asked.

"A few weeks, I'm sure. It'll take time to do all the transfer paperwork, shut things down properly, and transport everybody."

"That's something, anyway. Gives us time to get our ducks in a row, huh?"

Mrs. Lewis smiled at him. Then she looked around the

office and frowned. "Where's Miss Gruden?" she asked. "Didn't she ride with you today?"

Sam took a breath. He had tried to think about what he'd say when he got to the office. "No," he said. "You see—"

The door behind Mrs. Lewis opened, and Harris stepped out. Sam wasn't surprised to see a dark bruise beneath one eye. Sam forced a broad smile. "Good morning, Captain!" he said brightly.

Harris ignored him. He dropped a piece of paper on Mrs. Lewis's desk. "Type this, two carbons," he said and retreated back into his office, closing the door.

Mrs. Lewis scanned the page, her face darkening as she read. She glanced over her shoulder at Harris's door and then turned to Sam, her jaw set and her eyes hard with anger. She pushed the page at him.

It was a brief handwritten letter to Sam, informing him that he was dismissed, effective immediately.

"So much for getting my ducks in a row," Sam said.

"You could fight it," she said. "Send a letter to the Provost Office in Washington."

"Over a few weeks of work? They're not going to override a camp commanding officer for this."

"Maybe you can get him to change his mind." Her voice was bitter. "Especially if you knew something, had some kind of information." She looked up at Sam. "I've been loyal. He's my boss. But I know things …"

Sam raised his hand and waved it back and forth, shaking his head. He couldn't bear to hear her say anything about Harris and Hildy. "I think I'll just get my stuff together and go," he said and turned away.

It only took a few minutes to pack his few personal belongings. He had some books and papers. He'd brought in his diplomas and hung them on the wall of his tiny office. Everything fit easily into a cardboard box he found in the supply room.

After bidding a final farewell to Mrs. Lewis and promising to call her, Sam walked outside. It felt strange, heading for his car when the morning sun was still low in the southeast sky.

A truck backed up to the gate leading to the inner compound. A dozen or so prisoners stood near the rear of the truck, apparently waiting to climb in. Sam recognized Henri, his head sticking up above the shorter men around him. Sam waved, but Henri didn't seem to notice.

"Henri!" Sam called out.

Henri looked up.

Sam walked over. "Going out today?" he said, smiling. "I thought you hated doing real work."

Henri shrugged, "It's better to be away from camp."

"Oh," Sam replied, remembering the incident at the gate with Gott. He realized that there was no longer anything he could do to help Henri. "I just wanted to say goodbye," he said, shaking Henri's hand.

Henri looked confused. He hadn't shaved, and his coat was unbuttoned even as an October wind swept through the compound. "Goodbye? Why do you say that to me?" he asked. He noticed the box tucked under Sam's arm. "What's that?"

Sam shrugged. "My last day. The camp is closing."

"What? So soon!"

Sam realized that the prisoners probably hadn't been told anything official. He should be more careful. Oh, screw it. What did he care now?

"Yeah, probably soon."

"But you're leaving today. Is that correct? Our little experiment in 'freedom of the press' has turned out badly. As I anticipated, you've been dismissed."

"No, no. That's not it."

Sam felt Henri's eyes on him, expecting an explanation.

No, it was more sordid and petty and mean than any grand issue of human freedoms. But he couldn't tell Henri the truth. He shook his head. "No, no, nothing like that," he said. "The camp could close today or next week, I really don't know."

"Today?" Henri whispered, eyes turning glassy. He started to turn away.

Sam put his hand on Henri's arm, pulling him back around. "Where's Edwin?" he asked.

"Oh, he's probably in the mess hall. Sitting by himself."

"Well, say goodbye to him for me. He's a good boy. I wish I'd been able help him more."

"Edwin. Yes, he's a good boy." Henri looked sad. "And he's been through so many troubles."

"All right! *Betreten sie* truck." Private Martini pushed his way through the crowd of prisoners, his rifle slung carelessly on his back. "We ain't got all day. *Schnell, schnell.* Hey, what're you doin' here, professor?" he said when he saw Sam.

Sam ignored him. He shook Henri's hand again, turned away, and walked to his car.

Late in the afternoon, Edwin stood in the center of the assembly area, staring at the inner gate with its two bored guards and the HQ building just beyond. The faint sound of a radio drifted down from the guard tower overhead. Edwin had been standing by himself for half an hour, waiting. Nobody said anything to him, or even approached him, and that was what he wanted. As he'd already done several times, he turned around slowly, his eyes searching for danger, and then he faced the gate again. It'd be hard for anyone to sneak up on him here. Edwin's knees bowed slightly inward, and he forced himself to straighten them. He had to pee.

Henri had gone out a work detail again, some kind of roadwork for the local government. Edwin couldn't understand why Henri would go out alone, without him.

The gate opened, and Sergeant Engels stepped through, his arms filled with boxes. He ignored the guards, and they ignored him. Edwin stared at the boxes, guessing they were supplies for the canteen, maybe even candy! His mouth watered at the thought of lemon drops. But just as quickly, the memory of Gott's lips brushing against his cheek washed over him, and his mouth was soon as dry as the dusty assembly area around him.

Engels strode past without a word, but his eyes betrayed the disgust he felt for Edwin—this weakling, this poor excuse for a German soldier.

The roar of a truck motor sounded on the other side of the gate, and the guards swung it open wide. An olive drab army truck backed up so its load of prisoners could climb out into the inner compound.

At last! Henri was back. Edwin was safe. Henri probably needed to go to the latrine after that long ride, and then they could eat dinner. Edwin smiled for the first time that day.

Martini climbed out of the front passenger seat and lighting a cigarette as he walked, came around to the back of the truck. He shouted at the prisoners, and one by one the tired and dirty men climbed down. Corporal Becker, the soccer player, was the last man out.

Edwin stared at the empty truck. He turned to Becker and asked, "Where's Henri?"

"You don't know?"

Edwin shook his head. "What?"

Becker stepped closer. "I'm sorry," he said. "Henri … No, I shouldn't speak of this."

Edwin whispered, "Did Henri escape? You can tell me. I'm his best friend."

Appearing sad and slightly confused, Becker replied, "So I thought. But if that's true, why didn't he tell you himself?"

He turned away.

Edwin grabbed his arm. "I thought you were my friend too!"

"That's all I can say," Becker murmured, pulling free. "My duty ..."

Tears welled up in Edwin's eyes, and he turned around so nobody would see them. He'd been betrayed—again. Just like Axel had abandoned him in that French apple orchard, now Henri had also left him behind here in America. How could he do this? Edwin had trusted him.

"Hey!" Martini called out, and Edwin jumped. Martini laughed and said something in English that Edwin didn't understand. Edwin knew Martini was making fun of him. He knew, of course, because Henri had paid him off. Martini gestured with his thumb to Edwin, pointing at the barracks. He snarled something in English, and Edwin turned obediently.

He wondered what he should do. Henri was gone. How could he be safe that night in the barracks? What about the Heilige Geist? What about Gott? Ahead, in the dusty street between the rows of barracks, he saw prisoners shuffling toward the mess hall.

Edwin would go there. He'd be safe for a while. Then after dinner—

The evening head count! That's when they'll discover that Henri was gone. The Americans will question Martini, and he'll get in a little trouble for not being careful, but that's why Henri had bribed him with his aunt's money. Then, they'd come for Edwin. They'd both be after him, the Americans and Gott!

Edwin turned and ran until he reached the end of the barracks street, and the inner fence stood tall and impenetrable before him. He saw nobody; the rest of the prisoners were at dinner. To his right, the gravel road led to the latrine and the shower building.

Edwin shuddered at the memory of Sergeant Spinkel hanging by an electrical cord, swaying slowly.

Doris wished the kitchen had a radio as she picked up a plate and carefully dried it. She reckoned it was too much to ask of Mrs. Gruden, who was so old-fashioned and old country. It was a good thing Hans didn't take after her, or they'd never have any fun. Not that they really did anyway. She sighed as she gently set the plate on top of the stack in the cupboard.

Dinner had been quiet. They were all there, even Hildy. She said very little as Karl and Hans talked about their plans for fishing the next day. Oskar was subdued, listening to his sons, and occasionally glancing down the table at Hildy. Once or twice, Doris thought she caught him looking at her, but then he quickly turned away.

Doris had tried to get Hans to talk with her, but he'd put her off. He wasn't exactly rude, but he seemed more interested in fishing than in her.

As Doris put away the last plate, she felt the presence of Gertrud behind her. Doris wiped her hands on the towel and hung it on its bar just so, the way she'd been shown. She turned around to face Gertrud.

"Come to the hutches with me," the older woman said. Doris swallowed as she saw that Gertrud carried her metal pail, a cloth covering its top and a wooden handle sticking out through it. Although the pail appeared to be clean, it was dented and stained.

Following Gertrud out into the backyard, Doris thought maybe she'd have a chance to ask Gertrud about life back in Germany. Maybe she could finally figure out this family's story.

There were five hutches, each with two or three rabbits.

Gertrud put down her pail and pulled a wooden stool out from under one of the hutches.

Still not saying a word, Gertrud bent down and looked inside a hutch containing three large rabbits. As Doris leaned over so she could also see them, she was surprised at the sweet and grassy smell. The rabbits were all the same brown color, with a few white markings. She reckoned they were probably brothers and sisters and that the parents were in one of the other hutches. All three jumped back and forth in the straw bedding, occasionally stopping for a second to stare up at Gertrud.

"Sebastian, I think," Gertrud said. There was a brick on top of the hutch. As she moved it aside and lifted the top, the rabbits jumped about more frantically. "Quiet, my children," Gertrud said.

Reaching inside, she put her hand on the back of the largest rabbit, holding it there until he quieted. Then using both hands, she carefully lifted Sebastian out of the hutch, and Doris lowered the top for her and replaced the brick.

Gertrud sat on the stool with the rabbit in her lap. Sebastian was still, his eyes wide and staring straight ahead, unseeing. Cooing quietly, Gertrud stroked its fur. "*Weich, weich,*" she whispered. Without looking up, she said, "So soft. Come, touch."

Doris leaned over and touched the animal's back. Sebastian trembled beneath her fingers.

"I have something to tell you, Doris," Gertrud said. She shifted the rabbit around in her lap. "Pay attention to me," she said, never taking her eyes off Sebastian.

"Yes, ma'am."

Quickly, Gertrud grabbed the rabbit's rear legs with one hand, and curled her other hand around his neck, stretching him out full length in front of her. He struggled violently, but Gertrud's strong hands and arms held him firmly. Doris stepped back.

"It is finished between you and Hans. *Kaputt! Es wird getan.*"

Gertrud's hand wrenched Sebastian's head around and there was a dull snap. The rabbit lay suddenly still.

Doris stared at her, gasping.

Gertrud pulled the limp body to her chest and held him. "*Ruhe jetzt, mein kind,*" she said. She lifted the rabbit's face; his eyes were wide open and still glistening with recent life. She kissed him on the top of his head.

Doris backed away, her eyes wide in horror. The world seemed to whirl around her. What was going on? What was this crazy woman telling her?

Gertrud stood, lifting the rabbit carcass by its rear legs, and let the rest of the body swing down in front of her. "And you must move out," she said. "You may sleep here tonight, but tomorrow you go." She moved to a spot against the garage wall between two hutches, pushing the pail into place with her foot.

"Why are you doing this?" Doris asked.

There was a hook screwed into the garage wall, approximately at eye level. Beneath it, the wall bore a faint, but unmistakable red stain. Gertrud jammed one of the rabbit's rear legs onto the hook, piercing it between the tendon and the bone. She lifted the cover on the pail from the kitchen and pulled out the knife, its blade thin and sinister. Grabbing the rabbit's ears, she stretched out the carcass, and with one swift motion, cut off the head. Blood gushed into the pail.

Doris felt the gorge rise in her throat.

Gertrud looked at Doris, holding the head up in front of her, dangling by its ears. There was a spray of blood across her cheek. "We don't want you here anymore," she said. "You're bad for our family." She dropped the head into the pail, and Doris heard the sound of a splash and a clunk.

"What are you talkin' about?" Doris asked, her voice becoming shrill. "How am I bad for Hans? I know that he's got troubles, but I'm tryin' to help him."

Gertrud shrugged.

Doris realized that Gertrud had not specifically mentioned Hans; she'd said that Doris was bad for the family. What did she mean? Was it Karl? Had he told his mother that Doris had talked him into enlisting? Doris doubted that. Was it Hildy? That couldn't be. In the awful incident with John Harris, Doris had clearly sided with the family. Even Gertrud could see that. Who else? With a sinking feeling, Doris remembered what Hildy had said, that her father had a little crush on her. Oh, God. Was that it?

"Please, Mrs. Gruden. I never wanted any trouble. Just tell me what I've done wrong, and I'll fix it."

"It's too late. Tomorrow, you go."

The woman was as stubborn as Doris's father. Doris remembered him standing in her way that night when William had come to the house. Well, not this time.

Doris jabbed her finger at Mrs. Gruden. "You can't tell me what to do," she shouted. "You ain't *my* momma, thank God." When her daddy had threatened William with a shotgun, her own momma had stood by, watching. "I'm gonna talk to Hans," Doris added, "and you can't stop me." She whirled around and started toward the house.

"Go ahead. It will do no good."

Doris stopped and turned back. "He ain't a boy no more," she said. "He's a growed-up man now, a soldier."

"Yes, Hans is a gute soldier. He follows orders."

"I don't believe you. That's not Hans." Even as Doris said this, she wasn't so sure.

Gertrud had cut off the rabbit's tail, the dangling rear foot, and the front feet. Most of the bleeding had stopped. She used the knife to slice into the skin just below the joint on the suspended leg. As she worked her way down the body, she said, without looking up, "Ask him."

"Oh, I'll do that!" Doris said. "Don't you worry." Again she turned toward the house and again she stopped and turned back. "What about Mr. Gruden?" she asked. "I can't right believe he approves of this."

"He does," Gertrud replied without looking up from her work.

Doris wondered if it was Mr. Gruden pulling the strings. He was the head of this family, after all. Doris watched Gertrud's face as she worked at cutting and removing the rabbit's pelt. And then, finally, she knew the truth.

"What is it with you people?" she yelled. "I swear the newsreels are right. All you care about is following orders. Is that what being German means?" She thought of the armband she'd found in the attic, the black swastika against the white and red background. "You're just a bunch of goddamn Nazis!"

Gertrud stopped her work, leaving the rabbit skin hanging, half removed. She slowly turned to Doris, knife in hand, red with blood.

"Nobody in this country understands the New Germany," she said.

Doris ran for the house, seething. So that was it. Oskar Gruden wasn't the Nazi; it was his wife.

As Doris slammed the back door behind her, she heard laughter, and the thought of someone finding something funny in this house made her even more furious. In the living room, she found Mr. Gruden in his easy chair, the big RCA Victor console radio beside him crackling with the tinny sound of laughter and applause. On the couch opposite him, Karl sat sideways, his stocking feet stretched out across the cushions.

Doris stalked into the room and put her hands on her hips. "Where's Hans?" she asked.

Oskar and Karl looked up.

"Hi, Doris," Karl said. "You want to listen to the radio with us? Jimmy Durante is on."

"Where's Hans?" Doris asked again.

"He's in his room, Miss Calloway," Oskar replied. He spoke quietly, his eyes returning to the glowing dial on the front of the radio.

Doris turned to leave, but then she stopped and walked over to the couch. Karl gazed up at her.

"Karl, listen to me," she said. "This here is important. In America, we think for ourselves. Got that? You promise me that when you come back from the army, you'll be all growed up." She glared over at Oskar and then turned back to Karl. "You won't have to do what your momma and papa tell you. Go to college, get a job, do what *you* want, okay?"

Karl nodded vigorously. "Sure thing, Doris."

Doris glanced at Oskar again, expecting him to say something. Instead, he stared at the radio, his face flat and immobile, but with a puzzling glimmer in his eyes.

"Good," Doris said, turning back to Karl. She reached out and pushed an errant lock of hair away from his forehead. Poor kid. Fighting his folks without any help from nobody. But he's winning, he's escaping. "While you're gone, we can write," she said. "And when you come home safe, we'll go out and have that dinner together. Okay?"

Karl swallowed and nodded. "That'd be swell."

Ignoring Oskar, Doris returned to the front hallway and bounded up the stairs, her anger returning with each slamming step. At the top, she saw only closed bedroom doors. She stood in front of Hans's and rapped loudly with her knuckle.

"Hans, I got to talk to you."

Silence. She knocked harder and longer.

"Hans!" she shouted.

"I'm not feeling well," was the muffled reply from behind the door.

"Oh, please. You're just scared to face me." She tried the doorknob, but it was locked from the inside. "Open this door so we can talk."

Silence.

Was he standing by the door, waiting for her to leave? Was he climbing out the window? Was he curled up on his bed, crying? All of these images made her even angrier.

"Open this damn door!" She slammed her open hand against the door, pounding over and over. She had let him kiss her. Right here on this spot! "You momma's boy!" she shouted. "You coward!"

A few steps away, Hildy's door opened, and she peeked out. "What's going on?" she asked.

"Are you part of this?" Doris said, wheeling around to confront her. "Do you know what your goddamn *Mutti* has done?"

Hildy stepped out into the hallway, her eyes red and her hair disheveled. "Don't talk about my mother like that. You've no idea what she went through back in Germany."

"I don't care!" Doris shouted at her. "Nothin' gives her the right to run y'all's lives like she does. All your lives. And now mine too!"

Hans's door opened. "Leave her alone," he said to Doris.

Doris whirled around to him. His face, normally dark from the South Pacific sun, was pale. "Why, Hans?" she asked, her voice only slightly subdued. "Why don't you want to see me anymore?"

"It's not up to me."

"Why sure it is. Like my papa says, you're free, white, and

twenty-one. You got a right to go out with any girl you want. This is America."

"Not really. Not in this house."

"So you follow orders. From your momma."

"You don't understand," Hans said, looking down at his feet.

Through the bedroom door, Doris saw Han's bed, neatly made, but with his duffle bag, still dirty, sitting incongruously on top of the chenille bedspread. That bed. She flushed at the memory, and at the same moment she realized that Hildy was still standing behind her, watching them. Doris pushed Hans into the bedroom, followed him, and slammed the door behind her. Hans backed up against the bed.

Doris took a breath and said, "What'd I do wrong? I know you musta seen awful things in the war. I surely understand that. But why can't you give us a chance?"

Hans met her eyes. "I don't think I can love anyone right now. After the last three years, nothing makes sense." He glanced at the duffle bag and then moved slightly so he stood between it and Doris.

"I just wanted to help you, Hans. See if we could … I mean, I thought that maybe … Is this all because of what your momma says?"

"It's just easier this way."

Easier? How could he not love her because it was easier? Her anger boiled back up inside her. That was it. It was time to go. She had to stop wasting her time here.

"Goodbye, Hans," she said. As she turned toward the door, she saw him look at the duffle bag. What was it with that damn bag? She stepped close to the bed, and as she reached down to picked it up, Hans grabbed her wrist. He held on tight, staring at her, but after a moment he dropped his eyes and let go.

"Go ahead," he said, his voice both embarrassed and

defiant. "Take a look if you want. It's Karl's birthday present."

Her hands shaking slightly, she struggled to unhook the clasp at the top of the bag. She peered inside and saw something gray, almost white, down at the bottom. She reached in, and her hand closed on a rounded surface, like a ball, but it felt waxy beneath her fingertips. Her index finger found a hole, she was able to grasp it, and she pulled it out of the bag.

"Oh, my lord Jesus!" she cried as the skull tumbled onto the bed. It lay there, its empty eye sockets staring at the ceiling, missing its jawbone and with only a few top teeth. "Hans! What is this? I mean …Christ, is there anyone in this family that's not crazy?" She grimaced and rubbed her fingers against her skirt.

"Doris, please, it wasn't—" he said.

The door opened and Hildy peered in, her eyes immediately focusing on the skull. She didn't seem surprised. "It's from a Jap soldier," she said.

Doris looked back and forth between them. "You knew about this?"

Hildy shrugged. "He's my brother. He talks to me. Look, don't go nuts, Doris. Did you see that picture in *Life* magazine last year? This girl was writing her boyfriend, thanking him for sending her a souvenir Jap skull. The skull was right there in front of her in the picture."

Like most people in America, Doris had seen that picture, and she remembered being appalled and disgusted. She also remembered that in the picture there was writing on top of the skull. Forcing herself, she leaned over the bed and saw the words "Happy Birthday Karl" written above the eye sockets.

Downstairs, the doorbell rang.

"You people drive me crazy," she said. "I want nothing more to do with any of you. I'm packing up and getting out of this house as soon as I can."

As she stepped through the door, she heard Karl's voice in the hallway below. *Karl.* The skull was for him. She looked back into Han's room.

"Karl refused to take it," she said to Hans. "He's the only sane person in this family. You understand that, right?"

Hans nodded, but Hildy just stared at her.

Karl appeared on the stair landing below them. "Hey!" he called up. "That Sam Demsky guy is here."

Hildy put her hand to her hair. "Oh," she said. "What should I do? Doris?"

Doris stared at her in disbelief. "If you think," she said, "I'm going to give advice on your love life—"

"Actually," Karl said, "he asked to see you, Doris."

Sam waited outside the Gruden front door, his hands in his pockets and his shoulders slouched. Karl had reluctantly asked him to come inside, but Sam had refused.

The door swung open, and Doris looked at him. She wore no makeup, her red hair stuck out at odd angles, and her eyes blazed. For the first time, Sam noticed that Doris's eyes were blue.

"What do you want?" she asked.

"We have some unfinished business."

Doris blinked at him. "I'll get my coat," she said, disappearing. A moment later, she stepped outside, pulling her coat around her and shivering.

"I'm so glad to get outta that house," she said. "Let's walk."

"Sure."

When they reached the street, Doris turned left and Sam followed.

"I heard shouting," he said.

"Oh, I reckon that was me," Doris said. She shook her

head. "It's crazy in there."

"Yeah?"

Doris glanced at him for a second, shook her head and said, "It don't matter now. I'm movin' out tomorrow."

"Oh. Well, that's probably for the best. You see—"

"Oh, Sam! I'm sorry," Doris said, interrupting. "I didn't ask how you're doin'. I mean after ..."

Sam knew she meant after the disaster with Hildy. "Well, I've had better weeks," he said. "This morning, that bastard Harris fired me."

"What a son-of-a-bitch. What're you gonna do?"

"I keep thinking about it. I know I should do something, but damned if I can figure out what."

"Hildy's miserable," Doris said. "If that helps."

"Really?" Sam thought about it. "Well, good," he said. "That does help."

Doris glanced over at him, and he saw that she was smiling.

They walked in silence for a while. There was no snow yet, but the air was hard with the smell of it.

"I've got the letters," Sam said finally.

"I figured. Well?"

"My mother found them, and it took a while for me get them away from her. It's a good thing she doesn't read German." Sam stopped walking and turned to Doris. "Look, I'm glad you're moving out. You're not safe in that house."

"What do you mean?"

"The letters were from Mr. Gruden's brother."

"Otto?" Doris said. "They were signed by someone named Otto."

Sam told her about the second letter, about Lena Bauer.

"So you think Mr. Gruden, uh, messed with that woman back in Germany?" Doris asked.

Sam nodded.

"As crazy as that family is, that just don't sound like him."

"It was over fifteen years ago. Who knows what he was like then?"

"I reckon. You're right, all the more reason for me to get out." Doris thought for a moment. "What about him being a Nazi? Anything like that?"

Sam shook his head. "Otherwise, it was just family stuff. No secret orders from Berlin, I'm afraid."

"That's good, I guess."

"I feel a little guilty about reading those letters," Sam said. "They're private, after all. I keep looking back over the last couple of months, since I met Hildy and went to work at the camp, and everything. I keep trying to understand what I did wrong that would bring down all this misery on myself. The only thing I've figured out so far is that I shouldn't have these letters, and it was wrong to read them."

"I don't see the connection."

"Neither do I," Sam said. He took two large envelopes from his coat pocket. "I'm just saying it's time to make this right. I could take them to Mr. Gruden, of course. But that might cause more trouble for you."

Doris stared at the envelopes for a moment, and then said, "Give 'em to me. It was wrong for me to take them. They're his property, no matter what might've happened fifteen years ago. Like you say, they're private."

He handed the envelopes to her, and she tucked them inside her coat.

"I'll make it right, Sam," she said.

They turned a corner. Sam realized they'd already gone around the block, and he saw the Gruden house up ahead. They were back to where they'd started. Gesturing at the house, he said, "You said it's crazy in there. Do you need some help?"

Doris glanced, and shuddered, and then shook her head. "I

ain't stayin' more than one night," she said. "I'm going straight to my room and pack. I'll take my stuff with me to work in the morning."

"What're you going to do?"

"I give up. I'm gonna quit work and go home to Kentucky."

"What? Are you sure?" Sam looked into her eyes, noticing again that they were blue.

Doris shrugged. "I reckon I got to settle things with my folks. And there's this boy. He's in Europe now, and I'm gonna go talk to his momma."

Wait, he thought. Her eyes weren't just blue. There was a touch of green in them.

"So I reckon this is goodbye." Doris continued.

Sam took a breath and then nodded. "I suppose it's best." He reached out to shake her hand, but Doris lifted herself up on her toes and gave him a peck on the cheek. Turning, she headed toward the house, and after a few steps, she looked back over her shoulder and waved.

Sam waved back. Then he stuck his hands in his pockets and slouched away.

Chapter Ten

The wooden beam where Sergeant Spinkel had hanged himself was just a few feet away, but the lights were off so Edwin couldn't see it. Water dripped from the overhead pipes and the shower heads onto the plywood floor, and he heard a faint trickle as it drained away into a nearby ditch. In a relatively dry corner, far from the door, he sat curled into a ball, his arms wrapped around his knees.

He wondered what time it was. He had no watch. A while ago, he'd heard the bugle call over the loud speaker announcing the evening headcount, but surprisingly, the escape siren hadn't sounded. While it wasn't unusual for prisoners to be absent at a count—they might have some special duty or be in the infirmary—this was puzzling. Someone must have made an excuse for Henri and Edwin. Who would do that? Who *could* do that?

But maybe it didn't matter; maybe he could find a way out through the inner and outer fences. The guards might be sleeping, which according to the rumors, they always did. But then what? Try to walk to Max Lohmann's farm? Edwin had no idea how to find it.

Feet crunched on the gravel road outside and Edwin strained to hear, pulling his legs tighter to his chest and peeking out over his knees. A flashlight beam swept around the shower room, wielded by a man standing in the doorway. Almost immediately, it settled on Edwin, and he squeezed his eyes closed, tight against the glare. The man shouted something in English. It was Martini. More men entered the room, their boots squishing on the wet floor.

Edwin opened his eyes a bit. Still, the flashlight blinded him.

"Engels, watch the door."

Edwin recognized Gott's voice. And his henchman Engels was obviously with him. Why were they with Martini? Edwin didn't understand. He tried to press himself deeper into the corner.

Through his squinting eyes, Edwin saw there was another man next to Martini, and he said something in English. Edwin recognized the voice. Captain Harris! Martini handed his flashlight to Harris, grabbed Edwin's arm, and hauled him to his feet. Why was Harris with Gott? Edwin tried to turn away, but Martini pulled him forward. Harris shined the light on his face, and again Edwin was blinded.

"Where's Henri Gelbert?" Gott asked. "We know you know, so tell us now."

Edwin put his hand up in front of his eyes, shielding them. "He didn't tell me, Staff Sergeant," he stammered.

"Liar!" Gott said. "Now is the time for you to prove your loyalty to the Fatherland. Are you a traitor? Tell me now, and it won't go so badly for you."

Dimly, Edwin realized that Henri had not told Martini his full plan. They didn't know about Lohmann. Edwin shook his head.

Gott stepped closer. "We know where your mother lives. Do you understand? After the war, do you want her to suffer? Tell me! Where's Gelbert?"

"I don't understand, Staff Sergeant. Isn't it Henri's duty as a soldier to escape?"

Gott grabbed Edwin by the front of his shirt and violently threw him back against the wall, knocking the breath from him.

"Captain Harris," Edwin gasped. "Help me. Please."

"Just answer the question," Harris said, in halting German. "Where's Gelbert?"

Gott leaned in close to Edwin. Water from an overhead pipe ran down on his face, dripping from his nose.

"Are you his little poncey-boy?" Gott asked, his voice curling with derision. "Does he climb into your bunk at night?" Gott pressed his body up against Edwin's, his breath smelling of lemon drops. He whispered, "Does he make you feel loved and safe?"

"No, no!" Edwin cried. "You don't understand!"

"Don't I?" Gott said. "Leave us!" he shouted to the others.

"Helmut ..." Harris said.

"Leave us!"

Edwin heard the other men moving away. Why were the Americans allowing this? Why wouldn't Captain Harris help him? As Edwin stood cowering before Gott, he saw that Martini stayed at the door, watching.

Gott reached out and unbuckled Edwin's belt.

Edwin, his back pressed against the wall, tried to squirm away, but Gott jerked him back around. Gott unfastened the button on Edwin's uniform trousers and slowly, deliberately pulled both the trousers and Edwin's underwear down below his knees.

Edwin tried desperately to cover his nakedness with his hands.

"Turn around," Gott said, reaching for the button on his own pants.

"No, please," Edwin pleaded. He dropped to his knees and bowed forward, his face pressed to the slimy plywood, and his hands stretched out above his head, clasped as in prayer.

"Is Gelbert big?" Gott said, his fingers curling through Edwin's hair and pulling him up. "I'm going to show you big." The fly on his trousers was open.

"Lohmann," Edwin croaked. "Max Lohmann's farm."

Gott's fingers tightened.

"I know where that is," Martini said from the doorway.

"All right, Gott," Harris said, stepping back into the shower room. "That's enough. We've got what we need."

Edwin felt Gott's grip loosen, and he fell over sideways, retching.

Sam stepped through the back door leading to the kitchen and found his mother, a full glass of amber liquid on the windowsill at her side, leaning over the pottery wheel. "Is everything okay?" she asked, not looking up and keeping her eyes on the wet clay as her fingers forced it into a tight, symmetric mass at the center of the wheel.

"Yeah, sure," Sam replied.

He watched her for a moment and then wandered into the living room, tossing his coat onto the couch. On the coffee table sat the book he'd been reading, a biography of Frederick the First. He picked it up and then dropped it, returned to the kitchen, and opened the Frigidaire door. There weren't any bottles of beer.

"You drank them all last night," his mother said.

Sam slammed the door closed and went back into the living room. Ignoring the book, he went over to the big Zenith radio in the corner. He flipped the power switch and then, not waiting for it to warm up, he twirled the tuning dial back and forth. Finally, the sound of WJR emerged from the static, and he recognized the host of *Stump the Professor,* a particularly inane quiz show that he detested. He twisted the dial some more, trying to find CKLW out of Windsor, but tonight there was too much static. Some station was playing Hawaiian music and another had a decent Brahms concerto, but again the static was too loud to enjoy it. Disgusted, Sam flipped off the power and stood up straight.

On top of the radio sat three almost identical vases. Sam gazed down at them, and obeying an urge he didn't understand, he picked one up. He weighed it in his hand. He glanced around, looking for some hard surface.

"Go ahead. Smash it."

Sam turned and saw his mother standing in the doorway, holding her drink and watching him.

"We've got plenty, after all," she added.

Sam shook his head and started to return the vase to its place on the radio. Instead, he walked over to his easy chair and plopped down, the vase cradled in his lap.

"I gave the letters to Doris," he said.

Blanch put her drink down on the coffee table and picked up Sam's coat. After hanging it in the hall closet, she returned to the couch and sat opposite him.

"So why did you rush out of the restaurant," she asked, lifting her glass. "That Mildred Johnson saw me, sitting all by myself."

He looked down at the vase. "I'm sorry, Mom. It's just that, well, one of the letters mentioned something about Oskar Gruden that seemed pretty bad."

"Really?" Blanch leaned forward.

Sam told her about Lena Bauer and his sudden fear that Doris might be in danger. Blanch pressed him for details, and he told her everything he knew.

"I think it's okay," he said. "Doris is going back to Kentucky tomorrow."

"I'm sorry to hear that."

Sam shrugged.

"I never liked Oskar Gruden," Blanch said after a moment.

"Gee, Mom. I never would have guessed."

"Don't say, 'gee'," she said, ignoring his sarcasm. "You remember last night at dinner, when I said I know more about him than you might expect?"

"Yeah."

"Your father thought Oskar was his friend."

Sam stared at her.

"They came from the same part of Germany," Blanch continued. "They used to play chess together. I think they mainly talked about being boys in the old country."

Sam tried to take this in. So Mikhail Demeshilo had been a close friend of Oskar Gruden. Why hadn't she told him this before?

"And," Blanch added, "They talked about their military service during the first war."

Sam's father had never told him very much about the time he spent in the army, part of the American Expeditionary Force in Europe. Oskar must have been in the German military at the same time. That probably led to some interesting conversations over the chessboard. Sam glanced at the framed photograph hanging on the wall above the couch. Now fading after sixteen years, it showed his father, stiff in his army uniform, staring straight into the camera.

It occurred to Sam that he'd seen no hints of Oskar's military service in his house. No photos of him in uniform, no souvenirs. Perhaps he had purged this aspect of his past from his life. But with Dad, it seemed Oskar had been able to talk about his experiences. And Dad was able to talk with Oskar.

"Then one night," Blanch continued, "oh, it must have been just a year or so before he died, your father came home angrier than I'd ever seen him. The two of them had gotten into a huge political argument about the 'new' Germany."

Sam could understand that.

"Your father never raised his voice to me, but that night he raged on about the Nazis, accusing Oskar Gruden of being a member of the German-American Bund. He fumed for days. And then, once he finally settled down, he never mentioned Oskar Gruden again. And as far as I know, they never spoke after that."

"That's kind of sad," Sam said.

Blanch shrugged.

"Did Mr. Gruden know Dad was Jewish?"

Blanch shook her head. "I don't think so. Your father wasn't religious, of course, and he was a private man in many ways. I doubt Oskar Gruden would knowingly have had a Jewish friend." She looked at Sam. "Did Hildy know?"

Sam nodded. "She said she didn't care. She says her father knows now, too, and he doesn't seem to care, either."

"That's difficult to believe," Blanch said, taking a sip from her drink.

Sam remembered the uncomfortable conversation he'd had with Oskar that evening after he'd found out about Hildy working at the camp. Oskar had genuinely seemed to like him and had not discouraged him from seeing Hildy.

"I think," Sam said. "Maybe Mr. Gruden accepted me because he felt guilty about Dad."

Blanch shrugged. "I suppose. Of course, that assumes that a Nazi feels guilt about anything."

Sam understood that it really didn't matter now whether Oskar Gruden approved of him. Things were over with Hildy.

"Mom," he said. "I just don't get it. If Hildy wanted to be with Harris, why did she keep seeing me? Why did she string me along?"

Blanch stood, stepped around the coffee table and perched on the arm of Sam's chair. She gazed down at Sam, sadness in her eyes. "Well, for one thing, she probably liked going out in public with you. You're such a handsome man and you've got a nice car."

Sam remembered how much Hildy had enjoyed being

taken to the Lighthouse, just a few nights before. She couldn't do the same with Harris.

"And some girls are just selfish, dear. I think maybe she couldn't stand the idea of losing you to someone else."

Someone else? Who? Sam realized that he still held the clay vase in his lap. He picked it up and set it on the coffee table in front of him. He noticed that his mother was also looking at it.

"I know they're a little silly," Blanch said.

"You enjoy making them."

"I do." She glanced around the room. "But we need to get rid of these. They make me look like an old crazy-woman. I need to give them away or something."

"You gave one to Doris," Sam said. "Just like this one."

"Yes, I did," his mother said, again looking at the vase on the coffee table. Then she turned to Sam. "Son," she said. "Maybe it's not too late."

What did she mean? Wait—

The telephone rang.

The quarter moon, visible through the army truck's rear opening, chased them across the sleeping Michigan countryside. Edwin stared at it as they bounced over the rough farm road, the moon bouncing along with them, sometimes dropping low and grazing the occasional treetop or jumping high into the clear, cold sky.

Edwin had been in this truck before, or one like it. He sat on the canvas bench that ran down one side of the rear cargo area, the canvas cover flapping over his head, and the engine roaring when Martini shifted gears. On the bench across from him sat Gott and Engels, with Gott leaning forward so he could see into the front cab. Edwin heard Harris, who sat up front in the passenger seat, arguing with Martini in English.

Gott leaned back and muttered to Engels, "That idiot

Martini is having trouble finding the farm in the dark."

Handcuffs pinched Edwin's wrists, and a part of him marveled at this. Previously, he'd only seen them in American gangster movies, and handcuffs seemed like something from another world. But of course the American army would use them for prisoners—especially for prisoners attempting to escape.

He tried to figure out why they'd brought him along. It made no sense.

After a while, the truck slowed and turned off the road. Martini said something, and it sounded to Edwin like he was relieved. Looking out the back, he recognized Max Lohmann's farm.

Gott leaned forward again. "The house is dark," he said. "We'll try the barn first."

The truck pulled to a stop, Martini cut the motor, and suddenly the world was silent except for the distant sound of a barking dog.

"Captain, please ask Martini to watch the house," Gott said in German, loud enough for everyone to hear. "If anyone comes out, he's to tell them the truth. We're searching for an escaped prisoner."

Harris translated for Martini.

"Sergeant Engels and Captain Harris will search the barn. Is that acceptable to you, Herr Captain?"

"Yes," Harris replied, his voice subdued.

"And you, my young friend," Gott continued, addressing Edwin. "You will stay here and remain completely silent."

Edwin nodded.

Gott and Engels clambered out of the back of the truck.

It seemed to Edwin that he waited for hours. He slid closer to the opening and peeked out. Max Lohmann's huge barn loomed over Gott, who stood nearby, his hands on his hips, scanning the area around them. His eyes passed over Edwin with barely a flicker.

Finally there was a shout from inside the barn. It was Engels. A minute later, Henri stumbled out wearing civilian clothes, his hands handcuffed in front of him, and bits of straw on his shirt and in his hair. His shoulders drooped in defeat.

"Get him in the truck," Gott shouted to Engels. "Then we go. Quickly!"

Gott stepped close to Harris, and they looked at each other for a moment. Then they both nodded.

Henri struggled to climb up into the back of the truck, encumbered by his handcuffs. His eyes fell on Edwin. "No!" he gasped. He tried to back out, but Engels gave him a shove from behind that sent him sprawling onto the floorboards.

"Leave him there," Gott said to Engels as they climbed in. Martini started the engine, and the truck lurched forward.

"You told them!" Henri said, his voice uneven, his face hidden in the dark.

"You left me," Edwin whispered, swallowing down a sob.

"Silence!" Gott said. Then to Engels, he added, "A lover's quarrel, how tiresome."

Edwin turned his head toward the rear of the truck, toward the quarter moon, still bouncing across the landscape. He tried to remember the moon as it was the night Axel had left him, back in that French apple orchard. Was it like this one? He thought maybe it was. And he remembered the next night. When the Americans had taken him into the woods. That night, he had also stared at the moon, concentrating on every detail, every shadow on its slim crescent quarter.

And now he realized something: tonight's quarter moon was still visible. They hadn't turned the truck around; they were still heading in the same direction—away from the camp.

Half an hour later, Edwin stood in a dark wood, bare tree branches arching overhead across the night sky, threading through the stars and the quarter moon. There was no air in his chest. No feeling in his skin. The branches rattled in the wind.

Henri stood next to him in the glare of the truck's headlights which, though partially covered with blackout tape, were still bright enough to make it difficult for Edwin to see the four men standing next to the truck cab. Edwin and Henri's hands were handcuffed in front them.

"What are you going to do?" Henri asked the men, his voice quavering, his eyeglasses slightly askew.

"You are escaping prisoners," Gott said. "Right, Captain Harris?"

Harris, standing with Martini and Engels, didn't reply. It appeared to Edwin that he and Martini were explaining the operation of a rifle, an American rifle, to Engels.

"They're going to shoot us," Henri said.

Gott did not reply.

Edwin turned to look at Henri. "Do something," he whispered.

Henri shook his head. "They have the desire to kill us, and they have the capability. There's nothing we can do."

Edwin stared at Henri. Why had he given up? Was he nothing but a coward who'd do nothing to defend himself—or Edwin? He was useless, and he always had been. Edwin turned back to peer into the truck headlights.

"Are you the Heilige Geist?" Edwin shouted.

Gott laughed and replied, "And what do you know about that?" He pointed at Martini and Harris. "Do they look like fellow soldiers to you? No, the rumors of the Heilige Geist were merely a convenient diversion."

"To cover up the murder of Sergeant Spinkel," Edwin said.

"Spinkel?" Gott replied. "What are saying?"

"You killed him, right? And somehow, you think we can prove it. That we can make trouble for you." Edwin tried to see Harris in the glare of the headlights. "For both you and the Americans."

"I killed him? Why would I do that?" Gott looked over at the others, shrugging his shoulders. "Or any of us? He was a good soldier, I think. You see my little friend, you and this fat slob standing next to you are too clever. You think you are detectives in an American movie."

"Staff Sergeant Gott is right," Harris said in clumsy German, coming to stand next to Gott. "Spinkel killed himself."

"Then why?" Edwin asked. "Why kill us?"

"Ask your friend," Harris said.

"What does he mean by that?" Edwin asked Henri, but Henri said nothing.

"This is pointless," Gott said. "Herr Captain, are the men ready?"

Martini and Engels stood with their rifles held rigidly in front of them. Harris nodded.

"I think it's best if you give the order, Captain," Gott said.

"No," Harris said. "I can't do it. Please, Helmut. Don't make me."

"I must insist," Gott said, his voice dark with menace and command.

It seemed to Edwin that Harris was trembling. Harris looked around desperately for some way to escape. Even in his own fear, Edwin wondered at the control that Gott seemed to have over this American officer.

"Now, Herr Captain," Gott said.

Seeing no way out, Harris attempted to pull himself up into some semblance of the position of attention. He called out, "Ready!" in English, his voice shaking.

Martini and Engels lifted their rifles.

"Stop!" Edwin shouted.

"We have no time for this," Gott said. "Carry on, Captain."

Edwin glanced at Henri again, but the big man stood slouching and silent, his face turned away.

"No!" Edwin shouted. He faced Gott and took a step forward, his voice shaking with rage. "You're ashamed of me. You hate me. I'm not a good German soldier. I'm weak, right? Well, I guess that I am. But what can you expect of me? *I'm only fifteen years old! Fifteen!*"

"Silence!" Gott shouted.

"Shoot me if you want, but first I want to say something to my friend."

"Give them a minute, Helmut," Harris said, sounding relieved.

Gott threw up his arms in frustration and turned his back. Martini and Engels lowered their rifles.

Edwin knew he had little time. "Henri," he said, "I didn't want to tell them. Gott, you see, he was going to—"

Henri interrupted. "Sam Demsky told me that the camp was moving. All my preparations would be for nothing. I thought today was my last chance. There was no way to tell you."

Gott turned around and shouted, "Enough! Captain, give the orders."

"Ready!" Harris called out, his voice steady now.

Martini and Engels raised their rifles again.

"Aim!"

There was the sound of a car coming through the woods. It got louder.

Sam had not met Max Lohmann before. When Lohmann telephoned Sam at home, he was guarded, mentioning that he was on a party line. He said that they had a mutual friend, and could Sam come out to his farm to help him? After Sam expressed his confusion, Lohmann whispered that the friend's name was Henri. It took a second to register that Henri must be outside the camp; that he must have escaped somehow. When Sam agreed to come, Lohmann gave careful directions, explaining that the lights at the farm would be turned off.

Twenty minutes later, when Sam pulled into the dark farmyard, Lohmann came running out of the house. He told Sam to move over, explaining that he knew the roads and could drive without headlights.

"Why would we want to do that?" Sam asked.

"I think they're going to kill Henri," Lohmann said. "We can stop them if we hurry."

"What? Who? How do you know? That's crazy."

"Soldiers—guards, I guess, came in a truck. They just left a few minutes ago, and they turned away from the camp. If I'm crazy," Lohmann said, "then we'll appear a little foolish. If I'm not crazy, Henri will be dead."

As they drove, Lohmann explained that he'd been trying to help Henri escape. As planned, Henri had gotten away from a work detail and walked to his farm, where Lohmann gave him civilian clothes and hid him in the barn. Later that night, Henri was to catch a slow-moving westbound freight train on the tracks that skirted the southern edge of the farm. But Henri had forgotten that the train only passed on certain days, and this wasn't one of them. When Lohmann had explained this, Henri panicked and convinced Lohmann to call Sam and ask for help.

As the dark blue DeSoto barreled through the night with no headlights, they peered through the windshield, barely able to see the outline of the road in the light of the quarter moon. Seventy-three-year-old Max Lohmann drove like a madman, and it occurred to Sam that perhaps all he owned was his farm truck, and this was his chance to drive a real car for a change. In any case, they raced down the rutted farm road with Sam bracing himself against dashboard.

After a while, Lohmann slowed the car and pointed. Up ahead, Sam saw the taillights of an army truck, distinctive as they were partially masked by the regulation blackout tape. They tailed the truck for several minutes. Then the taillights disappeared. Lohmann drove on for a while before deciding that the truck must have pulled off the road. Saying he remembered a trail, two ruts through the woods, he turned the car around, and they doubled back.

Now, bouncing up that trail through a tunnel of overhanging tree branches, Sam saw the taillights again. As they drew near to the truck, he made out two men standing a short distance away, squinting into the glare of the headlights with their hands together in front of them. With relief, Sam saw that the tall one was Henri. They were in time. And the short one? Oh, God, it was Edwin.

"What should we do?" Sam asked.

"I should've brought my shotgun," Lohmann replied as he slammed on the brakes and stopped the car just behind the truck.

"What? Are you nuts? They're soldiers. They've got guns!" Sam gestured at the two uniformed men holding rifles in front of Henri and Edwin. "This doesn't make any sense —"

But Lohmann was already out of the car and striding past the truck. Sam jumped out and followed, trying to take in the scene before him. The men with the rifles were Martini and, incredibly, a German prisoner, whom Sam recognized as Sergeant Engels. Captain John Harris stood nearby, and Staff Sergeant Gott stood next to him.

"Stop right there!" Harris shouted. "This is official government business, and you're interfering. I can arrest you both."

"If that's so, then why is that prisoner armed?" Lohmann

asked, pointing at Engels.

"They're going to kill us!" Edwin cried out in German.

"Silence!" Gott shouted.

Sam stepped closer to Harris. "Captain Harris," he said, "what's going on here?"

It was hard to see Harris's face in the reflected glare of the truck headlights, but Sam was sure he saw confusion, and maybe fear.

"You shouldn't be here," Harris said, his voice unsteady.

Martini stepped forward, his rifle raised and aimed at Sam's chest. Engels followed him, his own rifle pointed at Lohmann.

"My wife knows we're here," Lohmann said.

"And my mother knows I was going to see him," Sam added.

"So you're threatening us with your *mother*?" Gott said with a sneer. "Is this correct?"

"You can't keep this secret," Sam said, staring at the muzzle of Martini's rifle. He knew his own voice was shaking. "Whatever you're doing."

Harris, sweat running down the sides of his face, glanced at Gott, and Sam was sure there was fear in his eyes. What in the hell was the matter with him? Was he simply pure evil, like Gott? Or maybe … *That's it!* Gott had some kind of control over the man. Something so awful that it brought John Harris, captain in the United States Army, out into the dark of night, deep in these isolated woods, with the intent to kill two innocent boys.

Sam took a step closer to Harris.

"John," he said. "Listen to me. You don't really want to hurt these boys, do you?" Sam reached out to touch Harris's shoulder.

Harris jerked back, snarling. He was breathing hard, and his eyes had a glassy look. "Keep away from me, Jew boy," he said. Then he stepped up close to Sam, his face an inch away. "I told Hildy you're a kike, did you know that?" he shouted. "I told her, and five minutes later we were fucking! So don't pretend that you're my friend."

Sam staggered back a step, stunned. Then he raised his arm, clenching his hand into a tight fist and swung at Harris's grinning face. Suddenly, his arm stopped, held back by Max Lohmann's strong farmer's grip.

"That won't help," Lohmann said quietly.

Harris had taken a step back, fear on his face for a second, but then he turned to Edwin and Henri. "He's a Jew," he shouted in German, his voice shrill. "Did you know that? A Jew!" He laughed hysterically. He turned back to Sam. "And the funny thing is that he thinks Fräulein Gruden is his girlfriend! He's crazy! She loves me and has been fucking me for weeks, and he never even guessed!"

There was nothing but silence for a second. Suddenly, a high-pitched scream filled the air, and out of the corner of his eye, Sam saw Edwin running toward Harris, his face contorted and his mouth open. "LIAR!" Edwin screamed as he barreled into the back of Harris's legs. They both tumbled to the ground, and Edwin managed to get his arms over Harris's head from behind, choking him with the chain of the handcuffs. "LIAR, LIAR!" Edwin cried as he lay struggling on his back with Harris on top of him, gasping.

Gott took a step back and looked at Martini and Engels. "Shoot, you fools," he shouted.

Sam saw both men raise their rifles. They hesitated, trying to get a clear shot at Edwin.

"Kill them both!" Gott shrieked. "Kill them both!"

Engels steadied his rifle, and there was a clacking sound as he pulled the trigger, but the rifle didn't fire. Next to him, Martini lowered his rifle. Then, aware that Engels was struggling to clear the jammed round in his rifle's breach,

Martini shook his head, lifted his own rifle again, and this time, pointed it at Engels.

"Drop it," he said.

Engels looked surprised. He glanced down at the apparently useless rifle in his hands and with a shrug, set it on the ground at his feet.

"Idiots!" Gott shouted.

Edwin and Harris were no longer struggling, and Sam guessed that Harris must have lost consciousness. Gott knelt down next to them, snatched Harris's Colt pistol from his sidearm holster, and jumped back. He aimed the pistol at Edwin who lay half beneath the unconscious Harris, and there was a soft click as his thumb disengaged the safety.

"It seems that this will be up to me," Gott said. He steadied his aim at Edwin's head.

Sam frantically tried to think of how he could help Edwin. Then he saw Henri, cowering alone, the glint of the truck's headlights caught in his eyeglasses. Henri raised his bound hands to awkwardly shade his eyes, and then with a speed that was surprising for a big man, he raced toward Gott, his face barely visible, but showing both fear and hatred.

Gott saw Henri coming at him, and he wheeled around to aim at him instead.

BANG!

Henri barreled into Gott, knocking him to the ground. The pistol spun away from Gott and landed nearby. Gott started to crawl toward it.

BANG!

Martini fired a second shot into the air and Gott froze. "Here," Martini said as he picked up Engels's rifle and handed it to Sam.

Sam Demsky, lame and 4-F, had never held a rifle before in his life. Remembering what he'd seen in cowboy movies, he lifted the barrel and pointed it at Gott, his finger groping for the trigger, forgetting that the rifle was jammed and probably useless. He looked questioningly at Martini.

"No Kraut's gonna tell me to shoot an American," Martini said, shrugging.

Henri seemed to be unhurt. At his feet, Harris showed signs of life, and Henri leaned down and rolled him off Edwin. Offering his hand to Edwin he said, "It's over, my little friend."

With Henri's help, Edwin climbed shakily to his feet and peered around. He saw Harris, who had managed to sit up and was coughing. Edwin snarled. He shook himself loose from Henri, and as he started to draw back his boot-clad foot to kick at Harris, he saw the Colt pistol lying nearby. In a flash, he grabbed it and aimed it at Harris, the barrel shaking.

"You *liar*," he snarled. "Fräulein Gruden would hate you."

Sam took a step toward them. "Stop, Edwin! Don't do it!" he shouted.

"Listen to Sam," Henri added, his voice pleading.

Edwin didn't seem to hear them.

Harris, still sitting on the ground and gasping, looked up at Edwin. "Go ahead," he said. "Pull the trigger."

Gott stood beside them, eyeing Harris with open disgust. Then he focused on Edwin who seemed to take no notice.

"Do it," Harris said.

The pistol barrel ceased to shake.

Gott edged closer. His arm reached out for the pistol.

Edwin swung around, his face hard and tearless, the pistol's muzzle inches from Gott's deaths-head face. He pulled the trigger, and Staff Sergeant Helmut Gott dropped like a hanged man after the rope has been cut.

Doris wished there was a better way to do this as she crept down the stairs from her attic room to the second floor, gripping Oskar's letters in one hand. It was after one in the morning, and the house seemed quiet enough. She continued down the main staircase, her palm damp against the broad oak banister, tiptoed across the entrance hall and through the living room, careful not to bump into the furniture, and stopped outside Oskar's study. The door was closed but not latched, and she pushed it open. Gasping, her hand flew to her mouth.

Oskar Gruden sat alone at his desk, the room dark around him, silhouetted by pale moonlight streaming through the window behind him. When he saw her, he quickly swept something from the desktop into an open drawer, closed the drawer firmly, and turned on the desk lamp.

Doris took a breath. She hadn't expected him to be there, of course. But it really didn't matter. She'd just give him the letters, apologize, and go. Then she noticed a brown smudge on Oskar's lower lip. In spite of everything, she smiled, remembering the candy bars she'd found in the top drawer of his desk.

"What do you want?" he said. "What are those?" He pointed at the letters clutched in her hand. He licked his lip.

"Look, I'm just tryin' to do the right thing," she replied, stepping into the room. "I'm going tomorrow, for good, and I wanted—"

"What? You're really leaving?" Oskar stared at her, his eyes like an owl's behind his wireframe glasses.

"Well, sure. Your wife made it clear I'm not wanted here."

"Yes, but—" he said, stopping himself. "I mean, wait a day. I can talk to her."

Doris shook her head. "Either way, you can't control my life. You two can't tell me who I'm gonna see and who I won't."

"I suppose that's true. But Hans is our son. He does as he's told. If he no longer wishes to see you—"

"But that's just it! He should figure that out for himself."

"This is a difficult time for him. His mother and I know what's best."

"You people drive me crazy!" Doris threw the letters on the desk. "Here! These are yours. I made a stupid mistake and took 'em. I'm sorry." She turned and walked out the door.

"Wait, please," Oskar said, standing up.

Ignoring him, Doris hurried into the living room, this time bumping into the heavy Victrola. She paused to rub her thigh, her jaw clenched.

"Miss Calloway, please," Oskar said, following, his voice like a stage whisper. "I've something to tell you. Doris, I *beg* you to stop."

She paused, the front hall and stairway leading to her room just steps away.

Oskar, glancing toward stairs, whispered urgently. "You think I am a terrible man. Please understand that this grieves me. You have no idea."

"You *are* terrible," she whispered back. "And your wife. She's a ..." Doris was going to say "monster," but the tortured look on his face stopped her. He took her elbow and pulled her gently toward his study.

"Yes, yes. You are correct," he said. "We can talk about it for just one moment, in private. Please."

Reluctantly, Doris followed him back into the study. He closed the door, walked back around his desk, but didn't sit.

"My wife is difficult at times," Oskar said. "She's had a hard life. Back in the old country, there was some trouble—"

"Oh, come on, Hildy tried that too, and I ain't buyin' it. I don't care what terrible things happened to her in Germany. That don't excuse what she says and does right now, today. Making excuses for her just lets her keep doing mean things."

"And you know everything about people. You're wise beyond your years. Is that correct?"

Doris turned to leave.

"You told me that you made a mistake," Oskar said, his voice urgent. "Well, so have I."

She stopped.

"I read in a magazine once," he continued, "about some famous old man. In an interview, he said that he had no regrets about his life. You've heard people say the same sort of thing, maybe?"

"I guess." She turned to face him, listening.

"Well, I don't understand it. Did he make no mistakes? Did he never hurt anyone? In my life, I've made mistakes, and I have regrets."

"You mean, like coming to America?"

"Oh, no," he said. "I think just the opposite. I wish that we'd come sooner. Perhaps then—"

"Yeah?"

Oskar shook his head. "Old business," he said. "Very personal."

"You mean Lena Bauer?" Doris spat out the words.

Oskar stared at her. "How do you know about her? You have no right ..."

Doris glanced down at the two letters still sitting on the top of his desk. He followed her eyes.

"The letters," he said, his shoulders drooping slightly. "Of course."

"So did you pay her off? Are you gonna to be able to return to your beloved Germany after the war?"

"That is none of your business."

"You're right, I reckon it's not." Doris turned again and reached for the door.

"Wait! Please don't go," Oskar pleaded. "Look, do you want to know what really happened?"

Doris paused and then turned back toward him. "What did she tell the police?" she asked.

"She accused me of attacking her."

"That's what Sam and I figured."

"Sam?" Oskar said. "Oh, of course. He translated the letters." Oskar sat down and covered his face with his hands. "So Sam knows. Is there no end to this?"

Doris was a little surprised that Oskar was so concerned about Sam. "What happened?" she asked.

"Lena and her parents lived next door. She was seventeen, so lovely, so bright and happy. I'm sure it's hard for you to imagine, but I was still a young man. I fell in love with her."

"But, let me guess, you were married."

"Yes," Oskar said. "Seven years and three small children. Gertrud, well, she had no time for me."

"And when you wouldn't leave your wife, Lena falsely accused you? Is that what you're telling me?"

"No, no. It never got to that point. I know it's a—what do you call it—a cliché, but you could say I worshiped her from afar. I hardly spoke to her." He glanced down at the book on his desk, the one Doris had seen when she'd found the letters. "Do you know Dante?" he asked.

Doris shook her head.

"He understood. But as I was saying, one night when Gertrud and the children were at some church function, Lena knocked at our door, asking to borrow something; I forget what. She came in. We talked. The radio was playing a nice madrigal by Heinrich Schütz. She liked me, I'm sure of it. I made advances. I was clumsy—and a fool."

"So she was right to call the cops."

"I don't know what to think any more," Oskar said.

"And you escaped to the States."

"Many Germans were leaving then. There was no work in Germany. I had a little money from Gertrud's father, so we came here."

"And Mrs. Gruden knew?" Doris asked.

"Yes. She stayed with me, of course, for the children. And

sixteen years later, she has not let me forget my sin for one single day."

Doris figured that his story was true. She knew one thing that was certain: the last part about Gertrud Gruden. It explained a lot.

She pointed to the letters. "Your brother wanted you to pay Lena a thousand marks. Did you pay her off so you could go back home after the war?"

"No. I sent her five thousand marks, about two thousand dollars, with a letter of apology. And, no, we'll not be going back. For my children, for me, this is our home now."

Doris thought for a second. It seemed almost fair. She looked at Oskar and saw that he was watching her, his expression expectant.

"Okay," she said. "I reckon you really tried to make up for things."

"Thank you for saying that, Miss Calloway."

His relief and gratitude seemed genuine. But it didn't really change anything. There was still Mrs. Gruden, and Hans, and —

"Mr. Gruden, like I said, I'm truly sorry about taking your letters. It was wrong. And there's another thing I did wrong. I found the key to the attic in your desk. I poked around up there."

Oskar stared at her, his face stony. Finally, he said, "And what did you find?"

Doris hesitated for a moment and then said, "A Nazi armband."

He sighed. "I know it's difficult to understand, especially now. But when the National Socialists were elected, and Hitler became chancellor, it was the beginning of a new Germany, rising again from a terrible war. We were afraid of the Communists." He waved his hand. "No, I'm not making excuses. But we didn't understand what was happening, what was going to happen. You see?"

"I don't care about none of that," Doris said.

"Ah, of course. You want to know if the armband was mine," he said. "If I wore it?"

"Yes."

"I am telling you the truth, and I hope you believe me. I never wore it. Not once. It seemed a little silly to me."

"So it was Hans?"

"Yes. It was like a boys' club. There were many such organizations in America then."

Doris remembered Karl saying how he'd seen people wearing swastikas in the house.

"And you encouraged this."

He shrugged. "Yes. We were proud of the new Germany."

They were silent for a moment.

"Miss Calloway, I know this has been difficult for you," Oskar said. "But please give us another chance. Please don't leave tomorrow. I can fix things with Mrs. Gruden."

Doris wasn't so sure of that. "Why should I hang around here, with all that's gone on? And with Hans still here? That seems just plain stupid."

"He leaves soon. Hildy needs you."

"Hildy's a big girl," Doris said. "I think she's proved that."

"Yes, I suppose that's true."

He was silent for a moment, his face illuminated by the desk lamp, his lips trembling slightly. "There is another reason," he said.

Doris waited.

"Miss Calloway—Doris," he said. "I'm forty-four years old, and since I can remember, I've felt like an old man, dried up, useless." He looked up at her. "Sad, yes? Pathetic?"

Doris didn't know what to say. She shrugged.

"Then you moved into my house," Oskar said.

Doris took a step back. What was he saying?

"No, no, you don't need to be alarmed. Please, Miss Calloway. I'm not saying I want …" He sighed. "I'm not a lecherous old man. I hate that idea. And besides, I'm not a complete fool. I do learn from my mistakes—even mistakes that happened fifteen years ago."

"So what are you sayin'?" Doris asked.

"I'm saying that my life is fuller with you as my friend. Having you around makes me feel like less of an old man."

Doris blushed. "You have three children," she said.

"And they've been the joy of my life. But soon they all will be gone, and I'll be alone."

"With her."

Oskar nodded.

Doris took a deep breath as she gazed at Oskar Gruden. He'd never been anything but a gentleman with her, but how could she stay in this house? What about Hans? Gertrud?

"Mr. Gruden," she said. "I'm sorry, but I can't—"

She was interrupted by the sound of a car crunching on the gravel driveway outside, its lights flashing across the study window. The car's motor cut off, and the headlights went dark.

Oskar turned around and looked out the window.

"That's Sam Demsky's car," he said.

Fortunately, Sam's big car had plenty of room on the floor in the back seat. Edwin crouched down behind the driver's seat with Henri hunched over beside him. They'd been driving like this for about twenty minutes, feeling the rough gravel country roads give way to paved streets a few minutes before.

Whenever Edwin was able to make out Henri's face, he saw that Henri was still staring at him with a look of surprise and perhaps awe, marveling at the knowledge that Edwin had shot Sergeant Gott. Edwin, still a little numb, remembered how the gun had jerked his arm up, surprising him with its explosive power. He had dropped his arm to his side, the heavy pistol still smoking as he stared down at Gott's lifeless corpse.

Nobody had said a word. Harris sat nearby, staring up at Edwin, his mouth open. His expression evolved as Edwin watched, changing from confusion, to fear, to understanding, and finally to something that Edwin thought might be exaltation. Edwin hated Harris with all his heart, but for that moment they'd celebrated together: Gott was dead!

Max Lohmann stepped close to Edwin and gently took the pistol. Edwin was happy to be rid of the thing.

"So, Captain," Lohmann said, turning to Harris, "just what was your plan? How did you think you could murder these boys and get away with it?"

Harris climbed shakily to his feet and—lost in thought— said nothing for a moment. Then he replied dully, "Tomorrow at the morning count, these two are missing. Before we left camp, Martini cut through the fences at a spot where the guards were sleeping. Everybody will assume they escaped. And they're never caught."

Lohmann considered this and then replied, "Okay, that's still the plan. Only there are three escaped prisoners who are never caught. Understand?" He pointed at Gott's body. "We bury him here."

Harris was silent.

"But," Sam said, "what's to stop them from sounding the alarm as soon as they get back to camp? Or from driving to the nearest farm and calling the camp and the FBI?"

"Is that what you want, Captain?" Lohmann said. "Do you want all of us—Sam, Henri, this boy, myself—all of us to tell the same story of how you brought prisoners into these woods to shoot them?"

Sam cautiously stepped closer to Harris. "John, think about

it. If you handle this right, nothing happens to you. You'll never see these two again." He gestured toward Edwin and Henri. "And Gott is dead. But if you turn us in, everything comes to light. Everything. Understand?"

Henri spoke up. "What about them?" he asked, pointing at Martini and Engels.

"They'll keep their mouths shut," Sam said. "They don't want to be involved in a murder either."

Engels nodded. Martini, who hadn't followed the conversation, as it was in German, looked confused. Sam quickly explained in English, and Martini, obviously relieved, also nodded in agreement.

Captain Harris looked at the men standing around him and then turned so that his back was to Gott's body. He said something to Martini, who turned to Sam and held out his hand, indicating Sam should give him his rifle.

Not knowing what Harris had said, Edwin held his breath.

Sam handed over the rifle, and they watched as Martini cleared the jam and unloaded both guns. He took them to the truck and returned with a shovel.

Martini and Engels took turns digging a deep grave. Harris himself rolled Gott into it, and they all flinched when the body hit the bottom with a thud. It took only a few minutes more to fill the grave, scatter the excess dirt, and cover it with leaves and branches. It seemed to Edwin that Gott would probably never be found.

At a gesture from Harris, Martini and Engels climbed into the front seat of the truck. Harris stood for a moment—looking at Sam, Henri, and Edwin—and Edwin saw that he was shaking slightly. But then, without a word, he turned and slid in next to Engels. Martini had started the engine, turned the truck around, and they drove off. A few minutes later, with Sam driving his big car, they'd taken Lohmann back to his farm. The old man had embraced each of them in turn and wished them well.

Now Edwin, kneeling in the back of the car, felt it slow down, turn, and then come to a halt.

Sam leaned over the back of the seat. "Are you all right, Edwin?" he asked.

"I'm fine," Edwin replied. And he meant it.

Sam looked at him a second longer and then shook his head. "I'm going to ask the man who lives here for help. I think we can trust him. But we're not going tell him about Gott. Understand?"

Both Edwin and Henri nodded. Sam got out of the car.

A moment later, Edwin heard an angry male voice speaking in English, but with a definite German accent. Henri lifted his head and peeked through the window, and Edwin did the same. The car was parked next to a house, and Sam was talking to a man and a woman, both wrapped in robes.

"Look!" Henri whispered. "It's that redheaded American girl from the train station and the corn field!" Henri began to translate. "The old man wants to call the police, and Sam is asking for just five minutes so he can explain."

The man finally nodded and pointed behind the house. Sam came back to the car, opened the rear door, and Edwin and Henri scrambled out. They all followed the man around to the back porch, in the kitchen door, and through the house, ending up in a small room with a desk and many books. The old man stood behind the desk.

Sam introduced them to Oskar Gruden. When Edwin and Henri reached forward to shake hands, he ignored them, continuing to glare at Sam.

"And this is Doris Calloway," Sam said.

Henri slid over to stand by her side. "We've met," he said. "Do you remember?"

She looked confused so Henri repeated himself, this time in English. She nodded to him, and to Edwin. She still looked confused.

Sam said something more in English to Oskar. Henri whispered to Edwin, "He's asking for help. For enough gasoline so we can drive to Chicago."

Oskar shook his head. In German, he said, "You should never have involved me or Miss Calloway in this. If we're caught, even now when I have done nothing to help you, do you realize what will happen?"

"I think," Sam replied, also in German, "it would not go well for any of us."

"Then why are you helping them?"

"They're my friends. I've tried to help them before, at the camp. That turned out badly. Now, because their lives are in danger, I'm trying again."

Oskar sputtered. "Their lives are in danger? But how? Hildy said—" He stopped, embarrassed, glancing at Sam for a second. Then he continued, "She said it's not so bad at that camp."

"Look," Sam said, "I don't know if I really understand all of this. But I do know that this German sergeant named Gott and the camp commander were going to shoot these boys just an hour ago. I was there—I saw it."

"But why? It makes no sense. The American commander of the camp and a German sergeant committing murder together? It's preposterous."

"Two months ago, a prisoner died at the camp," Sam said. "Hanged. I think Gott killed him. Maybe they thought Henri or Edwin knew about it."

"But why would an American officer—" Oskar said.

"Actually," Henri said, interrupting. "Sergeant Spinkel committed suicide. He was much more deeply troubled than we could have known."

Edwin, along with everyone else, turned to look at him.

"And how do you know that for sure?" Sam asked.

"Because I took his notebook when Edwin and I found him."

Edwin stared at Henri. He'd had the notebook all along!

"There was a letter to his wife," Henri said, trying to avoid Edwin's eyes. "He left instructions in the notebook, and I am happy to report that I mailed the letter to her. I am not so happy to also tell you that I also read it."

"And that was your big mistake," Hildy Gruden said in German as she stepped into the room. Edwin gawked at her. Her face was sallow, and her dark hair was unkempt and stringy.

"Hildegard," her father said, "go back to bed."

"Wait!" Sam said. "What do you mean by 'big mistake'?"

"There is so much going on at that camp," Hildy said as she gently closed the door behind her. "Sam, you never had a clue."

Everybody looked at her, waiting. Henri was whispering to Doris, apparently translating Hildy's words into English.

"Gott was some kind of criminal in Germany," Hildy continued. "He was also a member of the Nazi party. He couldn't avoid going into the army, but he was able use his Nazi connections to become a sergeant. It appears that he was pretty good at it. Anyway, you should know that he doesn't really have any fighting experience. He was captured in Tunisia just a few days after he arrived."

Edwin turned to look at Henri, who smiled at him. Gott was a bit less terrifying now. At least, the stories he'd told about himself were filled with lies. He'd probably learned a little Arabic from other prisoners.

"All that crap about serving under Rommel ..." Sam muttered.

"Yes," Hildy said.

"And you know all this because?" Sam asked.

"I looked at his file." She finally looked Sam in the eye.

"And yes, Sam, I know because John told me."

"And what's the significance of all this?" Oskar asked. "What does it have to do with these two?" He gestured at Edwin and Henri.

"I'm getting to that," Hildy said. "Gott and John were skimming the profits. That's what John called it. He said that hiring out prisoners to farmers and factories is incredibly profitable for the government. It more than pays for the whole POW system. So he and Gott worked out a scheme to doctor the records. It's kind of complicated, but basically they report fewer hours than the prisoners actually work. They charge the full amount, of course, and keep the difference."

"But the accounting, the books!" Oskar said. "There must be auditors."

"Not as much as you'd think. There's a war on after all, and the government has other things to worry about. Especially since this camp was still making a profit."

"Mrs. Lewis," Sam said suddenly. "She knew."

"I think she suspected," Hildy said.

"But I don't understand," Oskar said. "How could Gott profit from this? Is he going to take a stack of American money back to Germany with him? Surely, the Americans will catch him."

"Actually, it's pretty simple," Hildy said. "And kind of clever. John opened a bank account for him here in town. He even used Gott's real name. Nobody at the bank would ever guess he was a prisoner. After all, Ann Arbor is full of people with German names. John even took the signature card to the camp so Gott could sign it."

"Are you sure?" Oskar asked. "How do you know this?"

"I made the deposits and then showed Gott the bankbook," Hildy said. "He has over six thousand dollars already."

Sam whistled. "And after the war," he said, "I'll bet he just writes a letter to the bank from Germany. Even if he loses the bankbook, he memorizes the account number and his signature matches. They wire the money back to him. Why wouldn't they?"

Hildy nodded.

Edwin smiled, knowing that Gott was in a place where he'd never see any of this money.

"And you helped with this," Sam said to Hildy. "You helped that monster."

"I did it for John," Hildy mumbled.

"It was the bankbook that he wanted when you two came to the house," Sam said. "He used you!"

"I know that now," she said, sighing. "Maybe I knew it then."

The room was silent for a moment. Doris whispered something to Henri, and he whispered back, apparently summarizing in English what had been said.

"So," Oskar said. "This Gott and Harris think our Mr. Henri Gelbert here discovered all of this." Turning to Henri, he continued. "They thought you might report it, and so they decided to kill you? And your young friend."

"But we didn't know about any of it!" Edwin said.

"There's more to it, isn't there, Henri?" Hildy said. "Tell them why Gott and Harris thought you knew about the skimming."

Henri hung his head. "Because I did. It was in poor Spinkel's letter to his wife. The night we arrived, Gott tried to force him to participate, but it was all too much for him."

Edwin stared at his friend, as did everybody in the room.

"Tell them the rest, Henri," Hildy said.

"And I tried to blackmail Gott with this information. I was a fool."

"What?" Edwin cried. "You almost got us killed because you wanted money?"

"No!" Henri said. "I was trying to make things better for

us. For you too. I thought we wouldn't have to work so hard. But mainly, we'd be safer. And maybe you'd have more of your lemon drops."

"You're an idiot," Sam said.

It seemed to Edwin that everyone in the room nodded in agreement, including Henri. In the silence that followed, the wind rattled tree branches against the side of the house.

Oskar Gruden shook his head. "I don't understand," he said. "Why would an American army officer try to murder these two boys? To protect this silly financial scheme? It still doesn't make sense."

"I know," Hildy said. "But there's something else you don't know about John. When he was wounded in Sicily, they gave him morphine for the pain. The stupid bastards gave him too much." She paused and took a breath. "He was addicted."

Sam looked at her, and it seemed to Edwin that a light went on for him. "Those times when he acted crazy," Sam said.

Hildy nodded. "In Sicily and on the ship coming home, he bribed the orderlies or doctors to get more morphine. If you've got enough money, it's easier than you might think."

"But he started to run out of money here," Sam said. "That's why he needed this skimming scheme."

"Yes. But in a POW camp, there really isn't much need for morphine. He was afraid that he wouldn't be able to cover it up."

"What did he do?" Sam asked.

"The camp dispensary has lots of Paregoric. It's used for diarrhea, and we've got plenty of that. You boil a pint of it, the water and alcohol evaporates, and you skim off the camphor. What's left is pure morphine."

"And you helped him with this," Oskar said suddenly.

"Yes, Papa. I thought I loved him."

Oskar shook his head.

"I remember once John smelled of mothballs," Sam said.

"It was the camphor."

"I'm sure it was," Hildy said.

"So this John person wanted to kill these boys because he was crazy from the morphine and to protect his money?" Oskar asked.

"It was really Gott who wanted to kill them, right, Hildy?" Sam said. "And Gott had some kind of control over John."

"John tried to bribe one of the German orderlies in the infirmary. They had easy access to the Paregoric. The orderly told Gott, of course, and Gott threatened to expose John. And he threatened to cut off his supply. John is so desperate and crazy, he'll do anything Gott wants."

"Gott wanted money and privileges," Sam said. "He got them, and then he wanted the ultimate power. He wanted to kill."

"He's a monster," Oskar said. By the look on the older man's face, Edwin saw that this was all Oskar needed to know.

Doris said something in English, and she and Sam talked for a moment. After she shook her head impatiently and said something else, Sam turned back to the group.

"Doris correctly asks what we're going to do now," he said in German for Edwin's benefit. He turned to Oskar. "If you call the police, we'll all get in trouble. And Edwin and Henri will go back to the camp."

"Papa," Hildy said. "Gott is an awful man. He'll find a way to kill them both, I'm sure."

Sam, Edwin, and Henri glanced at each other, and it was clear to them that Sam had been right in warning them not to mention that Gott was dead.

All eyes were on Oskar. Doris stepped around the desk and touched his arm. She spoke to him in English.

Oskar listened and then said, "Miss Calloway says I should help. She says this even though she's accused me of being a traitor, a Nazi, of being disloyal to my adopted country. Still she thinks I should jeopardize my family by helping two escaped German prisoners."

"Please, Papa." Hildy said. "You know it's the right thing to do."

Oskar came around the desk, stepped close to Edwin, and said, "You're the one reading my Karl May books, right?"

Edwin nodded.

"And you're fifteen years old."

Edwin nodded again.

"Fifteen," Oskar said, shaking his head. He looked into Edwin's eyes, perhaps seeing his sons, or perhaps searching for something of his own youth. As he put his hand on Edwin's shoulder, Edwin flinched. Not removing his hand, Oskar said, "It's going to be all right."

Edwin pulled himself up straight, returned Oskar's gaze, and nodded.

Oskar took a handkerchief from his pocket and blew his nose. Then he turned to Henri.

"I do this for him, not you," he said. "Sam is correct. You're an idiot."

Henri shrugged and said nothing.

"Right, then." Oskar pulled a key ring from his pocket and removed a key. Handing it to Sam, he said, "You remember the storage shed behind my store, where we got your new tires? There is a tank of gasoline inside, and you'll find some empty gas cans. Take whatever you can fit in the car. That should get you to Chicago without stopping and attracting attention." He stepped around the desk and opened a drawer. "Here, take these gas ration coupons. They should get you home again."

"You know," Hildy said, "I think some of Karl's clothes might fit Edwin." She left the room.

"What if someone stops us?" Sam said. "We need some

kind of story."

"Fräulein Calloway goes with us," Henri said. "You and her are recently married, you see. You're on a honeymoon trip to Chicago."

Doris asked for a translation, and Henri explained. She said something.

"She says she'll go," Henri said. "But how do we explain two men in the car with us?"

"It's better to have a full car," Oskar said. "With the rationing, it's common for people with cars to take strangers."

Sam explained this to Doris, who said something in response.

"She says she has her factory ID card," Sam told them in German. "And I still have my ID card from the camp. They might help if we get pulled over."

Oskar nodded and then turned to Sam.

"Before you arrived," he said, "Miss Calloway and I were talking about regrets. I was telling her some of mine. Now, I'll speak of one more, and I want you to hear me, Sam. Your father and I were friends. We played chess. We argued politics."

"I know," Sam replied. "My mother told me."

"I'm sorry that he and I never resolved our quarrel. It was my fault."

"Is that why—"

"Is that why I approved of you seeing my daughter? Out of guilt? No, Sam. I approved of you because I know you are a good man. Like your father."

Before Sam could reply, Hildy came back into the room, and it seemed to Edwin that she hadn't heard what her father had said. She handed some clothes to Edwin, who blushed as he saw two pairs of underwear on top.

Hildy turned to Sam, stepped close, and whispered to him as she slipped something into his hand. He pulled away, looking confused.

Oskar, who had been watching, went back behind his desk and reached into the top drawer. Returning to Edwin's side, he handed the boy a stack of candy bars.

The faint smell of gasoline seeped into the back seat of Sam's car. An hour before, behind Mr. Gruden's store, Edwin had helped fill the three gas cans that were now stowed in the trunk, and a few minutes later—as they left Ann Arbor, driving west on US Route 12—Edwin had devoured all the candy bars Oskar Gruden had given him. Now he shivered on his side of the seat and on the other side Henri did the same. Sam and Doris talked quietly in the front seat.

Edwin leaned toward Henri and whispered, "What are they saying?"

"Oh, she's just telling him about what it was like in that house." Henri sounded sleepy. "She lived with them, the German family."

"With Fräulein Gruden?"

"Yes."

Edwin thought for a second. "So will I go to school in Chicago?" he asked.

"I hope so. We may need to hide with my aunt for a while, and you'll need to start learning English first."

"What're American schools like?" Edwin asked.

"What do you mean?"

Edwin swallowed. "Will there be girls in the same school? In the same classrooms?"

Henri chuckled. "Oh, yes. Many American girls. And where we'll be, many will speak German."

"Like Fräulein Gruden," Edwin whispered.

"Yes, I think so," Henri replied. "But perhaps a little younger, your age. That would be good, eh?"

Edwin nodded and slouched down, trying to imagine his

life in the coming year.

In the front seat, Sam and Doris began to argue. Henri gave a little shush to Edwin and leaned forward slightly. In response to something Doris said, Sam took something from his coat pocket and handed it to her.

"Sam," Henri said in German, speaking over the sound of the wind and the rumble of the tires on the rough road. "Did Fräulein Gruden give you that?"

"Yes. It's Helmut Gott's bankbook. It's the proof we need to get Harris."

Henri laughed, and Edwin joined him.

Doris said something, her voice serious and urgent. Sam replied in English, and when Doris spoke again, Edwin saw she was upset.

"Doris says," Henri whispered, "that it's too dangerous to use the bankbook against Harris and Gott. Too many people will get into trouble. Sam says he can handle it so that won't happen. It appears we're still not going to tell her what happened to Gott, at least for now."

Sam began to talk again, and as Doris listened to him, she slid around in her seat, her back to the door so she could watch him. When Sam was finished, she didn't reply. Even in the dim moonlight, Edwin could see concern and anger on her face.

"Sam?" Edwin said.

"Yeah." He kept his eyes on the road ahead.

"But what about Fräulein Gruden? She was part of it, wasn't she? You'll get her in trouble."

Sam said nothing for a moment. Then, in a voice so quiet that Edwin could barely hear him, he said, "She knew what she was doing."

"No! That's not right," Edwin said. "She's young. Like me. She made a dumb mistake."

Doris watched Edwin as he talked. Edwin knew she didn't

understand German, but he thought she followed what he was saying. Then she looked back at Sam.

He drove in silence for a while. Edwin peered out the window, but the quarter moon was dropping low in the western sky, and he could hardly see anything.

"All right," Sam said finally. He added something in English for Doris, and she smiled. She turned back around on the seat, looking forward again. To Edwin, Sam said, "I guess we'll have to wait. Someday, though, maybe years from now, I'm going to do something about that bank account," he continued. "But I'll protect Fräulein Gruden."

Edwin yelled "Hurray!" and Henri laughed.

After a few minutes of excited conversation in both German and English, Doris peeked over the seat at Edwin and said something.

"She says," Henri translated, "we should get some sleep."

Edwin, although feeling drowsy, ignored her. "Sam, this is a very nice car."

"It's a 1936 DeSoto Airflow. Did you—"

Doris interrupted him, saying something in English, and Sam looked over at her, surprised and pleased.

"She said that only five thousand were made," Henri translated.

"Perhaps someday I can drive a nice car like this ..." Edwin said, his voice trailing off as he curled up in the seat, wrapping his arms around his body and trying not to shiver.

"Sam," Henri said. "Is it true what Captain Harris said? Are you a Jew?"

"On my father's side. What do you think of that?"

Henri was silent for a moment. "I think it means you're not really a Jew, if your mother is not."

"And you know Jewish law because ..."

"Because my mother *is* a Jew. And finally, in America, in this car, away from the camp and my countrymen, I can say out loud that this technically makes me a Jew."

Edwin tried to see Henri's face, but the moonlight was almost gone. Looking out the window, he whispered, "You know, I don't think I like it out in the country very much. I think I'm a city boy."

"Well, we're headed for one of the biggest cities in the world," Henri said.

Edwin slid over on the seat and leaned against Henri. "I think I'll never go to the country again. And especially not into a dark wood."

"That's fine," Henri said, reaching out to drape his arm around Edwin. "Now sleep."

Edwin settled into place, feeling the warmth from his friend's body through his clothes. As his eyelids drooped, he saw Doris slide over next to Sam and rest her head on his shoulder. And through the windshield, far ahead, the slender moon slipped below the horizon. And the monsters left him alone.

Epilogue

As Doris turned the DeSoto onto the tree-lined street that she used to walk every day going to and from the bus station, she mused that this lovely blue car was a major benefit of having married Sam just over a year before. Well, she figured there were other benefits. As she let the wooden steering wheel swing back around, its bottom rim grazed against her belly, now swollen big with her pregnancy.

Sam always said that they had to get married. He didn't mean it in the usual way, of course, as it'd taken six months for her to get pregnant after the wedding down in Brooksville. Thank God for that. While her daddy still hadn't accepted Sam fully, her momma and meemaw adored him. It sure had been an interesting evening at the house after the ceremony, watching Blanch Demsky trying to make conversation with Doris's kin. No, when Sam said they had to get married, he said it because they'd already had their honeymoon in Chicago. Doris still blushed at the memory.

As they had so often before, the big oaks shielded the afternoon sun, and since the train wasn't due for another ten minutes, Doris slowed down to remember. When she'd walked this stretch so many times before, almost two years ago, she'd noticed the service stars displayed in the windows of so many houses. Mostly they had been blue, some were gold. Now, in the summer of 1946, they were gone.

The car approached the intersection where she'd need to turn right if she wanted to go past the Gruden house. She sped up a bit and continued straight. Too many memories. She knew that in the window next to the front door, there still hung two service stars. And one was gold. Her happiness drained away, and she felt tears slipping into the corners of her eyes.

During the last month of the war in Europe, Karl Gruden's P-51 fighter plane had been shot down near Berlin. When his body finally came back to Ann Arbor, Doris and Sam had gone to the Lutheran memorial service, and Doris had cried on and off for days.

But not today, Doris told herself. This is a happy day. She pulled a handkerchief from her purse next to her on the seat and dabbed her eyes, forcing herself to smile. Today, sweet Edwin Horst was finally going home.

Sam had promised he wouldn't be late, even though he was busy with all the classes he taught. There were so many returning servicemen, and as a result of the new GI Bill, the University of Michigan was bursting at the seams with freshmen and sophomores. The History Department had been delighted to offer Sam an assistant professorship, and now they could afford to rent their little duplex apartment out in the new Pittsfield Village, just a mile southeast of the campus.

As she pulled the car into the parking lot next to the train station, she saw Sam and Oskar Gruden standing on the platform. She beeped the horn, and Sam came rushing to the car, his face both happy and concerned.

"Hello, Green-Eyes." he said as he pulled open the driver-side door and helped Doris out. "How are you feeling?"

"Oh, I'm just fit as a fiddle, darling," Doris said. "Please don't fuss so much." She put her arm through his, and they walked up to the station platform to join Oskar.

"Mr. Gruden," she said.

"Mrs. Demsky," he replied, lifting his straw homburg hat.

She hadn't seen Oskar since the memorial service. He looked much older now, thinner, almost gaunt, and when he'd raised his hat, she had seen nothing but gray.

Impulsively, Doris reached out and took his hand. "I'm right glad to see you, Oskar," she said.

Oskar cleared his throat, and as he let go her hand, it seemed that his hand shook. Doris wondered if he was thinking about Karl. Then he smiled. "It's a good day," he said. "A happy day, don't you agree, Doris?"

As both Doris and Sam nodded, the sound of a train whistle sounded far off to their left, from the west, from the direction of Chicago.

"Here it comes," Sam said.

"Three minutes late," Oskar added, looking at this pocket watch.

Soon the big diesel engine chugged past, and with the air-brakes squealing, the first passenger car rolled to a stop in front of them. The conductor stepped off and hurried back down the platform, opening the train car doors, and pulling out battered wooden steps. Sam, Oskar, and Doris looked up and down the platform, searching.

In the second car, standing in the door, Edwin Horst—now seventeen years old and sporting a trim little mustache—paused. He wore a cheap dark suit and a white shirt with no tie. As he climbed down the steps, Doris saw that he'd filled out, his chest, arms, and legs were heavier, and it seemed that he'd grown an inch or two. Edwin searched the platform and, as he caught sight of Sam, a big smile spread across his face.

"Sam!" Edwin shouted as he grabbed a battered suitcase and rushed toward them.

They all gathered around Edwin. Sam embraced him, and Doris kissed him on the cheek, which clearly embarrassed him. Oskar ushered them away from the train to an isolated corner of the platform.

"I'm glad to see you," Oskar said, shaking Edwin's hand formally. "I trust dear Marthe is well."

"Thank you, sir. Yes, she told me to say hello to you. And to tell you how much she enjoyed your visit."

Doris looked questioningly at Oskar.

"I visited Chicago last month to finalize the arrangements. And to get Edwin's picture made."

Edwin looked up and down the station platform. "Fräulein Gruden is not coming?"

Oskar shook his head. "I'm sorry, she's unable to be here."

Edwin's face fell.

"It's too bad we won't see Henri," Sam said quickly.

"We agreed," Oskar said, "that there was no need for him to come today. We cannot take any additional risks."

"We said goodbye at Union Station," Edwin said. "He's happy in Chicago. And he has a girlfriend, a Jewish girl! She works at the library where he spends so much time."

Doris thought that Oskar rolled his eyes slightly at this news. Did he not like that the girl was Jewish? Then she figured it was because Oskar simply didn't think much of Henri.

"Edwin, your English is very good," Sam said, and the others agreed.

"I hope so," Edwin replied. He glanced at Oskar. "Our plans depend on it. Do you have the papers?"

Glancing around a bit furtively, Oskar took an envelop from his inside suit pocket. He pulled out a green booklet and handed it to Edwin. Doris looked over his shoulder and saw that it was a United States passport. As Edwin opened it, she saw Edwin's picture, including the new mustache, and below it the name "Karl Virgil Gruden," along with additional information that must have been Karl's.

Doris nodded. The picture was good; it was all very official looking. She figured this just might work.

"Here," Oskar said, handing Edwin the envelope. "There is Karl's library card and an old ration book. Put them all in your pocket.

Edwin did as he was told. "Everything is arranged?" he asked Oskar.

"Yes. I have the train tickets to New York. And the boat tickets. We sail aboard the Queen Mary for Amsterdam. From there we should be able to cross into Germany. Düsseldorf is only about one hundred and fifty miles away. We can hire a car to take us if the trains aren't running."

"And in a couple weeks, you'll be reunited with your mother," Sam said.

"And my brother! Her last letter says that Stefan is home! He was wounded. Well, one leg, it's gone. But he's alive."

"Oh, Edwin," Doris said. "That's wonderful."

Sam patted Edwin on the back.

"So the passport will get him into Germany, right?" Doris said to Oskar. "What about then? Ain't he gonna need some kind of German papers?"

"His mother surely has papers for him," Oskar replied "Baptismal certificate, school reports, that sort of thing."

"But how'll he explain what happened? If the Americans in Germany ever find out he's an escaped POW, won't they arrest him?"

"And what'd be the point of that? All the prisoners of war who came to America have been sent back now. Besides, hundreds of thousands of German soldiers returned home after the armistice, and many will have lost their army papers. Now, while things are still chaotic in Germany, is the time to go."

"Oskar, this is a marvelous thing you're doing for Edwin," Sam said.

Oskar shrugged. "Well, it's not just for him. After he's settled, I'll go on to Leipzig to see my brother and the rest of my family. Things are bad in Germany. I have a little money; I hope to help them. And perhaps I'll see Hans. But probably not, as he's still stationed in Berlin."

Doris looked at Oskar evenly. "I hope Hans is well," she said. She felt Sam stiffen slightly beside her. "Please tell him that I've married and couldn't be happier."

"Of course," Oskar said.

"It's too bad Mrs. Gruden can't go with you," Sam said.

"It's best," Oskar replied. "The trip will be difficult. And perhaps, well—"

The train whistle blew, and they all started.

"We must hurry," Oskar said, perhaps happy to have been interrupted. "But first, I have some news. At my request, Sam gave Gott's bankbook to me. Hildegard took it to the bank and withdrew five thousand dollars. She forged Gott's signature on the withdrawal paper, and since she'd made the deposits, they knew her. And they know me, as it's also my bank. It helped that she didn't take out all the money. So I have four thousand dollars for you, Edwin. It's a great deal of money; it'll help you get started in Germany. Against my better judgment, I've sent five hundred to your friend Henri in Chicago, care of his dear Aunt Marthe. Perhaps he'll marry this Jewish girl, and it will be a wedding present. I've kept five hundred to pay for your tickets and other expenses. I hope this is satisfactory."

They were all stunned, Edwin most of all.

Oskar turned to Edwin, put his hands on the boy's shoulders, and spoke quietly and directly. "It was dangerous for Hildegard to get this money, illegal in fact. She did it for you, Edwin. She understands you have feelings for her. You understand she doesn't feel the same, yes?"

Edwin said nothing; his face was tight.

"It's hard, I know," Oskar continued. "You may have trouble believing this, but once I was young, and I loved a woman who could not return my love."

Doris knew that he didn't mean Gertrud.

"All aboard! All aboard!" the conductor cried.

Edwin picked up his suitcase, and after formally shaking hands with Doris and embracing Sam, he climbed the steps and entered the train car. Sam helped Oskar with his suitcases, and the two men shook hands.

"Goodbye, Oskar," Doris said, stepping close to him. She gave him a quick peck on the cheek. "Take good care of him."

Oskar seemed flustered, unsure what to do. Finally, he clumsily embraced Doris and then quickly climbed aboard. Looking down from the doorway, he called out, "Sam, did you know that your father and I talked about going back to Germany on a trip together?"

"I had no idea. I wish I could be going with you today. I know Germany; maybe I could be of some help."

The train started to move.

"No, Sam," Oskar shouted. "You have your responsibilities here. Family! It's everything!"

The rest of the passenger cars and the caboose rolled by, gathering speed, and then the train was gone. Sam and Doris turned to each other.

"Edwin looks so grown-up," Sam said. "I hope he finds a good life back home. Some happiness, after all of this."

"And a girl who'll love him. Like I love you!"

Sam grinned and took her hand. Together, they walked toward the parking lot and the DeSoto. "Want to drive?" he asked.

"Nah, that's okay. You go ahead."

He opened the passenger door, helped her in, and then went around and climbed in behind the wheel.

"Did you see," Doris said as he pressed the starter button. "Karl's middle name on the passport is Virgil?"

"Yeah, another Dante reference."

Doris frowned and then she remembered. "That's right! Oskar had some Dante book on his desk."

"*Die Göettliche Komöedie*, that's *The Divine Comedy*," Sam continued. "Hildy's middle name is Beatrice, did you know that? Beatrice is also a major character in the book. And Dante, in his own life, loved a real Beatrice he met when he was young. He never spoke to her."

"He loved her from afar."

"Yes," Sam said, sounding a little surprised. "Idealized love. Dante believed that it was the truest love of all."

Doris thought about this as they pulled out of the parking lot and headed towards home. She remembered how she'd loved William from afar when he went into the army, and before Hans came home, she'd felt something like the same for him too. And what about Oskar Gruden and that German woman? What about Oskar and her, for that matter? Near as she could tell, this loving from afar business seemed to always turn out poorly. She reached over, slipped her left hand into Sam's and rested her right hand across the top of her bulging belly.

"Personally," she said. "I don't think this Dante guy had a lick o' sense."

About the Author

Prisoner Moon is John Van Roekel's second book, succeeding his epic historical novel, **Braver Deeds**. A retired software engineer, he lives in sunny San Diego with his wife, Pam.

John recently published his third novel, **Lorenzo's Assassin**.

For more information about John and his books, please visit **JohnVanRoekel.com**

Made in the USA
San Bernardino, CA
17 September 2017